MURDER
IN
BIG HOPE

A Novel

by

JJ Brinks

PRAISE FOR MURDER IN BIG HOPE

"Easily one of today's finest American storytellers."

Kim LeMasters, Past President CBS Entertainment, LA

"JJ Brinks' sequel to his first novel, "Murder on the Whiskey George" is a completely captivating winner. Cage and Luke and Wes....and Jamie and a whole cast of new characters are vibrantly believable. The syntax and phrases are precisely correct for the persons speaking and the story line is a heart stopping tale of small town treachery, bigotry and the determination to uncover hidden secrets (that) are destroying others. The perseverance of Cage, Luke and Wes, to discover and reveal what is unspeakably entrenched in this small Southern town will keep you on the edge of your seat. READ this book! You won't be sorry."

JB King
Kindle Edition.

"Hard to believe that Mr. Brinks could top his first book Murder on Whiskey George, but he has with Murder in Big Hope! His continuing development of his characters is OUTSTANDING! I place Mr. Brinks writing right there with the old master WEB Griffin. His writing I find similar to Harlan Coben's Myron Bolitar series. I could not put this book down once I started. The only

problem is I want more.... Anxiously awaiting the next Cage Royce, Luke Carey book!"

Geno Reddick
Kindle Edition.

"I can't wait for the next book in the series. Mr. (Brinks) makes you want to keep on reading. Great job."

Kim Stileson
Kindle Edition.

"This is a sequel to Murder on the Whiskey George; This story is full of deceit, action & suspense - I could not put this book down!"

Mary Ellen Garza
Kindle Edition.

"Murder in Big Hope" brings back Cage, Jamie, Luke, and Wes, and I was happy to have them back! Brinks not only got my "who done it" mindset working, but also flared up my righteous indignation. The twists and turns, revelations and discoveries are what makes "Murder in Big Hope" a great read. It was hard to put down. Brinks does an excellent (job) in character descriptions, and the plotline never bogs down. I highly recommend this but, suggest you start with Murder on the Whiskey George. You want to get to know the characters as they develop. I love the series and can't wait to see what Cage, Jamie, Luke, and Wes are up to next!"

Kat Vickers
Kindle Edition.

For Adam and Amy. A father's joy.

ISBN 978-0-9836784-3-4

Copyright J.J. Brinks 2015.

All rights reserved.

Empire Mystery Press

PROLOGUE

HIS SENSES SENT confirmation racing to his brain although he'd never heard it before, never *felt* it, his ear and nerve endings instinctively identifying the sound and tremor of flesh against metal.

Robby Cain brought his truck to a skidding stop fifty yards past the point of collision, the beam of the aging Silverado's right headlight angling skyward through the ground fog like a lazy eye while the left shot a straight path along the obscured stretch of roadway.

He sat in the darkened cab for a minute, brooding. It wasn't the damage to his vehicle; it was the idea of death that weighed him down each time he drove to Atlanta and visited the nursing home where his grandmother fought the pain of her last days.

Robby switched on the overhead light and opened the glove box, pulling out a flashlight and automatic pistol. If the animal he'd hit had survived it would be badly injured. He wouldn't let it suffer.

He left his truck and walked slowly back along the edge of the Alabama road that ran between Phenix City and Eufaula, sweeping the ground with the flashlight as he went, cutting deeper into the scrub at the first traces of blood.

Thirty yards further on, the deer lay on its side, bloody foam coating its muzzle, its exposed flank rising and falling in labored breathing. Robby shined the flashlight over the animal's heart and fired a single shot through its hide.

A S HE RETURNED to his truck, the shape of a man leaning against the front fender stopped him in his tracks twenty yards short. The hour was late, the road deserted. "Something you need, mister?"

"Deputy Sheriff," the figure said. "What say you move this way. Hold that light over your head with both hands. I'm not mistaken, that was a gun shot I just heard."

Robby stood his ground. "How about some identification? I don't see a cruiser anywhere."

The figure straightened. Robby heard a chuckle. "Smart one, aren't ya. That's good on account of I'm in no mood to deal with drunk and stupid." The officer walked to the front of Robby's truck. "Ridin' a cycle. See?" A beacon began to rotate, sending out a blue pulse of light.

In the staccato flashes Robby saw the officer clearly and did as instructed, noting that the sheriff's holster was unsnapped and his hand rested on the butt of his revolver. "The pistol," Robby said. "I have a permit for it. Gun's tucked in the back of my jeans."

"Just leave it where it is, boy, and tell me what this is all about—although from the looks of your Chevy I got a pretty good idea."

Robby explained what had happened while the deputy checked his driver's license and the pistol permit, then pulled the handgun from Robby's belt and examined it.

"Damn things scoot out of the dark like bad dreams, don't they?" the deputy said. "I'll call the boys at Highway to come cart the carcass off before the meat goes bad. There's folks around here can use all the help the law allows and the Good Lord provides. Now why don't you sit in your truck while I wander up the road and check this thing out."

Robby got back in his truck as ordered; the deputy sheriff started up the road and disappeared into the dark.

This, he flat out didn't need. He'd had a few beers along the way to help pass the miles—enough so that he might not walk the straightest of lines or touch his nose squarely on the first try. What if the cop had looked in the truck and seen the empties on the floor? One more ticket and he'd lose his license for sure. And that would put him out of work. Then what? How would he support his grandma?

Without giving himself a chance to think it through, Robby made an impulsive decision. He started the truck, and took off.

THE DEPUTY HEARD the engine turn over and the sudden screech of spinning tires. "Shit," he muttered. "Here we go."

He jogged back to his motorcycle. The truck had no more than a minute's head start on him by the time he mounted the Harley. Where the hell did this kid think he was gonna go? He turned on the beacon and the siren; a sharp twist of the throttle sent the bike up over seventy. The ground fog had thickened. He never saw the armadillo that lay dead in the road until it was too late. When he came to, he was lying in a ditch, gravel embedded in his skin, the truck long gone.

TWENTY MILES OF highway remained before the road would bring him north of Eufaula. To Robby, it felt more like a hundred.

His one good headlight cut a narrow path that traced the ribbon of road as it wandered through the rolling countryside, curving left and right in a series of turns. He'd seen nothing of the motorcycle cop in his rearview mirror. Good. The lazy bastard hadn't bothered. He knew it had been a stupid move taking off like that, but he was home free. Chalk one up to luck.

He slowed as he came to a patch of mist gathered in a deep hollow, then pulled the truck off the side of the road and stopped, badly needing to relieve himself. He got out and started for the tree line. Forty feet in from the road's edge, he came to three waist-high markers—simple white crosses made of wood and placed in memory and in warning that recklessness carries a penalty far greater than the laws of man.

Thin clouds lay across a harvest moon like gauze on a wound, playing amber light off the vapor that swirled around him as he walked, making him think of ghosts—as though he'd chanced on a cemetery and interrupted a gathering of spirits.

He passed the markers and headed toward the woods, aware of the coolness of the night air against his skin, a sensation that brought on a sudden shiver.

When he'd emptied his bladder he walked back by the crosses, stopping for a second to have a closer look—a man regarding Calgary, the bodies of the Innocent, the forgiven, and the non-repentant long since removed. It struck him as an odd thought; he was not by nature what his grandma would call a *true believer*.

"So who died here?" he asked in a curious whisper, not sure that he really wanted to know.

In reply came a throaty sound at his back. Startled, he spun on his heels. His eyes widened at what he saw: A large buck stood pawing the earth with its head lowered.

Robby took a cautious step backward. It was January; the animal was in rut. A dangerous time. Sweet Jesus, he thought. The buck's after me for hitting that deer. It couldn't be, but the ironic thought scared him badly and set his heart racing.

The animal reared, eyes intent; Robby backpedaled, struggling for balance.

The deer dropped its forelegs to the ground and advanced; Robby frantically groped the small of his back for the pistol. In a flash he saw the motorcycle cop stick the handgun in his waistband as he'd headed up the road. *Shit, man, is this bad!*

Then he saw a chance. The buck retreated a few feet to mount a full charge. As he did, Robby made a blind dash to his left, only to collide with the markers, an arm of the center monument burying in his groin. He crumpled to the ground in agony.

The animal stood motionless, its eyes on Robby. With a violent shake of its antlers the buck raised its head to the sky, its shoulders tensing.

Robby drew himself into a ball, expecting the worst. But nothing came. When he finally opened his eyes and looked up the buck was slowly moving away, melding with the darkness until it receded into the night.

As the pain lessened, Robby got to his feet, listening for anything that might signal that the animal was still out there waiting in the darkness. Cautiously he began walking back toward his truck.

Damn things scoot out of the dark like bad dreams, don't they?

He shook the thought from his mind as he picked up his pace.

From behind him, came a heavy thud.

Robby froze, blood pumping. What now? He turned warily, his skin shrinking in patterns of gooseflesh on his bones. The center cruciform had fallen to the ground, a smoky light rising upward from the spot where it had stood. He watched transfixed as the light gathered into what might have been a human shape, or the shape of nothing at all.

Nothing, until it spoke to him. *Who's going to bear the weight of the sin, Robby? Can you tell us that? Can you please just tell us that?*

And then as the deer, the image slowly vanished until the light was extinguished.

***

HE DROVE ON through the night with his internal systems charged and his mind in overdrive. He'd imagined it, had hallucinated the whole thing. Too much stress for one day.

With the first rays of dawn showing on the horizon, Robby reached Panama City Beach. As he pulled into his trailer park he should have felt relief. He was home. But he knew he was in trouble. Big trouble. You don't run from a cop. And the handgun. Now, how totally dumb was that?

As he dragged himself from his truck, he tried to figure out how he could set it straight. But he was too exhausted to think. He'd need help on that issue, anyway. Christ, he thought as he put the key in the door, if I could just start this damn day over.

And get that creepy image and that weird question out of my head.

ONE

None speak false, when there is none to hear.

—James Beattie

CHAPTER 1

66 **A**SPIRING TO FOUR hundred dollars per hour in this Godforsaken trade, Cage my boy, calls for the padding of one's won-loss record. A matter of avoidance, really. Allow controversy and the crassest criminals a wide berth. Forage instead in the troughs of the industrialists. Boring, but far safer. Forget all the other cockywaddle I've babbled on about over these past months. The money, lad. Head straight for the money."

Inspired words spoken years ago in a smoke-filled pub in Boston's Back Bay by an aging law professor, four Beefeater Gibsons bolstering his cynicism, a twice-removed subject of the Crown who at one time swayed jurors with his manufactured British accent, but in the end used its flavor to shield his ego.

He'd been a celebrated trial attorney until he'd stood in defense of an accused cop killer, a black youth whose arrest and confession seemed too convenient. He'd prevailed on defense, but not in the press. Tenure was all that saved him at Boston University.

AS A YEARLING lawyer, I took his advice and abandoned any thoughts of a career built on trials with Perry Mason endings, opting instead for a shot at the big bucks that lay within corporate coffers.

Billing four hundred an hour, it turned out, was not my calling nor ever my fee. Half was more like it, the boredom double the professor's dispirited calculations.

I reached my late-thirties as a partner in a respectable New York corporate law firm where I slogged along day to day. Bored but making a good buck. Until Billy was murdered— shot in the head and dumped like garbage on a patch of Florida swampland.

IT TOOK A year but I'd found my brother's killers where the authorities hadn't, and in the process unearthed a desire to live a freer life where I'd soon learn to regard the rules of law in a slightly different light.

So, here I am, transplanted and transforming, on most days practicing a simpler brand of law with my partner, Luke Carey, whiling away the sunny days amid DUI defenses, divorce decrees, personal injury claims, the structuring of wills and the filing of bankruptcies—the lot of man, not corporations; in part running *The Ship's Hatch Cafe*, a beach bar inherited from my deceased brother whose continued success I credit in my truest moments solely to my beautifully Irish, unwedded love, Jamie.

JANUARY ON FLORIDA'S Panhandle is a pleasant blend of cool days and cooler nights. The earth has moved to a point along its orbital path so that the sun sets well off shore in the Gulf of Mexico, setting fire to the sky by late afternoon.

I sat at a table on the deck of *The Hatch* near the outside bar beneath the warmth of a pole-mounted gas heater that Friday, blissfully sipping Ketel One on the rocks, watching in silence as the big orange ball slipped below the surface of the darkening water.

At four, Luke had shown up. He ordered a beer in clipped words, then drew deeply on the last of his cigarette and tamped it out in a glass ashtray as twin flumes of smoke streamed from his nostrils like a bull snorting a warning on a cold winter day.

I turned my attention from the palate of colors spreading slowly across the horizon and fixed my eyes on Luke. "Something bothering you?" I asked.

"Robby Cain. He's in some kind a' fix."

"Not surprising," I said.

Luke rested his tree trunk-sized forearms on the table. He flicked the top open and closed on the old dented Zippo lighter that seemed his talisman. "Had a run-in with a cop up on 431 near Big Hope last night. Messed up pretty good, he says."

"In jail?" I asked.

"Might a' been, he said, if he'd a' stuck around."

I sipped my vodka. "Charged with . . . ?"

"He didn't say much on the phone. Sounded shook, though. That much came through."

Robby Cain worked for the contractor who'd renovated *The Hatch* shortly after Jamie and I had taken title and moved in. He was a skilled framer and accomplished drinker, a redneck prone to participate in the local chapter of the Friday Night Fights.

Luke lit another cigarette. "He's not bad a kid, Cage. Works a full day. Most times, anyway. Takes care of his grandma. He had a rough go of it early on. That's all."

"And how many times have how many lawyers heard that excuse?"

"Not everybody's daddy in the Gulf War caught a bullet in the spine courtesy of some hopped up enlisted felon posin' as a regular troop and had the gears stripped on his legs and his nuts ."

"In war, not everyone's father *comes* home," I said, sorry that I had as soon as the words passed my lips.

Luke glared at me. He'd done two tours in the Army to my none. Timing. Age. The Lucky Sperm Club. Pick one. "It's true. Difference is, I didn't know 'em like I did Robby's daddy."

AT FIVE-THIRTY, ROBBY came through the wooden door with the brass portal and worked his way through the crowd to where Luke and I stood at the bar.

Robby was built like a middle-weight, every ounce as hard as the nails he pounded for a living, his brown hair shaggy, his face marked by sun damage that had aged him beyond his late twenties.

Luke watched him closely as he approached.

"I need a beer," Robby said. "And a lawyer. And my head shoved up my ass." He stuck out his hand. I shook it. "Cage, what's up?"

"My question," I said.

"It's not good. I freaked out and left a motorcycle cop with his dick in his hand. I'd had a few and, well, you know what my sheet looks like."

"Doesn't sound terminal," I said. "I think we can handle it. You sure he got your license and all that before you eighty-sixed him?"

The bartender brought Robby his beer. He took a long pull. "Doesn't matter. I gave him a gift to remember me by. My pistol. It's registered."

"What the *hell*?" Luke said.

"I hit a deer. Went looking for it and finished it off. Guy seen my truck sittin' there and heard the shot. I get back, he wants answers. He takes the gun and goes up the road for a look see and I take off. Brilliant, huh?"

Luke knuckled him on top of the head. "You'd had more than a few. Anything else, Einstein?"

Robby looked out the wide window, across the deck to the waters of the Gulf of Mexico, eyes narrowed as if the images of the previous night had followed him here and now floated somewhere on its black surface. He turned back to Luke. "Like that's not enough?"

"No," Luke answered, "like, if you hold anything back—anything at all—I'll put my boot up your scrawny ass."

Robby finished off his beer then set the bottle on the bar and picked at the label. "Shit. Alright. But you're gonna want me committed," he said. "Deal is, I stopped to take a leak. It was near some a' them crosses—the ones for roadkill? Anyway, I finish up, then nearly get attacked by a horny buck. I run balls first into one a' them things tryin' to bolt and end up on the ground with my scrot in my throat. He finally wanders off, I haul ass for my truck, and guess what? Cross that took out my joint hits the ground behind me. Then— Come on Luke, this is as embarrassing as hell and don't mean squat."

"Size thirteen, and it's got a reinforced toe, Robby."

He signaled for another beer. "Goddamn if you ain't worse than my old man was."

Luke waved it off. "Son, if you haven't figured that out after all these years then I truly do give up."

"Fine," Robby huffed, his finger tracing a line of rivets in the copper top bar. "So, if ya gotta know, this . . . this light 'er smoke 'er somethin' farts up outta the ground and wants me to tell it who's gonna bear the sin. For what the hell, I have no idea. There. Happy?"

"More than a few," Luke said. "Sounds to me like you drank the whole friggin' case."

PRESCIENCE TO MOST people is the stuff of King novels. To me, it's all too real—a micro-burst that blows a hole in your vision and gives you a glimpse of something you'd rather not see. I've experienced it twice: the death of my parents by plane crash; the murder of my brother by gun shot. But we had blood-ties. If what Robby had witnessed was fact or fiction was beyond me.

Luke would chalk it up to beer and fatigue. He defines the world in terms of blood, bone, and supportable fact. For me, it's not that easy. The dead speak in too many ways.

I'd left Luke with Robby and gone out to the deck. Jamie was drawing a draft, the fluorescent light under the bar top painting her face with an iridescent glow, a pale hue set against the blackness of her thick, cropped hair.

She motioned me over with a quizzical expression. "You guys looked awfully serious in there."

I gave her a recap and asked her to apply her psychologist's brain to the mystery.

"As far as an hallucination," Jamie said, "it's chapter one stuff. Seeing his dying grandmother . . . killing the deer . . . the crosses . . . being tired, drunk—all of it. As for the sheriff? That's your area, Counselor. But this kid's going to end up in big trouble one of these days. "

"I'd say this qualifies, wouldn't you?"

"Can't save them all, sweet cakes."

"We can try, can't we?"

"As lawyers? Sure. But that's all you owe, him, Cage. That's the extent of it." With that she turned away and went to the aid of a customer who'd signaled his urgent need for more alcohol.

CHAPTER 2

WESLEY HARLAND SHOWED up at *The Hatch* a few minutes later, the bulk of his heavy muscle tight against the confines of his sweats, a white bandana stretched across a forehead as dark as coal.

Wes had been the Chief of Police in Panama City Beach, a good cop who'd grown tired of the increasing restrictions placed on his ability to deal with situations that required him to jump through too many procedural hoops.

Billy's murder had pushed him over the edge:

While my brother hadn't been a complete innocent, he was far from a hardened criminal. He'd made one mistake, and in the end received the death penalty at the hands of some truly bad guys while the law kept Wes's trussed firmly behind his back. He resigned shortly after the mystery finally unraveled and came to work in our law office as an investigator.

"Who called in the heavy artillery?" I asked Luke as Wes joined us at the bar.

"Nobody," Wes said. "But we need to talk. And I do mean now. In private. I came lookin' for the two of you. Havin' Robby here's a bonus—kind of."

WE CRAMMED OURSELVES into the small office off the kitchen.

Wes closed the door behind him and leaned against it. "I just had a talk with one of my old charges over at the station." He turned his eyes on Robby. "Good thing I got contacts. You're knee-deep in shit, sonny."

"We know," I said.

"How much of it you tell 'em?" Wes asked Robby.

"All of it. Everything."

"Everything you *know*. Assumin' you didn't totally lose your goddamn mind last night."

Robby looked confused. "But, you couldn't know about . . . . What the fuck?" he said to me. "You go and call Wes? Think my brain fart was that funny?"

"I didn't call anyone, Robby."

"Pardon me, gentlemen," Wes said, "but what the hell are y'all jawin' about? Trust me, there's nothin' funny about it."

"About what?" I asked.

"About a shot in the heart."

"The deer, you mean," Robby said.

"*What* deer? I'm talkin' about a man. Guy name of Raymond Lintz."

Robby turned pale beneath his tan, his eyes nearly doubling in size. "What the hell you tryin' to say? You think *I*—?"

"Slow down," Wes said. "I don't think anything. You go ahead and tell me your side, but then you're gonna need to hear me out."

***

WES'S FORMER SUBORDINATE, also a friend of Robby's told Wes that the Sheriff's Department in Big Hope, Alabama, had made an urgent request of the Beach P.D. to pick Robby up and hold him pending extradition proceedings. They wouldn't say why.

The young duty officer called Wes who tapped his sources and uncovered two bits of disturbing information: a Missing Persons Report for a Raymond Lintz had been filed with the Fulton County Sheriff's Department in Atlanta on Tuesday; a body had been found early this morning near the town of Big Hope, Alabama.

"The body is that of a white male, approximate age, thirty. The description given by Holly Rhetman, twenty-eight, girlfriend of Lintz, thirty-four, when she filed the report, fits." Wes flipped open a spiral-bound steno book. "With a couple of notable exceptions. She described what Lintz had been wearing when she'd last seen him on Sunday, but the body had been stripped naked. The second point of interest is the bullet hole in his chest—a distinguishing mark we can assume was *not* known to her at the time she filed her report, if in fact the body is that of her boyfriend."

Robby shifted a nervous gaze from Wes to me. "And they're thinkin' they can pin this on me? I'm serious as I can be when I tell y'all I had not one goddamn thing to do with this other than bein' a dumb shit. Period."

"What caliber is your pistol?" Wes asked.

"Nine millimeter," Robby answered.

"Same as the slug they cut out of Lintz," Wes said, paying the words out like links in a heavy chain.

"The fuck am I gonna do now?" Robby said, struggling to keep his composure.

"I might have a suggestion," I said.

AT NINE THAT evening we parked in the lot at Destin Harbor, several miles west of Panama City Beach, and made our way along the dock.

The Free Spirit sat in her slip, her sleek white hull floating in the glow of footlights. She's a fifty-two foot Hatteras Convertible that had been owned by my brother—the spoils of his crime—fittingly named for his outlook on life. Now she operates as a fishing charter captained by Brian Martin and his girlfriend, Deanne.

The night air was crisp, scented by the thin smell of diesel fuel mixed with the stronger essence of steaks cooking close by on a stainless steel grill clamped to the stern rail of a handsome sloop, the water below her dark as pitch.

I introduced Robby as we boarded and went into the salon. Deanne and Brian live aboard and have added those personalized touches to the interior that convert space into a home.

"So I'm just 'sposed to take off on this luxury liner here like nothin's happened?" Robby said as he popped open a can of beer.

"We need time, son," Luke said. "Couple days and we'll know more about what we're dealin' with. If you were nothin' more than a person of interest and they wanted to fire a few questions your way, okay, we could go with that. But that deputy knows what really happened. So you're bein' set up by these characters and they're plannin' on closin' the lid down tight, seems to me. Why, is the question. We're gonna need that answer. You got the truth workin' your side, but they got timin', a body, and your gun."

"Thanks for the pep talk," Robby said.

"Our job now idn't about bein' cheerleaders," Luke said.

Brian went topside and started the engines; Luke and I helped with the lines, then watched *The Spirit* ease out of her slip at idle and turn to starboard, heading for the East Pass. From there she'd enter the Gulf of Mexico—destination, nowhere in particular beyond the jurisdictional limit.

T RAFFIC ALONG ROUTE 98 was light for a Friday night, and we were back at *The Hatch* by ten-fifteen.

We had a good crowd both inside and out, the deck-dwellers huddled together at tables under the glow of the propane heaters.

I skipped out on my usual late shift at the bar and accompanied Luke on the fifteen minute walk west along the beach to his Gulf front home, kicking off my shoes and leaving them at the bottom of the stairs that lead down from the deck. The sugar-white crystals felt cold underfoot and looked like snow in the pale moonlight.

While I trusted Wes's judgment in things connected to badges and warrants, I kept turning corners in my head and colliding with the same nagging thought: What if Robby *had* murdered someone? He was a hothead. Pour booze on a fire and funny things can happen.

"What's your gut tell you, Cage?"

"That the Red Sox will win it all again next year."

"You know damn well what I'm askin'."

"That he's innocent, I suppose."

"But you can't accept it on simple faith."

"It's not so much a matter of faith," I said, "as it is ignoring the circumstance."

Luke extracted a cigarette from a near-empty pack, produced his old Zippo and lit up in a flame that bent and danced like a miniature shaman in the faint breeze blowing in from the Gulf. In the flicker of light, I saw his familiar, crooked grin.

"Well, you can't just dismiss it, for Chrissake," I said.

"No, you can't. But if you dwell on it for too long it'll fuck with your head 'til you freeze up and don't know *what* to believe. You'll end up bein' no damn help to anybody."

We walked without words for several minutes.

"So then," I said finally, "I take it you're settled on his innocence?"

"Yep."

"And if you're wrong?"

"Partner, I been a one-man Boy's Club to that pup ever since his daddy passed when Robby was fifteen. I'm not wrong. But if

it turns out that I am . . . ? Why'd you suggest sendin' him off on The Spirit?"

We stopped at the foot of the deck stairs. "For his benefit— so no one can get to him before we're ready."

"And . . . ?"

"And, *what*?"

"Oh, I don't know . . . maybe so he couldn't run out on us? Just in case?"

"That's . . . bullshit."

"There's nothin' wrong with doubt, Cage, so long as you don't allow it to get in the way to where you go and trip over it."

"What's that supposed to mean?"

He turned to face me. "It means that after your own flesh and blood got caught up on the wrong side of the law, to you the word *trust* doesn't have the same ring to it."

Part of me found Luke's insight intrusive, wanted to tell him to fuck off. But I let it go.

He started up the stairs to the house then stopped and turned toward the darkened water. I watched the arc of his cigarette trace a path against the lightless sky as it tailed to the sand below.

"Life's a Petrie dish, Cage. Whole goddamn thing's an experiment. That's the fun of it, and that's the hell of it. Now that you're witness to it, keep your eye on the glass. Study what's under it 'til you can pick out the good from the bad on your own. Otherwise one day you'll find yourself knocked flat on your ass and never know which mutant on this crazy fucking planet it was punched your ticket."

I JOGGED TOWARD *THE Hatch* along the tide-pack, dodging small waves that lapped the shore with a tongue of winter-cold water, upped the pace until my heart pounded and my breath ached in my chest; until I felt I could outdistance the ghost of my brother and the obsessive thought that I'd mortgaged a measure of my mortal being in seeking vengeance for his murder.

On the night breeze came the haunt of Billy's voice. *Tell me big brother, who'll bear the weight of the sin? Can you tell me that?*

CHAPTER 3

CLAYTON W. VERNON, Sheriff of Big Hope, Alabama—town and county of the same name—was not a happy man when he received a call late Friday night from the Panama City Beach Police Department informing him that the subject in question, Robert R. Cain, had not been in residence at his trailer.

Wes relayed this bit of news on Saturday morning over our traditional weekend breakfast, cooked by Luke and served on the Careys' deck—a meal built from all things bad that taste good, accented by a pot of LuAnn's famously strong coffee.

The body in question had been confirmed as that of the missing Raymond Lintz.

Holly Rhetman had traveled by private limousine to Big Hope on Friday afternoon, made the identification, then returned to Atlanta.

Officially, we couldn't know anything. Our first point of contact, we decided, would be Holly, the grieving girlfriend.

The job of talking to her was assigned to me.

EARLY THE NEXT morning, I caught the short flight to Atlanta.

The weather in the Southeast had cleared leaving the city below looking fresh and peaceful, washed clean of trouble and sin as we flew the approach into Hartsfield-Jackson International.

I rented a car, then drove north on the interstate to Buckhead.

The address I had for Holly Rhetman put me on a tree-lined drive in an area of inflated real estate where the streets were festooned with Range Rovers, BMW's and jogging strollers pushed by fit and stylishly attired young mothers.

We'd gambled that she'd be at home at ten on Sunday morning just two days after she'd identified the remains of her boyfriend; judging by the late-model Jaguar that sat on the circular drive under the spreading limbs of an enormous oak, she was.

I pushed a button that rang a bell that sounded too big for the bungalow house, waited, then pushed it again.

Seconds later, the door swung open.

I am in love and I am loyal, but through and through I am Man. If the young woman in the doorway was the lady of the house, she was anything but the grieving girlfriend I'd expected to encounter.

She stood five-seven in a white terry cloth robe that hung open at the front, her black bikini visible beneath. Her small feet were set in puddles, toenails manicured and painted dark red, her trim ankles base to perfect legs ending in gently flared hips that in turn surrendered to the concave of narrow waist, flatness of stomach, fullness of breast, broadness of shoulders and the elegance of a long neck. All this I noted in the blink of an eye without, I was fairly certain, ogling or drooling on myself.

She'd piled her thick dark hair atop her head and fastened it in place with tortoiseshell barrettes. Her deep blue eyes shone with energy; her smile was inviting. "Hi, there," she said brightly.

"Are you . . . Holly Rhetman?" I asked like a schoolboy.

"That's me. Come on in. Careful not to slip on the floor. You got me out of the hot tub."

The house seemed bigger on the inside. Hardwood floors gleamed underfoot; skylights set in the cathedral ceiling of the living room cast the morning's glow on rich furnishings.

"Ms. Rhetman, I'm—"

"Call me Holly. I know who you are—not your name, of course. It's . . . ?"

"Cage. Cage Royce. I'm here—"

"You're here about Ray. They said an investigator might stop by today. I thought probably later, though. How about some coffee? Grab a seat. Be right back." She was off before I could answer.

She returned a minute later holding two mugs. "Black, right?" She handed one to me then plopped down on the couch holding the other.

"Black. Yes. Fine. Thanks."

"Okay. So, what is it that I can tell you?" She sat attentively, smiling pleasantly. People act oddly in the face of death, I allowed.

She hadn't asked me for any identification. To her I was a cop. I decided to forge ahead before she had a chance to consider caution. "You and Mr. Lintz were in a relationship?"

"Yes, and no. We *had* been, but , well, we were sort of . . . moving apart. We hadn't officially broken it off, but that wasn't long in coming."

I N HOLLY'S WORDS, Ray had of late become, *like . . . totally moody.*

They'd begun dating a year earlier. She'd met him at a party at a bar in Buckhead. He was adopted with no living family, which Holly found touching. He was handsome and sweet.

"I thought we were doing really well, you know? We shared a lot of the same interests, did fun things. I thought everything was fine up until a few weeks ago. He kinda became distant and starting finding reasons to break dates at the last minute.

"When I tried to get inside his head, he said he'd fallen behind at work and his boss was all over his butt about it. He needed time alone to catch up."

"What kind of work?" I asked.

"He was a reporter for the *Atlanta Daily Chronicle*. Anyway, he promised things would get better, but nothing improved. We started fighting."

"Did he tell you anything specific about the trouble at work?"

"That's one of the things that upset me the most. I mean, the man was sharing my bed! You're supposed to confide in each other when you've gotten that far, right? Well, he was a real clam—said it was confidential stuff and he had to 'protect his sources, protect his journalistic integrity.'

"Then, like all at once he started to get really depressed. He couldn't . . . . Before the end, the intimate part? Well it just stopped."

Holly sat on the edge of the bed while I made a cursory pass through Lintz's belongings—much of it already boxed up.

There was little to paw through, other than some clothing and toilet articles.

We left the bedroom and drifted back to the living room.

"I felt sorry for him," she said. "I was worried about . . . well, about his mental state. That's why I filed the Missing Persons Report when I did. He was supposed to call me. He didn't. Then, I couldn't get him at his apartment. I even went there. I thought, you know, maybe he'd . . . ." She let the thought tail off. "It was like, he just became this sad sack person for no reason and I couldn't help him. I had this strange feeling that he wanted to love me, but . . . . It was like he was drowning, and he wouldn't take my hand."

I stood to leave. "Thanks for your time, Ms. Rhetman."

"Holly. And I hope I was of *some* help at least," she said, getting to her feet.

"You were." I pulled open the door and turned to say goodbye.

Holly looked past me as if I'd already left. "Daddy liked him okay in the beginning, but later he worried that Ray was all wrong for me. And he's a great judge of people. Maybe he was right. But I didn't wish Ray dead. Really, I didn't."

"I'm sure not. What happened wasn't your fault."

Her eyes gained focus and found my face. "That's sweet of you to say." Then a little smile appeared at the corner of her mouth. "You're not a cop. Cops aren't soft that way. When I said my dad was a great judge of character, I meant just that. He *is* a judge. I've been around law enforcement types all my life. How did I miss it?"

"I didn't intend to give you the impression that I was—"

"Of course you did." She flushed. "I'm a pretty good judge of character myself. That is, if you discount Ray. Anyway, I don't think you meant any harm. Now . . . tell me who you are."

"A friend of someone who's about to be arrested for Ray's murder. I'm an attorney. I'm digging for anything I can."

She nodded as if coming to terms with something. "Will you tell me when you find out?"

"*If* I find out—yes. And . . . if you wouldn't mind? . . . when the police—"

She laid a hand on my forearm. "I won't mention a word to anyone that you were here. Promise." Then her shoulders slumped. "She's lucky, you know—your wife or girlfriend or whoever. You're a prize. And I'm feeling . . . alone and sorry for myself. I thought for a minute there you might try. But you didn't."

"That bad, are we?"

"As a breed? Yeah. I'm afraid so. Especially cops."

"Which I'm not. But if I were . . . ."

She stood on tip-toe and pecked me on the cheek. "I hope you find whoever it was that killed Ray."

I handed her my business card. "And I hope you find just who it is you're looking for."

"Me, too," She said. "To date, I'm about oh-for-ten."

Impossible, I thought as I closed the door behind me.

CHAPTER 4

I'D PACKED AN overnight bag on the chance that my interview with Ms. Rhetman might for some reason keep me in Atlanta beyond Sunday. When I found out that Lintz had been a newspaper reporter with troubles at work, I went in search of a bunk.

At eleven, I checked into a chain hotel on Piedmont, then called Jamie.

I lay on the bed using the remote to flip idly through the channels on the TV. "Lintz was a fool to give her up," I said.

"More often than not, it takes two," Jamie said. "And why was he a fool?"

"Let's just say that Holly is . . . mildly attractive."

"Shallow beast."

"It's the cop in me."

"The what?"

"Nothing. But I can tell you this. There's no question whatsoever that I am committed to you to the end of time."

"Gee. Aren't I the lucky one?"

I found a theatre in a plaza in Buckhead and spent the afternoon watching a mindless movie, then hit some art galleries and had an early steak dinner, all the while sidetracked by trying to identify what I'd found strange about Holly Rhetman.

It might have been my ego, but I could have sworn that she'd propositioned me. That had I wanted to take her to bed she would have led the way, turned back the covers and thrown me down and gotten on top.

Could she have been that callous? Cared that little about Lintz being murdered? She'd filed the Missing Persons report out of concern, she said. Afraid that he might kill himself. It might have been that she'd written him off as a lover, but not as a friend.

Whatever the reason for the way she'd acted, I didn't think that she was connected to the murder. She'd been far too at ease.

IN MY DREAMS that night I returned to the house where Holly lived. It was abandoned and in need of repair. When I pushed the doorbell, my hand punched a hole through the wood.

Something inside grabbed my wrist. I couldn't pull free.

I awoke with my right arm pinned beneath my body, the phone ringing. It was Brian. He'd tracked me down through Jamie. We had a problem, he said. I switched on the light. It was a little before six.

"He couldn't even keep water down. He was dehydrating. All I could do was make port and get him to a hospital. He'll be okay in a day or so."

"Where are you?"

"Tarpon Springs."

I called Luke who told me in deadpan that he'd been up watching *A Perfect Storm.*

"Those slow rollers are the worst," he said. "The good news is where he's at. They'll probably get in and out without anyone takin' notice."

I hoped Luke was right. Tarpon Springs was not a buzzing metropolis.

"I'll let Wesley know," Luke said.

I showered and dressed, then went down to the lobby and bought a copy of the *Atlanta Daily Chronicle,* poured a cup of complimentary coffee and perused the paper front to back. It ranked somewhere between the *New York Post* and a check-out counter tabloid.

A T NINE, I drove to the address listed on the newspaper's masthead.

The *Chronicle* did business from a four-story brick structure with dirty windows set in a neighborhood of warehouses south of Turner Field, home of The Braves. A guard waved me through a chain link gate that squeaked loudly as it moved slowly on its track.

I entered the lobby and checked the location of the gentleman I wished to see with the receptionist who pointed with disinterest toward a set of stairs. "Second floor, left side," she said.

I waited while Gerome Gerard—Lintz's editor—finished what his secretary said was an assignment meeting with his reporters. I watched him through the slats in the blinds of his glass-sided office as he admonished his charges with hand gestures and changes in facial expressions. He wrote quickly and heavily on a whiteboard as he talked.

When he'd finished, he opened a door that had been secreted in the geometry of the cubicle, followed his reporters out onto the main floor and marched in my direction. "Royce, is it?" he asked, his voice sounding as if his throat had come loose, the words banging around inside his neck before rolling out of his mouth.

I shook his rough hand. "Cage Royce. I—"

"You a cop?"

"No, I'm a—"

"Lawyer?"

"Yes. I'd like to—"

"Got a beef with the paper, take it up with Sol Lipschitz. He's a bigger prick than I am. Number's in the book. Best goddamn libel attorney in the city. You'll grow hair a foot long on your ass before you get a nickel. Good luck." He turned away and started walking back toward his office.

"I'd like to talk to you about Ray Lintz," I said evenly.

He stopped and looked at me. "Lintz was a putz, may he rest in peace."

"Holly thought he might have been suicidal," I offered. It worked. Shameless name-dropper. Newspapermen and judges. Crime and politics. Four short strides and he stood in front of me again.

"Where's your suit, Counselor?" he asked. His breath smelled of peppermint.

"I don't normally wear one. Unless I'm in court. And that's not often."

"Should I trust you for any particular reason?"

"Yes, you should," I said.

"This off the record?" he asked.

I assured him it was.

He stood for a moment as if weighing the investment of his time against any possible return. "Five minutes—max. Fuck with me, Mr. Royce, you won't make thirty seconds."

Sitting in Gerard's office was akin to hunkering down inside of an ashtray. I could feel the residue of nicotine and old smoke gathering on my skin and seeping into my pores.

"Charming, isn't it?" he said.

"What's that?"

"The fucking stink, what else? It's not me. I quit the crappy habit two years ago. But I don't have the balls to make my renegades out there do the same. If I did, nobody'd work here. Fuck the health department and fuck OSHA. They want to enforce the law, fine. Shutting down this rag sheet ain't gonna change a thing anyway. "

"Mr. Gerard, I'd like to—"

"Gerry. Mr. Gerard was my father. He's dead."

"Then we have something in common," I said. "And 'Cage' would be preferable."

"What the hell kind of a name is that?"

"Family," I said. "My mother's side. Her grandfather's."

He unwrapped a pink and white striped mint for himself and tossed another to me. "Let me guess. Bluecoat. New York, Taxachusetts—New England someplace, right?"

"Florida, now . . . but, yes, you're correct."

"The no suit bit. Florida. Now I got it. Okay, let's talk."

I had the impression that I'd passed some kind of cursory interview and checked out okay. But I knew enough to be careful. "We do agree that 'off the record' goes both ways?"

"Let's see if I got this straight. I'm a newspaper hump. You're a lawyer. We got Lintz shot dead. You come all the way up from Florida to ask questions and I'm supposed to sit on whatever you might know or find out? Geez, I mean . . . I gave you a mint and everything." He leaned back in his chair and smiled.

"I didn't know what his occupation was or that he wrote for your paper until yesterday so I have nothing to trade."

He shrugged. "But now you do know and you're here, so what's the difference?"

There wasn't any, and I knew it. "None. So . . . ?"

"So, I'm not running the fucking *Atlanta Journal Constitution* here. If you've read us, you know that. They got all the goddamn money they need. I don't. Whatever sells papers, I do—within reason. Lintz worked for the *Chronicle*. Anything you come across related to his passing that makes for good ink should be printed here first, yes?"

I was in no position to argue. "Within limits."

"Limits. Everybody's got fucking limits. Okay, deal. But if you blow smoke up my ass, we're through. Got it?"

According to Gerard, Lintz hadn't been a putz during his first months as an investigative reporter with the paper. Putz came later—near the end.

"His early stuff was good, decent enough to sell a few extra papers and cause an uptick in our circulation. Later, he gets this hair up his ass about wanting more inches, like my telling him that his work isn't too shabby fertilizes his freakin' head. I hold him off. I tell him I got other reports I'm trying to keep happy too, ya know?

"Okay, so a few more weeks go by and he starts leaning on me again. I throttle him. We argue, but I win. He pushes it to the limit, but I got it in control. Then? Bam. The wife and I go to Europe. I get back and the shit's sticking to the walls in big brown lumps.

"He tells the associate editor I approved more space before I left. We'd discussed the *possibility*, but not the *when*. Now, I gotta save face. So I take back half the inches he stole which still gives the little prick more than what he had before. *Still* he's not satisfied."

"Why didn't he get fired for what he did?" I asked.

Gerard looked at me as though I were dim-witted. "We're talking press here, not Bloomingdale's. He's got readers—your basic political types. We got letters ten-to-one in favor of the stuff he writes. We're talking circulation on one hand, ad revenues on the other.

"So Lintz gets all pissed off and goes to the publisher. I get called in for a little *Come to Jesus, what-the–fuck's-this-all-about* meeting with the Old Man. Control him. Save him, he says. If I can't? Well, that's my problem. Anyway, so now with what happened to him, I don't have a problem anymore, right?"

"Before he was killed, how were things working out between the two of you?"

He unwrapped another mint with great study. "That's the thing. Couple a days before he gets nicked he apologizes for what he did while I was gone. Says he'd been having troubles with his *girl*, he calls her. *He* doesn't know that *I* know he's shacking up with the judge's daughter. Tells me he wasn't thinking straight. But now he's over it. Now, he says, he's working on something important—so whatthefuckandkissmyass huge that it's going to win him an award.

"But it wasn't sincere, the apology. More like a threat, you ask me. Like if I dinged him he'd take whatever he was working on across the street and I'd regret it, the little putz." Gerard sat back as if he'd been running on quarters and the meter had timed out.

"That's it?" I asked, breaking the silence.

"That's it. Next thing I hear, he's dead. Now, I got work to do. And, no, I didn't kill the little bastard or have someone else do it so if it's there, wipe it outta your head."

We exchanged cards at the top of the stairs. He fixed his eyes on mine. "Maybe you should talk with Zachary Rhetman," he said flatly, then walked back to his office.

I watched a young reporter light a cigarette and follow him into the glass cubicle then descended the stairs to the lobby. The treads were covered in hard green linoleum, scuffed and thinned as though the footfalls of those whose duty it was to gather and report the news of the day bore a heavy weight.

Could the heft of whatever story Lintz had been investigating been enough to bring him down?

I had several more questions for Gerry Gerard.

Five minutes, he'd said, and that's exactly what I'd gotten.

CHAPTER 5

A T FIRST, GETTING a same-day appointment with an
active judge of an appellate court seemed too easy; but
then I reasoned that Gerard would have called Rhetman's office
out of respect for whatever relationship existed between the
judge and the paper as soon as I'd left the building. He'd sent
me calling, and it's not nice to surprise those with high standing.

At one that afternoon I entered the Elbert P. Tuttle Building
on Forsyth Street, the home of the United States Court of
Appeals for the Eleventh Judicial Circuit. I cleared security
and was escorted to the offices of The Honorable Zachary L.
Rhetman, III.

After a ten minute wait I was shown to the Judge's chambers
by an officious, matronly woman whose humorless expression
looked as if it were ironed on her face.

I shook hands with the Judge who thanked his assistant and
closed the door behind her as she left. "Please," he said, "have
a seat, Mr. Royce. May I offer you some coffee, or a bottled
water, perhaps?"

"No sir, but thank you." I felt the force of his presence,
of his civility, my years of practiced discipline automatically
engaging decorum.

We sat on opposite sides of a large mahogany desk.
Matching wood paneling wrapped the room with the feeling of

warm, aged elegance. Sunlight washed in through tall arched windows that opened onto a central courtyard below and settled on accent pieces and photographs whose common theme was the game of golf.

"I appreciate your seeing me on such short notice, Your Honor. My apologies for the casual attire. I'm traveling light and hadn't anticipated the appointment."

"Quite alright," he said. "And please, let's dispense with the formality." He tented his fingers and touched them inquisitively to his chin. "It may interest you to know that no attorney outside of this court has ever been granted an invitation to my chambers, or that of any of the judges to the best of my knowledge. Only a few close friends and not many of those are allowed access to the inner sanctum. However, my daughter mentioned you at dinner last evening."

I was duly humbled and did my best to cover my surprise in learning that Holly had mentioned our encounter to her father. "Your daughter, sir, is . . . very nice. And I'm honored to be in a circuit court that has so much history to its credit—the Elian Gonzales case. Bush v. Gore."

He chuckled. "You're respectful. And studied. And, yes, Holly is quite . . . special." He leaned back in his chair. "Are you a married man, Mr. Royce?" His question seemed casual and unassuming but carried a protective tone.

"Not in the legal sense. But morally, I'm just as committed. Given what goes on in the world today, perhaps even more so."

"That's good to hear. Now then, how did you come to call me? And what interests you about my daughter and the late Raymond Lintz?"

"Lintz, sir. For starters, that he's dead," I said.

"I assume Holly shared with you her feelings about the man?"

"She did. To a point. I didn't probe."

"I take it then that you have a vested interest of some sort in Mr. Lintz's death?" the judge asked.

"I'm mindful, Judge, that we're both officers of the court. My being here is of a personal nature. For the record, as of this moment I represent no one associated with the Lintz murder in a legal capacity although that may soon change."

"Your candor is commendable, as is your regard for my position. So then, I'll view this conversation as informal chatter between colleagues although I'm not quite sure what there is of any substance that I can offer."

I eased back in my chair. "Your daughter mentioned that you were somewhat distrustful of Ray."

Rhetman considered my statement. "Naturally so—or for that matter, wary of *any*one in close contact with Holly whom I don't know well. It annoys her to no end. But as you say, she's very . . . nice. My daughter is also more than a bit over-trusting."

"I don't have a daughter. But if I did, I'm sure I'd feel the same. It seemed to me, though, that she felt there was something more specific that bothered you."

Rhetman picked up a golf ball from a miniature stand on his desk and tossed it slowly from hand to hand. "My solitary hole-in-one. An eight iron. One hundred and fifty-three yards. Elevated green. The shame of it is I never saw it go in," he said. "Do you play the game?"

"No sir, I don't."

"You should take it up. It's a gentleman's game and to my way of thinking the truest test of honesty. No one is there to look over your shoulder on every shot. Either you play by the rules, or you don't. There simply is no middle ground." He replaced the ball. "Young Raymond ignored the rules, Cage. He was not to be trusted when backs were turned. I'm afraid that some of what he wrote in his column found its roots as a result of my faulty judgment."

"In what way?" I asked.

"My error lay in the fact that I favored him with a round or two at my club. His game was solid and his banter and etiquette on the course generally appropriate," Rhetman said. "My partners enjoyed his company and so he was invited to play with us twice more. And later, by others."

"But you inferred that he cheated."

"Not on the course."

"I'm sorry, sir, but I'm not following you."

Judge Rhetman removed the prized ball from its stand once again. It was an act I envisioned his repeating several times a day. "There are *two* sets of rules in golf, Mr. Royce—those that are written, and those we accept and understand as fellows. The latter denotes Mr. Lintz' failing. What's said during the course of play, or more befitting the point, later in conversation over cards and cocktails in the clubhouse is expected to stay within the confines of the grounds. And mine, Counselor, is a very old club whose walls have absorbed countless stories. Many of which are quite true and perhaps damaging."

THE SUN WAS perched low on the horizon as the Delta jet cleared the runway in Atlanta and lifted into a deep blue sky devoid of clouds.

I ordered a vodka on the rocks then eased back in my seat and allowed my mind to sift free-form through the gathered intelligence of the past few hours.

Lintz was dead, but it seemed that nobody much cared— his legacy, a boss whom he'd made to look like a fool, one who dubbed him a putz; an influential judge and prominent patriarch marred by social embarrassment as Ray let indiscretion supplant trust courtesy of his investigative and opinionated writings; an ex-girlfriend whose face would command the pen of Shakespeare, but whose heart he'd let slip away without explanation.

I began to mentally assemble a list of questions and suppositions, to build hypotheses and construct theorems. But the combination of travel fatigue and the vodka did little to aid the cognitive process, and my thoughts became jumbled.

So I put my mind on hold and drifted upward where the air thinned and reason disconnected from consciousness—to a place where suddenly, *Holly appeared before me, naked, her terry cloth robe lying in soft folds around her ankles, her eyes fixed on a point over my shoulder. I turned to see the decomposing body of my brother Billy as he lay dead on a stainless steel table that spun slowly, as if he were on display for someone's morbid purpose.*

WHEN I DEPLANED at the Bay County Airport fifty minutes later, Jamie was waiting at security.

We detoured on the way to *The Hatch* and stopped at a local restaurant on Thomas Drive that, like a few others, had shunned the old tradition and reacted to the area's growing population by remaining open during the off-season.

As I picked over my dinner, I shared with Jamie what I'd learned in the last two days, but said almost nothing about Holly nor referenced my disturbing vision of my dead brother. It was uncomfortably strange, almost deceitful how I avoided both subjects.

I had a sense that Jamie felt the uneasiness in our conversation, but she let it pass.

THAT NIGHT THE blades of the ceiling fan turned slowly in the currents of cool air that seeped through the partially opened sliding glass doors of our third floor bedroom above *The Hatch*.

Below, waves broke on the shore, their misty spray illuminated with the cast of radium by a chalky moon set high overhead.

Next to me, Jamie slept, the white linen sheet resting lightly on the contours of her body.

Our sex had been long and slow. She'd clung to me, her legs and arms enfolding me, her hands drawing me into the deepest part of her as though she sensed a challenge to our relationship, or a coming separation and perhaps felt a need to protect us from it.

More probably, the thought was of my own making. Residual guilt for stunting the conversation at dinner and failing at full disclosure.

In half-sleep, I reached for Jamie, splayed my hand across the small of her back and watched strangely from a dream-state as I measured the reality of our existence and the depths of our bond in the rise and fall of her rhythmic breathing.

CHAPTER 6

JAMIE SHOOK ME awake, holding the portable phone extended toward me as though it were burning her hand, the blanket pulled high around her neck to ward off the cold air that filled our bedroom like frozen breath.

I'd been watching a faceless Ray Lintz hit golf balls at Judge Rhetman who stood bound to the oak tree in front of his daughter's house while she knelt at his feet collecting the dimpled white orbs, dropping them into a canvas bag as they'd first thudded into his body, then fell to the ground covered in blood.

"It's Brian, hon," Jamie said. "Something's wrong."

I spoke into the receiver. "What's up?"

"He's gone," Brian said. A simple statement of fact that brought me fully awake.

It was just past seven. "What the hell happened?"

"I checked him out of the hospital an hour ago. He seemed fine. The next thing I know, he's coming up the passageway with his duffel bag. Said he couldn't go back out on the Gulf. He's heading for the Beach—hitched a ride over to Tampa with one of the marina mechanics. Said he'd catch a Greyhound back home from there."

***

ALERTED LUKE, THREW on jeans and a sweater and twenty minutes later parked in the alleyway behind Carey, Royce & Associates.

Our law offices occupy what had been Luke and LuAnn's first house—a one-story cinderblock building tucked in among the T-Shirt shops, tattoo parlors and daiquiri bars on Front Beach Road across from the Gulf of Mexico that, in the light breeze of a sunlit morning, had taken on the look of shattered glass.

Luke and Wes were already there. I poured a half-cup of reheated coffee and propped a haunch on a low bookcase in the conference room. "Now what, gentleman? Put him on a plane to China?"

"It's on the wire," Wes said. "Big Hope cops got a bench warrant for his arrest on suspicion of murder, 'though of course we're not supposed to know that until they grab him and he calls us. But that's not the worst of it."

"Then just what the hell is?" I asked.

WHILE I'D BEEN in Atlanta, Wes had done his homework—the subject, Big Hope, Alabama, a speck of a place with a couple of thousand full-time residents spread across a few square miles.

Statistics at the State Capitol in Montgomery showed the scant piece of real estate north of Lake Eufaula to be a jurisdiction with a nearly perfect record of conviction. It seemed that the accused had been found guilty in ninety percent of all court proceedings—not that it was the Nation's crime center: The court dockets catalogued a handful of assaults—the neighbor-on-neighbor variety—plus six counts of statutory rape, five of incest. The rest of it was standard issue misdemeanors comprised of drunken disorderlies, speeders, DUI's, and a smattering of petty thefts.

What had gotten Wes's attention were the three counts of murder within the past ten years. One: A wife who'd been charged with stabbing her husband to death in a domestic dispute. Two: A janitor who apparently caved in the head of a retired schoolteacher with a length of two-by-four. Three: A seventy year old veteran who allegedly blew away his eighty year old friend with a shotgun in a fit of anger over a game of Scrabble. All had pled not guilty.

"Same prosecutor, same judge, and Sheriff C.W. Vernon were involved with each complaint," Wes said.

"Three convictions?" I asked.

Wes stood and paced the room. "Hardly," he said, "and this is where things get interesting. All three died before they got to trial. The woman apparently had a heart attack. The janitor burned up on his jail bed—fell asleep with a cigarette stuck in his mouth. And the old vet slipped and fell in the shower. Cracked his head and died of a cerebral hemorrhage."

"And this, apparently, bothers no one?" I said.

"You're talking about a burg the size of a blister in a state infected with problems. Who's gonna care about three inmates dyin'?"

"Then it really adds up to six killings over ten years—seven, including Lintz," I said. "They were all townspeople. Maybe there's a connection."

"We know for a fact that Lintz wadn't a townie," Luke said. "That makes it a good bet he stuck his nose up the wrong hole."

"And Robby's the fall guy. This is just great," I said. "Any bright ideas up for consideration on what the hell we do now?"

Luke and Wes exchanged knowing looks.

"It might sound a little nuts to begin with," Wes said with a crooked grin, "but hear me out."

At first I thought Wes belonged in a padded cell, all safely locked up in a nice sanitarium somewhere, not in the jail he had in mind.

"Robby can't be there on his own," Wes said. "We need to snoop that place from the inside. My bein' there is the best way to do it. Hell, it's the only way."

"And what about Tisha and the kids?" I asked. "They don't mind Daddy taking a jailhouse vacation?"

"Part of the job, Cage. It's what y'all pay me for."

"That's not the point," I said. "I'm talking about your safety here, Chief."

"I appreciate that. But Robby needs us—badly. The way I've got it planned, nobody will find out who I am. And I'll be pullin' maybe ten days, tops."

I didn't like the idea. But Wes was right. Robby was in serious trouble. "Then let's hope a few days is time enough."

CHAPTER 7

ROBBY'S TRAILER HAD been placed under twenty-four hour surveillance. If he made it back to the Beach before we able to intercept him, he'd wind up sitting in the Bay County lockup before daybreak awaiting extradition to Alabama.

A call to check on bus schedules provided departure times from Tampa to Panama City. The bus Robby would most likely catch was scheduled to make a stop in Tallahassee early that evening.

We left for Florida's Capital at three and headed north on Route 79 where we connected with the Interstate at Bonifay.

Luke cracked his window and lit up, the smoke drawn out through the narrow opening as if being peeled away from his words as he spoke. "I can hear the gears meshin'. What's on your mind, Cage?"

"Jamie doesn't buy it. We got into it after Brian called."

He shook his head slowly. "Okay, so let me hear it."

I'D BOLTED FROM the bed and hit the shower. Jamie came into the bathroom, her arms crossed in front of her, a predictable signal that she intended to drive home a point.

"He's running, Cage."

"He's on his way here. How can you label that running?" I said through the spray of water.

"Then what's the big hurry in sending out the call to the Three Musketeers?"

I stepped from beneath the stream of water and glared at her. "Don't."

"Why not say it. It's the same thing you're thinking, isn't it. He takes the bus to Tallahassee—maybe—and then, who knows where he's headed after that?"

"You're wrong. That is *not* what I'm thinking," I said.

"And if he's on the bus? You'll encourage him to turn himself in?"

I shut off the water. "I can't answer that."

She tossed me a towel. "You helped him elude the police once already. You're a *lawyer*, for God's sake. Doesn't that mean anything to you anymore?"

"Of course it does. Only . . . it's different now."

"Since Billy, you mean. Since you met Luke. And since we hired Wes."

I threw the towel on the bed. "Goddamn it, Jamie, I'm my own man."

She looked at me. "Okay. So that was a cheap shot and I'm sorry. But when you and Luke and Wes got together and we set up the fund in Billy's name, I thought . . . ."

"That we'd be getting back at your father by using his own money—by writing checks off your trust and firing them off like bullets to help nail the bad guys. And what else? That we'd go skipping along in the fucking sand and live happily ever after? I'm trying. But sometimes it gets personal."

"Yeah, I know." She sat on the edge of the bed. "Like finding out my real father's a terrible person. A real live criminal. But, damn it to hell, Cage, I haven't let it change who I am."

"Good for you, kiddo. I'm glad," I snapped. "Just don't expect the same from me. You'll be disappointed."

L UKE TAMPED OUT his cigarette. "Wesley and I'll handle this on our own if that's what's right for you and Jamie."

"This isn't *about* Jamie," I said. "No, this is fine with me. It's what we set out to do. To nudge the rules a little and help weed out the scum."

"Truth is, it might be more than a little."

"It was with Billy. And you and Wes stood by me all the way."

"You don't owe either of us a—"

"Drop it, okay? Let's see what we can do to help Buddy's kid."

T HE SUN SAT low in the five-o'clock sky looking as if it might come to rest on the wide pavement of Tennessee Street, then roll down the gentle slope of the boulevard and stop at the foot of the small hill near the entrance to the Tallahassee Bus Terminal where we'd parked.

I bought two Cokes from a vending machine and joined Luke in the passenger waiting area where he sat thumbing through a second-hand copy of *USA TODAY*.

"Cliff Notes for the Millennium," he said, shaking his head as he put the paper down. "Like CNN. It's all headlines. Mostly doom and gloom with no real context or substance."

"Unlike the *New York Times*, or CBS?" I said.

"No. Unlike the *St. Petersburg Times*, or PBS," Luke countered.

"There's nothing like diversity of opinion to stimulate the Populous."

"Oh, sure. Then I 'spose we could all read the *Atlanta Daily Chronicle* for our morning ration of intelligence. That'd enlighten the masses and make the world a better place, now wouldn't it? Or maybe spend the better part of our lives online eatin' up the crap that the bloggers dish out."

"Things change, Luke. I'm not saying it's right, but you can't stop progress."

"I'll be goddamned if you call what's happened to newspapers 'progress.'"

There are certain things I'd learned not to argue about with Luke, so I let it pass.

He picked the paper back up and hid his face behind it, waited a ten count and got up and made a show of throwing it in the trash.

"Sports section is pretty good," I said.

The bus from Tampa pulled in a few minutes behind schedule. Luke and I both glued our eyes to the door as it swung open and a line of passengers disembarked and gathered around the cargo bays waiting for their baggage to be unloaded.

Robby stepped off the bus a moment later and came into the terminal, looked around and then headed for the men's room.

When he came out, we were waiting.

"Shoulda figured. Okay. Let me grab my bag." He dashed across the pavement and re-boarded the bus.

Two uniformed officers appeared from nowhere and climbed the steps behind him.

A minute later, Robby was led off the bus and to a waiting patrol car in handcuffs.

"Hospital, probably. Or might be he paid for his damn bus ticket with a credit card," Luke said. "Hell, we couldn't a' kept him on the run much longer, anyway. He'd a had to go in sooner or later."

We headed west on Tennessee Street and picked up Interstate 10 a few miles later.

I called Wes on my cell and brought him up to date on Robby's arrest.

"Okay. I'll find out where they plan to park him," he said. "I'm pretty well set here, anyway. I suppose I coulda' used a day or so extra, but I can go in by tomorrow and it'll be alright."

Given what he'd learned about the law and how inmates had a habit of meeting with unfortunate accidents before they went to trial, Wes planned to be jailed in Big Hope on a misdemeanor charge—a drunk and disorderly that carried a few days' sentence at the most. He'd arranged for a bogus identity and would enter Big Hope County as Maurice Pickett, a dullard, an unemployed auto detailer from Bartow, Florida, hitchhiking his way to Atlanta in search of a job with only a few dollars in his pocket which meant that he'd be unable to pay a fine in lieu of jail time.

Once inside, he'd become the perfect prisoner—contrite, friendly, ready to please—establish a rapport with his jailers and fellow inmates, keep his eyes and ears open and relay to us anything that might be of use in planning a defense for Robby; or, we hoped, in finding out who'd really killed Lintz.

WE SWUNG DOWN the alleyway and parked behind the office a little before eight in the evening. The wind had picked up and the sound of waves breaking on the shore carried across the street on air flavored with salt.

Wes was on the phone as we came into the conference room. He finished his conversation and sat down at the table. "That was Tallahassee. They're shippin' Robby back here at the request of the Big Hope Sheriff's Department. He'll be in the Beach lock-up in a couple hours."

"Might as well hit *The Hatch* and get some chow and kill some time," Luke said.

"I'll buy," I said.

"Count me out," Wes said. "Tisha's holdin' dinner for me."

"Not a last meal, I hope," Luke said, a big grin on his face.

"Shut up, Luke, will ya? I'll pick you two thugs up about ten-fifteen."

***

WES SWITCHED OFF his lights and pulled in behind the Panama City Beach Police Station at ten-thirty. Robby was in the house. The new chief was home in bed. The duty officer was a friend of Wesley's. Another break of the rules would go unmentioned.

"I never thought you could lose a tan as good as yours in only a couple of days," Wes said to Robby as we walked into the office.

"Try pukin' your guts into the drink all day. But what the hell, thirty years on a road gang and I'll be darker'n you," Robby said, his humor a thin cover for the fear he must have been feeling.

Wes sat down behind his old desk and looked up at the ceiling.

"That's not in your future. Not if we can help it," I said.

"Anyways, I'd just as soon get on with it," Robby said. "I already told them that I wouldn't fight that . . . whatchacallit?"

Luke picked at a finger nail. "Extradition. They'll come get ya in the mornin'."

We sat quietly for a time, Luke finally breaking the silence as he sketched an outline of Wes's planned incarceration.

"Y'all 'er crazy," Robby said. But, he was smiling.

We drove back to the office. Wes had some details that would need to be expedited—one having to do with building a profile for the fictitious Maurice Pickett in the Florida DMV's main frame.

Luke and I worked a schedule with Wes for the next day, then walked out back. A mist had settled on our vehicles. Luke drew a finger down the hood of his truck and held it up as if he expected to see blood. "Lead counsel's shapin' up. Got a decent referral outta Eufaula."

I opened the door of my Landcruiser. "The way things are stacked, does it really matter *who* we get to defend Robby?"

Luke lit a cigarette and leaned against the fender of his pickup. The wind had died and smoke gathered like fog around his head. "I've seen things happen to the human body when it takes a hit that you can't imagine. The image and the name stays with you awhile, then you tend to find a way to erase it. But I keep thinkin' about Robby's daddy—most honest, hard workin' sonofabitch I ever knew. Never deserved his fate. Buddy was a square-up soldier and human bein'. Watched Robby grow up from a wheel chair. Raised him hisself when his momma cut out." He let his cigarette fall to the pavement where he crushed it under a hiking boot. "Yeah, partner, it matters. It matters so fucking bad it hurts."

CHAPTER 8

W E REACHED THE outskirts of Big Hope County at one in the afternoon. Wes—aka Maurice Pickett—had taken on the appearance and redolence of a down-on-his-luck drunk. He'd dirtied his stubbled face with a swipe of road grime, ground grit into his denim coveralls and consumed enough Jack Daniels to produce a sweet-bourbon odor that tainted the air inside my SUV.

I pulled onto the shoulder of Route 431 a hundred yards short of the truck stop where Robby said he often stopped for gas and coffee on his way to Atlanta and gradually slowed to a stop.

Wes opened his door and stepped out. "Whatever happens, stay cool."

"Good Luck, Wesley," Luke said. "We got your back."

"No, you don't. You can't. But I appreciate the thought just the same."

We drove on ahead, parked the SUV in the dirt lot out front then went in and took a booth near the lunch counter in the truck stop's restaurant.

A bubbly waitress with teased blond hair and too much makeup set rolled up flatware in front of us on the table and handed us plastic-covered menus. "Whatcha havin'?"

We looked over the choices, then gave her our order.

"Up in a jiffy," she said, then padded off.

I expended some nervous energy cleaning my fork on the paper napkin.

"You know," Luke noted, "they say if you don't let a few germs into your gullet now and again, it screws up your immune system—weakens it so it can't fight off bacteria and viruses and such."

"Is that right?" I said, giving the tines a final inspection.

"It's why so many kids can't fight off the common cold— why antibiotic drugs stop workin'."

"Not to worry, doc. We'll just alter their DNA and it won't matter anymore."

Luke glared at me. "Don't get me started on that, partner."

"A race of infection-free super-kids running around without defect or blemish. The—"

That was when Wes came through the door and sat down heavily at the lunch counter.

The same moment that it struck me that there were no other blacks in the place.

For several minutes, Wes was ignored. No menu or dirty flatware were set on the counter in front of him. It was as if he were invisible.

"Get me some hep over here?" he asked at length, his request directed at an obese woman who busied herself rearranging glasses and plates with no apparent purpose.

She stopped what she was doing and walked down the counter in a huff and stood opposite Wes, her stubby hands set on wide hips. "The only *help* you're gonna get around here is out the door, mister."

Wes swayed slightly on the stool. "There a problem. ma'am?" He made a show of looking around the restaurant. "It ain't that y'all 'er sold out." Then, "Oh . . . I *see*. Well my good woman, that don't matter none to me. I need to eat, and this is the place I'm gonna do jus' that."

"I don't care on Aunt Jemima's cane what you think you see," the waitress said. "What *I* see is that you're stone-ass drunk. And I don't serve drunks in my place—black, white, or purple—'specially one the size of a bear gonna bring on nothin' but trouble. Now . . . head on out that door, and be on your way."

Wes didn't budge. "I b'leve I'll have the special of the day, long as it don't cost no mo' than . . . let me see here . . . ." He fumbled with a wad of papers and money he'd extracted from his pocket and laid a five and three ones on the counter. "No mo' than eight dollars."

The woman fumed, the color rising in the sweaty folds of her fat neck and spreading in pink splotches across her bloated cheeks. "Mister, if'n you ain't gone from my place by the time I get back from the kitchen, it ain't my problem no more." With that, she pushed her way through the double doors and disappeared.

Wes stayed put, money spread out on the counter in front of him like a birthright, hands tucked between his knees, shoulders hunched.

I saw movement to my left and realized with a sinking feeling what was about to happen.

Luke narrowed his eyes at me across the table. "Let it be," he said quietly.

Two men moved to sit on either side of Wes, their bellies hanging over their belts. Both were dressed in denim work shirts and baseball caps, the bills dark-stained and oily.

The one to Wes's right said something.

Wes reacted by swiveling his stool around to face him.

That's when it happened.

The man he was facing shoved Wes in the chest, causing him to lose his balance and fall against the one who was now at his back and who slipped a forearm around his neck.

The man in front jumped to his feet and swung at Wes's jaw. Only it was more than a fist: I heard the smack of the weighted leather as the sap connected with the side of Wesley's face.

Wes shook his head clear and kicked his attacker in the kneecap, then rolled off the stool taking the other man to the floor where he caught him in the head with an elbow.

Blood flowed freely from the man's nostrils as he covered his face with his hands.

There was a squeal of tires in the parking lot. Seconds later a pair of young police officers moved in to break up the fracas. They separated Wes from the other two men; one officer ordered him to remain splayed face down on the floor while the other led Wes's limping and bleeding adversaries to a nearby table.

The fat lady came out of the kitchen a moment later with a smirk stitched smugly on her face as though she'd known what would happen in the minutes before the police responded to her call, and took pleasure in its aftermath.

The officer who'd been talking to the men who'd attacked Wes addressed the restaurant's sparse patrons. "The way it looks, the gentleman on the floor started it. That the way y'all saw things?"

"That's it. Yessir, that nigger sucker punched Coy." The voice came from the rear of the room.

"Thank you kindly, Dooley. That'll do just fine." He turned to his partner. "Read him his rights and let's get his sorry ass out of here. Coy says he wants to press charges on him for bustin' his honker."

Wes was pulled roughly to his feet and handcuffed. The officer repeated Miranda from memory then guided his prisoner to the door.

As he passed us, I could see the swelling in Wes's jaw and the stream of blood that ran from the corner of his mouth, down his neck and beneath his coveralls.

He caught my eye long enough to wink, then spit out little pieces of broken teeth that pinged off the glass door like BB's on marble.

CHAPTER 9

RACIAL EXPLETIVES PUNCTUATED the loud conversation that filled the truck stop's restaurant following Wes's arrest. The man named Coy pressed a handkerchief to his bloodied beak and slapped high-fives with the other men.

Tammy, our cherubic young waitress, came by the table with iced tea and refilled our glasses. "How 'bout some dessert?"

"Good as that barbecue pork was? We've got no room for it," Luke said.

"Momma cooks it up, don't she?" Tammy said brightly as she tore our bill off her order pad, set it on the table and began clearing dishes. "Y'all can pay me, or pay up front when y'all are ready."

"I feel like we oughta leave somethin' extra for the side show," Luke said. "That boy the town drunk, is he?"

"You mean that nigger fella? Never seen him before," Tammy said. " 'Course, we don't get many colored in here."

"Busted that fella's nose pretty good," Luke said.

Tammy added the last plate to the dishes stacked in a line on her forearm. "Tell you what. That spook's got any sense, he'll do his time and haul clean on to Canada—don't care how mean he is." She tapped her temple. "Coy's not right."

"Wind up in jail for a spell, will he?" Luke asked.

"You betcha. Sure as Christ was on the cross. County'll work him on the road for a month or two—hard enough so's he'll know he earned his keep and don't fancy comin' back. And that's fine by me. They give me the creeps. 'Specially the really black ones. What I think is, the deeper color means they's the worst of the lot."

"Truth be told." Luke had opened a fresh pack of cigarettes as Tammy explained her theory on how evil and pigmentation were linked. He paused for a second to light up. "Might be it was one a' his kind kilt that white boy a week or so back."

Tammy leaned in close, having found kinship with Luke. "You'd think so, wouldn't ya? But Randy—that's the taller of them two deputies was just in here, the handsome one?—he says they know who did it. Some white boy from Florida. Says it was a sissy fight." A blush rose in her cheeks.

"You don't say? Randy . . . he's your boyfriend, that right?"

Tammy's painted lips broke into a wide smile. "Now, how'd you know that?"

"Well," Luke said, "girl pretty as you's got to have caught the prize. And not just anybody's gonna know about the details of a killin'—stuff like . . . well, like him bein' queer and all."

Tammy stifled a giggle. "Randy says . . . he says, 'Tammy darlin', I swear some rump ranger rode that boy hard enough so's I coulda drove my cruiser right on up the Butthole Tunnel.'" Her giggle intensified, threatening to upset the precarious balance of the dishes on her arm.

The woman behind the counter called to her sharply. "Tammy, girl?"

"Yes 'm?"

"You cut your flirtin' and get on to your other customers, hear?"

"Yes ma'am," she said, then turned back to us. "Momma's fixin' to pitch a fit, so I gotta move on. Nice to meet you both. Stop back, 'kay?"

"Same here," Luke said. "We'll do that. Stay safe, now."

I handed her a twenty and a ten. "The change is yours," I said.

"The pretty one here don't say much, does he," she said to Luke, "but there ain't nothin' wrong with his math." She stuck the nail-chewed fingers of her free hand into our iced tea glasses, then picked them up off the table and headed for the kitchen.

I CLIMBED BEHIND THE wheel of the Landcruiser and pulled the door shut with a thud.

Luke sat heavily in the passenger seat, then flipped the butt of his cigarette out the window. "We got us a minor concern, Cage."

"I'd say two months in jail for Wesley instead of a few days qualifies nicely—not to mention the tolerant attitude of the upstanding people of this fine community."

"Don't worry, partner. Wesley'll be able to handle himself. Meanwhile, back on out 'a here so Momma can't see the license plate."

I saw Tammy's rotund mother standing at the window. "That's what you get for chatting up her daughter." I shot backward across the lot, angling for the road. "Next thing you know, she'll be accusing you of hauling Tammy into the backseat of a fifty-seven Chevy with her uniform up around her neck."

I headed south.

Luke kept his eyes fixed on his side mirror.

"That little Tammy's a charmer, isn't she? The rest of them, too," I said. "Christ, I thought bigots that bad went out with Disco."

"You know better than that."

A half-mile later I passed a slow-moving log truck. When I checked my mirror before re-entering the southbound lane, I noticed that we had company and alerted Luke.

The police cruiser hung back several car lengths for the next quarter-mile.

"Randy and his buddy, most likely," Luke said. "Probably runnin' the plate right now."

A few hundred feet further on, the cruiser's red and blue strobe lights came on.

"So we've been up in Atlanta pricing restaurant equipment, if anybody asks," Luke said.

The police car was now on my bumper. Two short bursts of electronically produced siren signaled me to pull over.

As I came to a stop, the front doors of the cruiser opened. Two officers emerged. They put on their hats and walked abreast toward the back of the vehicle, then split up. I lowered my window.

Randy spoke from over my left shoulder. "License and insurance card, sir."

I produced the requested documents. "There a problem of some sort?"

He studied my license, giving the insurance card no more than a quick glance. "'Bama's full of problems, Mr. Royce. Headed back to Florida are you?" He framed himself squarely in the window then bent down to look across the front seat and give Luke the once-over.

My reflected face stretched comically across the lenses of his sunglasses. "That we are," I said brightly.

"Your partner there got some I.D. does he?"

Luke reached into his back pocket. He removed his license from his retrieved wallet, then reached across me and handed it to Officer Randy who looked at it closely.

"Mr. Carey, your driver's license has expired. Now, how 'bout that."

"Good thing I wadn't drivin' then, idn't it?" Luke said with a smile.

"Yes sir, it is." He rested his hands on the window track and looked straight at me—or that's what I imagined his eyes doing behind his Ray Bans. "Tell you the truth, I've had my fill of troubles with folks from Florida today."

"Sorry, Officer, I don't follow," I said.

Officer Randy stretched his lips wide and clacked his teeth together. "You don't, do ya? Well now, you was there, right? Saw that *colored* boy—the one that sucker punched Coy?"

"What about him?" I asked, all innocence.

"He's from Bartow." Randy was starting to look a bit piqued. "Bartow, Florida."

I addressed him by the name on the breast of his uniform. "How would I have known that, Officer . . . Becker?"

He ignored the question. "That is what happened, right?"

"What? That the . . . *Negro* started it? No, sir, matter of fact it's not," I said.

"That so?" Randy rocked on his heels, then squatted down to eye level and leaned in close to my face. "Maybe y'all want to come in and be a witness for him, then. Y'all wanna do that for that nigger fella, do ya?"

I smiled pleasantly. "What we'd like to do, Officer Becker, is be on our way. Frankly, neither one of us gives a particular shit about what happened. All I know is that the barbecue pork platter was the tits. I'll recommend it to all the boys back home. Now, if you'd kindly explain why you stopped us . . . ?"

Becker stood up and adjusted his hat, then passed my license and the insurance card back through the open window. "Ya'll have a nice drive home, hear?"

Luke reclined his seat, his eyes closed. "He did everything except coil up and rattle his tail," he said when we were once again headed south.

"I hope he steers clear of Wes," I said.

Luke opened one eye and grinned. "He will, if he's got any smarts."

CHAPTER 10

W E WERE CLOSING in on Eufaula when my Blackberry chimed an incoming call.

"There's twenty of us in line for the phone," Wes said. "I've got exactly three minutes."

"Twenty prisoners?"

"Brothers. Blacks. Monkeys. Man, I was called everything in the book by the guards in the first five minutes inside. Anyway, I found out that they got Robby in a cell by himself and the rest of us locked up in threes. I haven't seen him, but there's talk about how we got a murderer in the house."

"We have a lawyer with a big reputation lined up. A guy named Russell Conklin. We'll get him up there as soon as possible. We're looking for his office right now. What about you? How's the jaw?"

"Swollen like a friggin' balloon—sore, but I don't think anything is broken. Good thing, or they might have sent me to a hospital. I go up before the judge tomorrow afternoon. I could be in for as much as sixty days. Listen, tell Tisha I'm fine. But don't mention my teeth, okay? Or the goddamn two months. I'll call her soon as I can."

"We'll see about Conklin getting you a good attorney. Maybe it'll speed—"

"I'm an indigent, Cage. They already assigned me half-ass defense—half in the bottle, half asleep. He's worthless, but in their eyes, so am I. Havin' Robert Shapiro wouldn't make any difference. Just take care of Robby. We get one hour three times a week for all of us. When the hour's up, the phone gets shut off so my gettin' to call out depends on where I am in line." I heard raised voices in the background. "Rest of the brothers are gettin' edgy."

"Keep your eyes open for Becker," I said with some urgency. "One of the cops that arrested you. He's—"

"Yeah. Got it. See ya."

The phone went dead.

CONKLIN'S LAW OFFICES were in a red brick house on a tree-lined street of historic homes. The plaque on the post set the date of construction as 1896. We climbed the steps of the veranda and opened a black-lacquered six-panel door with hand-tooled hardware.

The receptionist led us to a conference room with walls hung in old Civil War photographs. I studied the portraits of Rebel soldiers and officers while we waited for Robby's lawyer to make an appearance.

"I collect them for inspiration."

I turned from a picture of ragtag infantrymen gathered around a cannon as Conklin stepped into the room. He was tall, with Lincolnesque features and long fingers that felt like talons when I shook his hand.

"Flea markets, estate sales, Internet swaps. I'm always on the lookout for more. The fakes these days are very well done, so you have to be careful." Conklin folded himself into a chair at the head of the table. "Please, have a seat gentlemen." He referred to his notepad. "I was impressed with the research your office provided, but not encouraged. Still, like the Gray, I'm a formidable adversary. However, I'm not sure how much that means on a battlefield like Big Hope. We have no basis for a change of venue, and not much to offer on defense with the unlikely exception of a favorable ballistics report." He looked at us over the top of his reading glasses. "Barring that, the best we might hope for is murder two or three, then go for an appeal."

"For the record," Luke said, "Mr. Cain is innocent."

Conklin raised his heavy eyebrows. "Well now, of course he is."

"No. He *is*," Luke stated.

"Then . . . that makes this all the harder, doesn't it. I'll register this afternoon with the court and go see Mr. Cain first thing in the morning. What would you like me to tell him?"

"To have faith," Luke said. "That the South shall rise again. Only this time, we'll get it right."

I PULLED INTO THE private driveway alongside *The Hatch* at six-thirty, changed to jeans and a heavy sweater and joined Jamie at a table on the deck.

The sun was well down and a reddish flush glowed on the horizon.

One of our staff waiters appeared with a Ketel One on the rocks and set it in front of me.

"It's a bitch," I said after a good hit of vodka. "Hopeless if it goes to trial."

Jamie sipped on white wine. "But you won't quit."

"I think that's the point, Jamie. We can't."

Her gaze went out across the water. "Do what you think is right. I've done a lot of thinking on what you said about my expectations, and about not being disappointed. The truth is, I am."

"In me."

She ran a finger around the rim of her glass. "No, hon. Disappointed in myself. Too many years of dealing with hurting kids and dysfunctional families. I guess I want our little corner of the world to be idyllic. Not very realistic of me, is it."

"It's something to shoot for."

"Of all people, we should know better. You're right— neither of us could possibly have anticipated what happened to Billy or anything having to do with it. It can't be the same as it was. For you, or for me either. Not as people."

"Maybe not," I said. "But it doesn't have to change us— not what we have together."

She looked at me with a touch of sadness in her eyes. "It already has. And it will continue to. It means acceptance, Cage. We have to learn to live with the changes in each of us. I can't tell you how many times I've said that to a kid in therapy. Now I'm reminding myself." She lifted my hand to her lips. "There are lots of days when I don't like you, or parts of you as much as I did before. And plenty of days when I love you more than I ever have. My guess is that you have those days, too. And it's okay, you know? We can't be at the senior prom forever."

CONKLIN CALLED THE office at eleven the next morning. I buzzed Luke and he picked up on his extension.

"He's putting up a good front but he's afraid, as you might expect. I explained to him the need for you not to be seen in Big Hope until Mr. Harland is no longer incarcerated, thanks to Officer Becker having pulled you over."

"Does he need anything?" I asked.

"Hope," Conklin answered. "Other than that, he's being treated well."

"Has he seen Wes yet?"

Conklin blew out his breath into the phone. "Only briefly. But long enough to cause a potential problem, I'm sorry to say. He passed the cell on the way to the lawyer's conference room. He was startled by the swelling in Mr. Harland's face and began to speak to him without thinking. Mr. Harland cut him short with a comment about Mr. Cain being the killer everyone was talking about. The guard responded that Mr. Pickett might want to keep his black nose out of white business, so perhaps it worked."

"Let's hope they don't try and make a connection," I said.

"Any idea of the trial date?" Luke asked.

"Thirty days. Voir Dire begins in twenty-one. It's as long as the judge will give us. The prosecutor will forward his evidentiary findings and his list of witnesses to me shortly. They finished their search of his residence last night. They're supposedly waiting on the ballistic tests. The autopsy report on Lintz is available now. In short, they are quite eager to proceed." There was a measured silence. "I've spoken with Mr. Cain about the possibility of a plea to a lesser charge. It may well—"

"You did *what*?" I demanded.

"Mr. Cain is my client. My duty is to—"

"*Our* client, Mr. Conklin."

"Our client, then. But semantics won't spare him, Mr. Royce. He must be made aware of all his options, wouldn't you agree?"

Conklin was right, of course. "Don't you think you might have consulted with us first?"

Luke interceded. "Mr. Conklin, my partner and I appreciate your qualifications. I share Cage's frustration, but I'm sure you did what you thought best."

"Yes, I did. My apologies if my actions seemed exclusionary."

"What was Robby's response?" I asked in a more civil tone.

"I thought he might fire me on the spot. Mr. Cain will entertain no such option. It has to do with honor, he said. But he realizes his situation is bleak."

"We all do, Mr. Conklin," Luke said. "But he's a scrappy one—just like those Rebs a' yours."

"Yes he is. Scrappy—but like them, as well, not bulletproof."

CHAPTER 11

TEN CELLS LINED a narrow walkway in the bowels of the Big Hope County Jail—five on each side. At one end of the corridor a flight of stairs led up to the exercise yard; at the other, a guard was posted in a cage twenty-four hours a day.

Wes lay on his bunk studying the web of cracks in the peeling paint on the ceiling eighteen inches above his face.

He'd been given two month's duty with the Highway Department, as it was known by the black inmates who'd been its exclusive members over the years. White prisoners—and there weren't many—drew work details of a less strenuous nature cleaning the jail and the courthouse above, or washing patrol cars and picking up litter.

Inmate Pickett had been transported to his crew after his court appearance and spent the afternoon with a pickax tearing up asphalt on a county road that had washed out when Big Hope Creek breached its banks in heavy winter rains.

Wes was a strong man who took pride in his conditioning; even so, busting blacktop for hours on end without a break proved a test of his endurance. He needed sleep. But with his mind working overtime, it was slow in coming.

By one-thirty in the morning, he'd at last begun to drift off when the pattern of shadow on the ceiling suddenly disappeared. The cellblock was thrown into darkness. Wes knew that something wasn't right. Because jails were never totally without light.

He lowered himself silently to the floor and moved to the bars where he pressed his face against the cold steel and craned his neck to look up and down the corridor. Pale light painted the far end for a brief instant as the access door to the exercise yard had been opened, and then closed.

He reached under the stained sink and pulled free the small mirror that his cell mates had taped there and used to eyeball their buddies up and down the line. Wes stuck the mirror through the bars and angled it so that Robby's end of the corridor came into view.

In the ambient light he saw the dark forms of two men. One unlocked a cell door, then both stepped inside. His pulse raced as he held his breath, listening.

A minute passed in silence. Two.

No good could come of the silence. He could wait no longer to act.

Suddenly, Wes let out a chilling scream as he began to thrash about on the floor of the cell, slapping at his arms and shoulders. "Get 'em off me! The bugs! Sweet Jesus get 'em off a' me!"

His cell mates shot awake; Pickett was having some kind of seizure. They called out for help. In seconds, the whole block was yelling. Still, the corridor remained dark.

The duty officer dozing at his desk on the first floor heard the commotion and bolted down the stairs just as the lights blazed on and the guard came out of his cage.

The duty officer strode quickly down one side of the corridor shouting at the men to be quiet. The guard walked the other side doing the same, stopping at Pickett's cell when he saw him rolling around on the floor yelling.

He looked with contempt at the black man. "Shut up! All 'a ya!" he hollered. "Fucking drunk chucker's got the hibbie gibbies. Ain't no bugs on his sorry—"

"Rollie! Open up number ten! Do it now! Cain's hung himself with his bed sheet!"

The frantic directive froze Wes in mid-convulsion. His heart sank. Without thinking he sat bolt upright, then quickly dropped his chin to his chest and began to spew a line of gibberish as he realized his mistake.

The guard looked at him warily, then ran down the line to open cell ten.

The inmates' shouting stopped abruptly.

In the stillness, Wes picked out a few critical words exchanged by the guards. " . . . get him down!" " . . . know CPR?" ". . . not breathing!" ". . . fucking nine-one-one!"

WES REPLAYED TO me what had happened in rapid-fire Thursday evening from the payphone in the yard of the Big Hope county jail. "Took the EMT's from Eufaula twenty minutes to get here. He was unconscious when they wheeled him out. Cage, we gotta do something. It's just like the others."

I was badly shaken by the news. "We'll need security at the hospital," I said.

"Find someone from my files in the office, or have Conklin handle it. You and Luke gotta keep away. I may have blown my cover. Leave a light on someplace and let me know where. And not a word about this to Tisha, hear?"

"Wes, wait. I—"

"Time's up and I got enough trouble as it is." The phone buzzed, the connection broken.

I WORKED UP A heavy sweat in the chilled evening air stealing ashore like a night thief as I ran quickly along the beach to Luke's house.

I'd told Jamie in a brief, handful of words about Robby but said nothing of my concern for Wes. If I had, the next time she saw Tisha the guilt in knowing and not saying anything would be too much. She can't stand to lie—a good quality maybe, but not always convenient.

I took the stairs two at a time and slid open the glass door, interrupting dinner. Luke stopped a fork full of salad in midair.

"They got to him," I huffed.

He narrowed his eyes. "Robby?"

"In the middle of the night."

I filled in the blanks.

Luke reached for a cigarette, dinner forgotten. We walked out to the deck.

"Christ 'a Mighty, this thing's goin' further down the crapper by the hour."

"They'll draw a line between Wes and Robby. I'm sure of it."

Luke flipped his cigarette over the deck rail. "We'll leave the light on like he asked. Trust me, he *will* get out." I followed him back inside where he bent over the table and kissed LuAnn on the top of her auburn hair. "Gotta go. Sorry about dinner."

LuAnn is Luke's second wife—ten years younger than he—our legal assistant, a woman who puts up with the actions of the man she loves without question.

She rose from the table and gave me a hug. "Go take care of whatever's come up. From the way you look, I think I better say good luck."

"Let's hustle," Luke said, already halfway to the door. "We got calls to make and then some travelin' to do before the night's over."

I REACHED CONKLIN at home.

"I learned of his attempted suicide from the prosecutor just now," he said.

When I told him what Wes had witnessed, his thought that Robby had been dispirited enough to take his own life vanished.

"I'll take care of security."

"The police will be watching," I said. "We can't tip our hand."

"I have some good people in mind," Conklin assured me.

The next call went to Montgomery, Alabama— to the man Wes had used to dig into the records of the Big Hope court.

"I don't know," he said in response to my question regarding the whereabouts of the records of the three people who'd been charged with murder then died themselves, "but I'll find out."

"There might be nothing useful, but it's worth a try."

The final call went to an employee of the State of Florida, a connection of Wes's who'd set up the profile in the DMV mainframe for Maurice Pickett.

"You're asking a lot," he said. "A license is one thing, but—"

"His prints are on file" I said. "He was a cop. The state's got a whole dossier on him. If they run him and find out who he is, it's going to get ugly up there."

There was a brief moment of silent contemplation on the other end of the phone. "Tell him he owes me a box of Havanas. I'll wipe the file out then put it back when he gets home. On second thought, make it two boxes."

THE DUFFEL BAG in the bed of Luke's pickup held everything Wes might need once he'd bolted from the Big Hope County Jail: clothes, money, his legitimate driver's license, a cell phone, and a Smith and Wesson .38 service revolver.

As we drove toward Eufaula, I phoned Conklin again for an update on Robby's condition without telling him where we were, or where we were going. The less he knew, the fewer questions he'd be able to answer if things didn't go as Luke predicted.

"Mr. Cain's security is in place. He's in a coma. No one is willing to give me an indication of his chances for recovery. Too early, they say."

I saw a snapshot of Robby with tubes protruding from his body and monitors bleeping away. "What about his grandmother? Has she been notified?"

"No," Conklin replied. "I didn't see a need at this point. Not until we know more."

WE SCOUTED AN apartment complex on the northern edge of Eufaula, one that was shielded from route 431 by a stand of pine trees, then drove to the Hertz office.

It was after eleven when we returned to the apartment complex and I swung the rental into the darkened parking lot. I spotted a space at the far end and backed in close to the shrubbery, concealing the license plate from easy view. I got out and took the duffel bag from the back seat and tossed it into the trunk, then placed the keys in a magnetic holder that I affixed inside the right rear fender.

I kept to the shadows as I walked away, looking one last time at the rental, hoping that Wes would get the chance to use it, wondering what the odds were that he'd find a way out of the Big Hope County Jail, or that Robby Cain would survive the attempt on his young life and come out of his coma.

CHAPTER 12

SATURDAY MORNING WAS unseasonably cold. I got an armload of wood from the outside storage bin and built a fire in the great room before I went into the kitchen to make coffee.

Jamie came down from the third floor bedroom fifteen minutes later. She poured herself some coffee and sat on the couch next to me where I held a mug of my lousy brew in one hand and the phone in the other. Her green eyes were filled with sleep, her hair tangled and looking as though she'd been out in a gale.

"Hey, mister, haven't you forgotten something?" She let her robe fall open, exposing her nakedness as she wriggled herself in next to me. "Or are you too pooped. Must have been the middle of the night when you got in."

"Almost three," I said.

I set the phone and the mug of coffee on the end table.

Jamie looked at me. "Problem?"

"Sure," I said. "Lot's of them. Why?"

"Funny face, that's all. Anything I can do?" Her hand drifted to my thigh.

"I've got a call to make first," I said.

She straightened. "Either I've lost my touch, or it must be seriously important."

"Your touch is just fine." I smiled at her as I tousled her hair, adding to the thick black tangle. "Go grab a refill of coffee. This should only take a minute."

"How about I make a new pot?"

"Better yet," I said.

For a dollar or two or whatever the going rate was, Information happily provided the phone number for the Big Hope County Jail.

I'd decided that if the cops believed that Pickett had family interested in his well-being—people who knew where he was, and why—it might give them something to think about and slow them down and give Wes more time to find a way out.

My call was answered by a deeply drawn voice. "Sargent Stansville speakin.'"

"Ah . . . yas sir. I was . . . I was wonderin 'bout my brother Maurice? Maurice Pickett? See, he call me and says I need to come get him when he gets out. Only, I ain't so sure when that is."

My accent was pathetic—unintentionally insulting should the sargent happen to be an African American. But then I doubted that there were any black cops to be found in Big Hope.

Jamie listened as she came back into the room, looking at me oddly.

"Can y'all hep me wit dat?" I anticipated a bombardment of questions. None came.

"Pickett? Hold the phone." I heard Stansville whistling. "Pickett. Yeah. Got it right here. Looks like he was processed out at dawn. Early release. Good behavior. Guess you missed him."

I clicked off without another word and immediately speed-dialed Luke's number. LuAnn answered, and went out to the deck with the phone.

"Yo. What's up?"

"Wesley's been given an early release. That's the word I got from the duty officer at the jail."

Luke's sigh was long and deep and weary. "Whatever happened, it can't be good," he said.

The Hi-De-Ho's—or, *Highway Department Homeboys*, a name passed from man to man in the rotation of black inmates at The Big Hope County Jail—had the weekends off. Two days to lay around and shoot the shit, play basketball on the dirt half-court where the hoop had no net; forty-eight hours to walk the yard smoking cigarettes and brag on the women; time to set your back against the worn vinyl of a rickety weight bench and pump iron while flecks of rust from the corroded bar sifted down into your eyes and mouth.

Inmate Pickett would share none of these pleasures with his cell mates on this particular Saturday morning.

Pickett was sent to the yard at six a.m. A truck was waiting. It was one of the dented panel vans used to transport inmates out to their assigned road work. A flatbed trailer loaded with an air compressor and jackhammer unit had been attached to the frame hitch.

Deputy Becker stood by the rear doors of the boxy vehicle, a shotgun held on his shoulder, the barrel gripped in his left hand and pointing down to his spit-shined shoes.

As Pickett approached, Becker unlatched the rear double doors and motioned him inside. "Got a pothole to chop out and fill before church tomorrow. Reverend Harnell's missus busted a tire rim on it last evenin' on the way to choir and she's bitchin' up a storm."

Pickett dropped his chin in docile compliance as he climbed into the back of the van. It was a cell on wheels with benches for seats, mesh bolted over the painted-out windows and a solid metal divider set between the cargo area and the front seat.

Wes felt the shift on the springs as Becker dropped into the driver's seat—felt an internal weight suddenly settle on his lungs and heart, then explode in shards of energy as his mind raced and his muscles became charged with adrenaline. *This was it*, he thought. *Lord Almighty, here it comes.*

Fumes from the leaky exhaust permeated the small space and filled his nostrils as the van bounced and rattled out of the yard.

Wes sat in the near darkness calculating the time and route Becker was taking, relating each twist and turn in the road to the points of a mental compass.

After what felt like ten minutes, give or take, they came to a stop. Becker got out, but returned after a few seconds and climbed back in. Then, they were moving again.

When the van stopped some minutes later, Wes's mental map placed them a few miles southeast of the jail. Once more he felt the vehicle shift on its springs as Becker got out, then heard the tapping of some hard object against the length of the side panel as the deputy walked to the rear of the van.

Becker slipped the key in the lock, pulled open the door and retreated several steps with the shotgun leveled at the opening. "C'mon, let's get to it."

Wes had positioned himself on the bench against the forward partition. He stalled for time as he waited for his eyes to adjust to the light.

Becker barked his order again. "Now, goddamnit! This has royally fucked up my day off and I'm not wastin' my time standin' here waitin' on your lazy black ass. Now move it!"

"Cain't, boss," came Pickett's dull reply. "Leg iron's got itself stuck on the bench."

Becker took a cautious step toward the rear door. Pickett was no more than a black form in the depths of the interior. "Don't you get ideas. I'll fuck you up one side and down the other, you get smart with me."

Wes believed Becker had it in mind to do just that anyway. Luring the deputy into the shadowy small space was his best chance. "Ain't got no problem with you, boss. But you have to hep me."

Becker tossed the keys toward his prisoner. The ring skittered across the floor like a metallic spider. "It's the one with the square head on it. Unlock yourself then unbind them things and bring 'em on out with you so you can put them back on for the work detail."

Wes was running out of time. What if Becker got pissed and shot him where he sat? So he unlocked the shackles, rose from the bench seat and held them dangling by one end. If he had the chance, he'd swing the heavy iron at Becker's head.

But Becker was no dummy. He stood ten feet away as his man emerged into the sunshine, his shotgun pointed at the center of Pickett's chest. "That's far enough. Halt right there. Put 'em back on and toss the keys over to me. And do it underhand, boy."

Wes did as instructed, looking dutiful as he tossed the keys to Becker although every muscle fiber and strand of sinew in his body was on fire.

Wes unloaded the trailer, set up the equipment and got to work.

The noise of the jackhammer was deafening. Becker wore ear plugs, but not Inmate Pickett.

The pothole to be jacked out and filled sat at the bottom of a sharp rise in the road. *When* it would come, Wes couldn't be sure. But come, it would. His ears were useless in defense; his eyes by the nature of the work were cast downward, glued on the wide chisel that bounced on the concrete looking for purchase, his foot a careless split-second away from a piston stroke that would embed the metal blade in meat and bone and pulverize both.

Becker sat on a stump at the edge of Wes's limited field of vision a good thirty feet away, the shotgun cradled in his arms. Wes chanced repeated, quick looks at him by shifting his eyes without lifting his head. Each time he stole a glance, Becker's attention seemed fixed on the crest of the hill.

It went on like that for five minutes. Then, suddenly, Becker jumped to his feet, his eyes directed on the road above Wesley's back.

On instinct, Wes dropped the jackhammer, dove to his left and scrambled for the roadside ditch.

Becker swung the shotgun in his direction and fired off two rounds as the speeding car careened down the last few yards of pavement and over the pothole, striking the jackhammer and bursting the car's front left tire.

The driver lost control; the car slammed sideways into Becker and sent him flying through the air and into the trunk of large oak tree. He was dead before he fell to the earth ten feet below.

Wes got to his knees and peered over the edge of the road. He watched as the car rolled twice and smashed violently into a stand of pines, saw the driver fly headlong through the windshield and into the woods beyond.

In the stillness that followed, the vehicle ticked and hissed its mechanical death throes, finally falling silent.

At first, Wes thought the blood on his hands came from the scrapes and cuts he'd suffered as he hit the pavement and clawed his way into the ditch. Some was. But most of what trickled down his wrists stemmed from the spray of buckshot that had taken him on his upper arms and back.

He stood up and stripped off his shirt. A pattern of pock marks burned in his flesh. The pain was severe, but bearable.

He hobbled to where Becker lay on the ground, face down. Wes had seen worse, but Becker was a certifiable mess. The impact of the car had wracked Becker's body so badly that no single part appeared linked in a natural way to another. Wes bent down and slipped a hand into the front pocket of the deputy's pants, feeling for the keys he'd watched Becker stuff there, but instead felt the sharp shards of shattered bone.

Wes searched the area for five minutes hunting for the missing keys, then finally gave up and stumbled his way back to the jackhammer. The compressor was still running, and the hammer had survived the blow from the car; in sixty seconds Wes had the chains cut and the shackles off.

He walked along the road forty yards to where the car had crashed into the trees and come to rest. The man whose name was Coy lay dead on a bed of pine needles, his forehead smashed flat. Wes rifled his pockets and came away with thirty-three dollars and a handful of change, then went back to the car and tore off a dangling mirror and used it to examine the welts on his arms and back. It looked as if he'd been hit with a board full of nails. The blood flow had slowed. Nothing near fatal, he thought, but he'd need medical attention to stem the bleeding and ward off infection.

Wes reasoned that the brief stop Becker had made before reaching the killing ground was to set up the *Road Closed* sign that had been in the rack on the van's side that morning. Still, he couldn't chance any delay in moving on: When Becker failed to call in to say that Pickett was no longer a concern, somebody was bound to come looking.

He turned his prison-issue shirt inside out, then moved several yards into the woods where he paralleled the road for a mile before coming to an intersection where the trees abruptly ended.

Across the road lay acres of partially turned field. An old tractor with a canvas-enclosed cab sat alongside a telephone pole where Wes had emerged from the woods, plow blades attached to the rear. He could see the nearest farmhouse in the distance across the furrows to the south.

Wes removed the pin holding the plow blades, then hot wired the ignition with a quarter. Once he'd figured out the clutch and the gears, he drove the tractor through the shallow ditch at the side of the road and was on his way, heading east.

Two miles further on, he found an abandoned corner store. The small building was faded and shuttered. Attached to the side of the building was a battered payphone with half of a weather-beaten phone book tethered to it by a rusted chain. Not a chance, he thought. Not a prayer.

He dug in his pocket for the change he'd pilfered. In went a quarter. Up came a dial tone. A minor miracle. He dialed Luke's number, depositing the required amount when the operator asked.

The phone rang in Florida. Then, Luke was on the line.

***

WE SAT AT the inside bar at *The Hatch* at three o'clock that Saturday afternoon, Luke replaying the call.

"They were gonna process him out, alright," he said. "He'd 'a wound up in a hole in the ground somewhere in the bottom land. Now, he's on his own. They'll set up roadblocks all around Big Hope. Us gettin' stopped in one idn't advisable. So, we wait. He'll find his way and let us know."

"No. We need to do more than wait. We need to spend our time tracking Lintz's killer," I said.

"Back to Atlanta," Luke guessed.

"I think so. It's Gerard. Why did he push me in the direction of Judge Rhetman?"

And, I didn't add, *what the hell was it that had me so bothered about Holly?*

I RAN THE BEACH with Jamie early Monday morning, then threw some clothes and my shaving kit in a carry-on, drove to the Panama City airport and boarded a flight to Atlanta.

I sat on the propjet reading the morning paper, awaiting the instruction to turn off anything electronic. When it came, I retrieved my bag from the overhead compartment and grabbed my Blackberry to hit the off button. The little red light was blinking and the screen told me I had one missed call. It was from Luke. There was no voice message.

I hit SEND to automatically dial the last incoming number.

"Sir? The door is closed. You'll have to switch off your phone and buckle your seatbelt."

I nodded my understanding, but ignored the request.

"Sir, *now*, please."

I started to plead for an extra minute or two, then considered the wizened face of a humorless flight attendant whose severe eyes said there would be no appealing the instructions. I depressed the OFF button, feeling as I did like I'd clicked off a life-support system.

The starboard engine began to spool up. Then the port. The pilot adjusted the pitch on the props; they bit into the air and the plane began to move.

CHAPTER 13

I ENTERED THE TERMINAL in Atlanta with my Blackberry glued to my ear, exchanging random glances with several of my wireless brethren, but making no real eye contact. A modern day ritual. I was calling Luke, but there was no answer. I left a message.

Then it was down an endless corridor to the long descending escalator and onto the shuttle train that would whisk me underground for a mile and spit me out at the foot of an ascending escalator that would bring me up and into the crowded main terminal where I'd be directed by signage to the rental car counter.

One man in a pack of moles.

GERARD GLARED AT me from inside his glass cubical as he spoke with his secretary. After a few seconds, he strode out of his office.

"Some people do the courtesy of calling ahead. This is twice now, Mr. Royce."

"Cage."

"Yeah, I know—on your mother's side. So what is it *this* time?"

I smiled a friendly smile. "Oh, I had nothing better to do so I thought I'd just fly on up from Florida and stick my head in and say hello."

He looked up at me, cheeks red, peppermint on his breath. "Jesus Christ on a fucking mule. Alright. Five minutes." He spun on his heels and headed back toward his office.

I sat across from him at his gray metal desk. The ashtray overflowed with cigarette butts. I moved it aside. "What do you know about a little town north of Lake Eufaula, Alabama—a place called Big Hope?"

"What is this? . . . twenty-fucking-questions? Read the papers. It's where Lintz got dead."

"And a few other people over the last ten years," I said. "Three victims, and three murder trials that never happened."

"Yeah, so? What's it got to do with Lintz?"

I gave him the background on the other cases, then finished with the attempt on Robby's life.

Gerard shot forward. "And you got a witness to this?"

"A damn good one," I said.

"Who?"

"Not yet. We're still off the record."

He slammed his desk with a fist. "*Fuck* off the record! You got something, you share it."

"In time, Mr. Gerard," I said.

The squall passed. "It's Gerry. Mr. Gerard was my father."

"I know," I said. "He's dead."

Gerard issued a grunt. "So what more is it you think *I* can do?"

I shrugged. "You're the newspaper hump—said so yourself."

A virtual trip to the electronic newspaper morgue turned up nothing. What happened in the history of Big Hope was apparently of no concern to the *Atlanta Daily Chronicle*.

"No way that we transferred everything from microfilm to computer files," Gerard said as he clicked his mouse and exited the program. "I suppose you could try the *Eufaula Tribune*. Closest daily rag to Big Hope. Probably be a waste of time, though. Would have been a couple of lines if they bothered with it at all. And the deaths were spread out, you said."

"They were. But the judge was the same. So was the prosecutor. And the sheriff."

"Small town politics. Get in, and you're as good as elected for life. And they all got a hand on each other's ass. Buzz around the wrong carcass and you get blown out of the sky. Or you get nothing you can use. Funny how it works." Gerard stood up. "I got a meeting." He walked me to the door. "Find me something *I* can use, will ya?"

"Two other questions."

He looked impatient. "Which would be . . . ?"

"How did Lintz write?" I asked.

"On his fucking hands and knees, for all I know."

I ignored the quip. "Computer? Notepad?"

"Both. Here, it's a computer linked so we can edit and send it right to the press room."

"Then he might have left some sort of—"

"Forget it," Gerard said. "Before he got clipped, he wiped his hard drive clean. I told you, I think he was gonna take what he had across the street if I didn't give him what he wanted. The putz." He folded his arms across his chest. "Okay. That's one."

"How did you know Lintz and Holly were a couple if Lintz didn't tell you?"

"I'm a newspaper hump, remember?"

"Yeah? Then tell me what you know about the judge."

"That's three." With that, he closed the door in my face and went back to his desk.

Why did I have the feeling that the only item so far that was news to him was the attempt on Robby's life?

I SWUNG THE RENTAL onto the expressway heading north to Buckhead.

Holly's Jaguar was in the driveway. This time the ringing of her doorbell and my repeated knocks brought no response.

As I was about to give up and come back later, she jogged up the driveway outfitted in a bright red warm-up, matching headband and gloves. Her cheeks glowed from physical effort and the effect of the cold, drying air.

She beamed out a beacon of a smile as she slowed her pace and came toward me. "Hey, there! What brings *you* back so soon?"

"You know, just . . . ."

". . . In the neighborhood?" She took my hand. "Walk with we me while I cool down."

The traffic on Lake Forrest Drive flew by with absolutely no regard for the posted speed limit. We walked the edge of the pavement shoulder-to-shoulder, the wind from the passing cars whipping against us at regular intervals.

"Okay. So let's have it," she said.

"I'm sorry if I'm being a pain in the butt, but I wanted to ask—"

"Stop with the apologies. And ditch the guilt trip, okay? Do I have to spell it out? I'm single—not a bad catch. You're a hunk, and I think a nice guy. They could sell the babies we'd make for a zillion dollars apiece. If you asked me to go to bed, I'd jump at the chance. You might never leave, by the way. But you won't make a run at me. So that's the extent of it. All in your head. The big one, I mean. Did I leave anything out?"

I cracked a smile. "I think you covered it."

"Good. So stop being such a tight ass. You've got blood in your veins that heats up once in awhile. So, who doesn't?"

I thought about the first time I'd seen Jamie. "Guilty."

"Well, hallelujah! The man is human." We started walking briskly toward the house. "I'd love to walk and talk with you all day, but I'm gonna be late for my yoga class."

"I don't want to mess up your schedule, but I have a couple of questions that I'd like to—"

"Nope," she said, "not now. Tell you what, if you've got any more questions, the answers are gonna cost you dinner. Deal?"

"I don't know if that's the best—"

"Be a hero. I could use the company. I've been in a downer the last couple days. I don't know if it's because of what happened to Ray, or because I'm just . . alone again. I thought I was fine. Then I found some more of his stuff—some clothes, and a couple of those computer things—those memory sticks?—on the floor in the back of the closet and for some reason it set me off on a pity jag." She squeezed my hand. "Anyway, I promise I won't bite."

The mention of computer flash drives cinched it.

"Deal," I said. "You've got yourself a date."

She stood on tiptoe and hugged my neck. "Be here about seven?"

"Should I make reservations?"

"Nope, this is my town. I know the perfect place."

I checked into the same hotel where I'd stayed a few days before, flopped down on the bed and punched in the numbers for our condo.

When Jamie didn't answer, I left a voice mail telling her about my meeting with Gerard and my brief chat with Holly. I was going out to some of the local bars, I said, to ask around about Lintz. Probably be best if I called her in the morning.

I left out the part about my upcoming dinner, bothered as I hung up by the fact that I'd purposely made the exclusion. What the hell was I so afraid of?

While I was in Atlanta, Luke had decided to go to Big Hope, and called to tell me later that afternoon.

"I thought we decided to stay away?" I said.

"I got a problem leavin' my wounded in the field."

"Find out anything?"

"Yeah. The service for Becker's tomorrow afternoon. Paper calls it an unfortunate accident. I hope to hell we're not still on the hunt for Wesley by then, but if so, I'll see if I can't get to our Tammy girl while she's tore up over Becker and not thinkin'. Loan her a shoulder'n and see if I can't talk a thing or two out of her between tears."

"You're all heart. Speaking of shoulders, with any luck I'll have a couple of Lintz's memory sticks in hand by tonight."

"Do tell," Luke said.

"Dinner with a debutante. But I think she might be planning dessert for two. Not good."

"Don't let it get to you, partner," he said. "Play along if need be."

"I thought you were my friend."

"I am—Wesley's too. And Robby's. No disrespect to Jamie, mind you, but keep your sights on the end game. There's lives at stake here."

***

WHEN I PULLED into the driveway at seven, the Jaguar was nowhere in sight and the house was dark. Had she changed her mind? I felt relief; but that gave way quickly to sharp disappointment as I thought about the memory sticks.

I went up the short walk and knocked lightly on the front door expecting no response. When it opened, I knew I was in trouble.

The inside of the house was dappled in candlelight, the drapes drawn. At the heart of the living room a stone fireplace pulsed with beckoning flames.

And there stood Holly; she was absolutely stunning.

She touched my face with the tips of her fingers then stepped aside. "Come in, handsome. Let me take your coat."

I sat on the leather couch in front of the fireplace while Holly went to the wet bar to fix drinks for us, watched her as she crossed the room, the light of the candles marking her path, reflecting off the gold threads of her black Kimono like trailing fireflies.

She spoke softly as she put ice in two tumblers, added Ketel One to both and a thin slice of lemon to hers. "I hope this is okay—I mean, having dinner in. I don't get the chance that often. I didn't mean to go over the top. You know, the candles and all."

She came and sat next to me on the couch, unstrapped her heeled sandals and pulled her bare feet up beneath her. We touched glasses, then silently sipped the chilled vodka.

"This is really special," she said, a hand resting lightly on my shoulder. "Thanks for being here. I feel alive again. Like I'm wanted."

"Holly, I'm—"

She pressed her fingers against my lips. "Stop," she whispered. "Don't spoil the mood, okay?"

"What I was going to say was, thanks for thinking of this instead of our going out someplace."

That brought new light to her eyes. She took another sip of her drink, then rearranged herself so that there was some distance between us. "Dinner will be awhile yet, so let's get it over with. Go ahead and fire away whenever you're ready."

I sat there, not sure of what she meant.

She cocked her head. "The questions . . . ?"

Ah, yes. The questions. My sole reason for being here, right? "Sorry. I guess my mind was somewhere else. So. Let's . . . let's start with a guy—newspaper editor—Gerry Gerard? Do you know him?"

"Well, yeah—I mean, you know . . . Ray worked for him," Holly said.

"How about other than through Ray?"

She thought for a moment. "Sort of, I guess. Not well, I mean, but, yeah. I tried my hand at reporting for one of the local TV stations. They hired me on my looks. Anyway, I basically sucked at it but they didn't want to fire me. I think it was because of my dad. So they offered me a weekend weather job where I could smile pretty and giggle and not hurt anybody. I said, no thanks, so that was that. But I'd made friends—gotten to meet several other people in the business. This is a big media town. Lots of social stuff. Actually, that's how I met Ray."

"Right. At a party, I believe you told me."

"It was one of those no-host things for an anchor from the station where I used to work. He landed a great gig in Seattle. Gerard was there. He asked if I was maybe interested in print news. I couldn't decide if he was just chatting me up, or if he was being nice because of, you know, the family name, so I talked with him and said I'd think about it."

"Did he say anything to you about Ray? Did he mention him at all?"

She shifted her weight on the couch as if redirecting her energy from talking to thinking. "Well . . . I guess you could say he sort of . . . pointed him out to me. He said he'd just joined the paper and showed real promise. A few minutes later, I was talking to some friends at the bar. Ray came over to order a drink. He said, hi, and that he'd seen me talking to Gerard and was Gerard trying to hit on me. He said it as a joke, so I said, yeah, I think he's really cute and we're going away for the weekend. Then he said, too bad, because he, Ray, was going to ask me to go to Palm Springs with him for the winter. We laughed, and just sort of hit it off. The rest . . . well, you know the rest." She stirred her drink with a long, slender finger, then looked at me. "Gerard set me up with Ray. It's what you're thinking, isn't it?"

"Given your father's position? I'll admit that it crossed my mind," I said. "So did Ray's approach seem . . . staged to you at the time?"

She laughed self-consciously. "Afraid I'm not that deep. I just thought he was cute and sort of vulnerable. Knockout combination for a girl like me."

"So you dated, everything was going fine, then it began to sour. What exactly started it downhill?"

Holly held her glass between her palms as she drank, then lowered the heavy crystal as if memory had added to its weight. "I don't know, things sort of began to shift. What I mean is, Ray's vulnerability started to disappear. It was like, all of a sudden he didn't need me anymore— didn't care about me. He made me feel . . .insecure. I mean, we'd gotten really close. We'd lie in bed and cut up the snobs and the power brokers. Joke stuff. Laughs. Talk about some of the people he'd met at my dad's club. My family has a lot of history in this town, which means I know way more than I should.

"Then, one night, he didn't want to talk about that stuff anymore. Said he'd had enough—that people could get hurt. It was really weird—like I'd given him all the dirt he needed." A shadow moved over her eyes. "That's it, isn't it—why Gerard got him close to me."

I took her hand. "We can't know that for sure, but . . . it's a possibility."

Her eyes moistened. "What a fool I was."

"Not a fool, Holly," I said, "just trusting by nature. It can open you up to a world of hurt."

Moist eyes turned to tears, then to gentle sobs. Holly excused herself and left the room.

I went to the bar and poured myself a generous helping of booze on ice. Now what? A real hero, you are. But I had to get all I could.

"Mr. Royce?"

I was startled by the accented male voice behind me. I whipped around so quickly that half the vodka flew from my glass; clear ice bounced across the bar like crystal dice.

Eight feet away stood a young man in a crisp red jacket and dark pants. He had close-cropped black hair, Asian features, and a white towel draped over his left arm. In his right hand, he held an open bottle of wine. "Apologize. Not mean to cause you alarm. Ms. Rhetman say please sit for dinner."

My heart slowed to a mild trot.

With a courteous little bow he said, "Follow, please."

Whatever expression I carried on my face as I rounded the corner into the dining room was enough to send Holly into waves of laughter.

"Van, give us a few minutes, please?" she said.

Van held my chair, then quietly disappeared.

I sat to Holly's left. "You could have at least warned me," I said. "I didn't see any cars out front. I assumed we were alone."

"My fault, sweetie," she said, barely holding her laughter in check. "Van cooks and drives and whatever for Dad. I stole him for the evening."

"So the good judge knows that I'm dining with his daughter?" I asked, doubting his approval—although I didn't need it, did I?

"I keep certain things to myself. And Van's a bud—he won't say a word." She raised her wine glass; I did the same. "Here's to no more surprises."

Dinner was exceptional—the cuisine, Cantonese; the wine, superb—a spicy Oregon Pinot Noir that smoothed by the minute and complimented the flavors of the food perfectly.

We finished with sherry in the living room—an unneeded additive to the pronounced buzz I'd built.

Van appeared as if from the shadows. He stooped to stoke the fire then rose and turned to where we sat again on the couch—much closer than before. "If nothing more, Ms. Holly . . .?"

"Thank you, Van," she said warmly. "Everything was perfect. Have a nice night."

A nod to me, the same to Holly, and Van was gone.

Holly set her glass on the coffee table, then put her arms around my neck. "Now," she said, her lips brushing my ear, "now my beautiful man, we are finally alone."

She snuggled against me on the couch, her hands pillowed together under her cheek like a praying child. Her hair smelled of herbs; her breath floated up to touch my face with the sweetness of too much wine.

Without thought, I stroked her hair, feeling as I did that my hand belonged to someone else.

I was rapidly losing my equilibrium.

Some minutes later, I was, without consent or complaint, coaxed into her bedroom.

Holly stepped into my arms and kissed me, then loosened the fastenings of her silken wrappings and let them fall to the floor in a whisper.

I guided her toward the bed where she slid in between the sheets. "Be right back," I said.

I stood for a long time at the sink staring into the bathroom mirror at someone I vaguely recognized—a college kid who'd scored the winning touchdown and now had the chance to bed the homecoming queen. A face from the years before Jamie when Billy and I kept count of our conquests and compared notes.

This was wrong. I couldn't go through with it. There had to be some other way.

I returned to the bedroom and sat on the edge of the bed. Holly's back was to me. I stroked her bare shoulder and whispered her name.

There was no response. Her breathing was deep and patterned. She was asleep.

I was too liquored up to drive, briefly considered the discomfort of the couch then stripped to my shorts and lay on top of the covers next to her, pulling the bedspread over me, the sheet a barrier between us as thin as my drunken resolve.

I'd face the morning when it came.

For now, at least, I'd gotten a reprieve.

CHAPTER 14

I AWAKENED SLOWLY, FEELING drugged, *drifting through a place where I trudged up a steep mountainside, my body assaulted at every step with the limbs and branches of a flaming forest. With great resolve, I made my way to the plateau of a sun-filled meadow,* shook the dream, and opened my eyes.

Holly was no longer next to me; in her place lay an envelope embossed with the shape of her full mouth formed from the gloss of cherry-red lipstick. By its shape, I guessed what must be inside.

I opened the envelope and extracted two flash drives, then a single sheet of linen notepaper embossed with Holly's initials.

You must have been so fantastic that you knocked me out! Ha!

Sorry, handsome. But there's always next time!

I dressed in my day-old wardrobe, then walked down the hall to the kitchen where I heard her clanking dishes, led there by the smells of frying bacon and browning toast.

I was not the least bit hungry and without question, not ready to play house. I considered slinking out the front door and out of her life. But I was still by some measure a gentleman. I would face her with a smile.

Then I would slither out into the morning light and beat feet.

I rounded the corner into the kitchen working up a great big smile. "Good—" It's as far as I got. It wasn't Holly who worked at the stove; it was Van.

"Miss Holly gone. Ask for me make food," he said, his back to me. "Then you go."

I stood there, nonplussed. "Sorry? I don't understand. I'm sure she's—"

He whipped his head around. "No coming back to house." His words were hard as stone. "Has appointments. Miss Holly very busy lady."

It left me somewhere between confusion and contrition. I felt unwelcome, strangely apologetic. My annoyance with Van's attitude and my own reaction showed itself. "Fine," I said. "And you can shove the chow. I'll just go."

Van set the spoon he'd been using to stir eggs in an iron skillet down on the black granite countertop. The tendons in his narrow jaw stood out like wire. "You no come back," he hissed. "No bother Miss Holly again. Not ever come here again."

The flow of blood quickened in my veins. "I doubt if my being here *bothered* Miss Holly—not that it's any of your goddamn concern. And as for not coming back, I hadn't planned on it. So if that's what she said, you may tell her I won't ever—"

"Judge say, too."

That stopped me. "You told him that I was here?"

Van's eyes narrowed into fine pencil lines. "No matter. You go. Leave house."

"I'm sure Miss Holly will be happy to know that you broke her trust."

He took a step forward, knees flexed; a mean grin stretched across his lips. "Go home. Explain self," he said. "You stay, maybe have more you need explain."

It seemed the judge had armed Van with a tidbit or two from our conversation. Like my comment about my relationship with Jamie. Van was taunting me. But I was suddenly unsure of whether it was a physical response he was after, or if he was digging around for some kind of information. I decided to test him—to bluff him and push back on both fronts.

"Van, Van, the Little Man. Tough guy. More to explain? About what Miss Holly told me in the dead of night between moans and groan—?"

I felt it almost before I saw it coming. Van turned sideways; his leg kicked straight out like a lightening bolt, catching me square in the gut.

I'd had only a microsecond to ready for the impact, but it was enough to keep me from potential disaster. I grabbed his foot, pulling him off balance, then dropped my full body weight on top of him, pinning his arms and torso to the floor.

I outweighed him by perhaps eighty pounds; without the advantage of distance and leverage, his martial art was useless. His temper and predicament betrayed him. He glared up into my face. "She tell you nothing—nothing!"

But of course, he couldn't know that. I smiled down at him. "She lies, you know," I said. "She doesn't play fair. Miss Holly told me lots of interesting things."

His gaze suddenly flicked past my shoulder; the tension ran out of his body. But I wasn't about to be fooled.

"No you don't," I said.

To my astonishment, he began to cry. I couldn't believe it, not until I heard Holly's voice behind me.

"What are you *doing*?" she yelled. "Get off him!" And then she was on my back, pummeling me with her fists trying her best to bite into my flesh through my shirt.

I scrambled to my feet, one eye on the Karate Kid; I expected him to be on me in a heartbeat.

Instead, he scooted himself across the floor and into a corner where he cowered, his hands drawn over his head. "Please! No hit! No more hit Van!"

Holly spun toward me, an incredulous look in her eyes. "Proud of yourself?" she asked, and then slapped me hard across the face. "Just who the hell do you think you are?"

For the first time I noticed her running outfit. "What about you, Holly? Are you proud? Proud of having me tossed out on my ass without a word? 'Miss Holly very busy lady. Have many appointments,'" I scoffed.

Her nostrils flared. "What? What are you *talking* about? You were asleep so I went for a run. I come back, and you're beating up on Van. What's going on here?"

"Why don't you tell me?"

She searched my face with a look of confusion. "I ... I only wanted to make you feel special—the way you made *me* feel." Tears began to fill her eyes. "I thought I was doing something nice for you. That we could share something that was ... that was ...." The sobs came in gulping breaths; she ran to her bedroom and slammed the door.

I turned on Van. "Get up you little shit. What the hell are you trying to pull here?"

Van remained glued by his ass to the floor in the corner, cold eyes once again trained on me. "No hit Van. No more hit Van," he mocked.

In three steps, I towered over him. I pulled young Van the Man to his feet by the back of his collar. "Why don't you get the hell out of here before I kick a towel up your scrawny little ass. The lady is upset enough without having to watch me use you for a floor mop. Clear?"

I shoved him toward a small alcove where a French door opened onto the driveway at the rear of the house. Parked next to the garages sat a black Cadillac limousine, shining in the early morning sun like polished onyx.

Van went out without another word, opened the driver's door and reached inside.

He turned to look at me through the window, doffed a chauffeur's hat then feigned a series of quick jabs and punches, kicks and chops. When he was finished, he bowed his little bow, then gave me the finger.

As he got into the limo, I noted the vanity plate: JDG NOT 1

I had not anticipated a return to Holly's bedroom under any circumstance. But I couldn't simply walk out the door without attempting to unravel the morning's chaos.

She was wrapped in the terrycloth robe that she'd been wearing over her bikini the day I'd first met her. She had her hair bound up in a matching towel. The room was steamy and smelled of scented soap and herbal shampoo—of freshly showered woman. She was barefoot, her face untouched by makeup.

I was armed with all my defenses and all my senses, and with no need to ply her with my charming self to gain information. I had what I needed—what I'd come for—with a bonus from Van the Man.

Holly unraveled her terry turban and shook out her tangled hair. Without speaking, she handed me a wide-toothed comb, lowered the robe from her shoulders and sat down on the bench in front of her dressing table, straightening her back, her eyes closed.

Obediently and with a practiced skill, I started at the ends of each snarl of black rope and worked upward toward the crown of her head until her mane was groomed into smooth wet sheets that fell like a curtain across her back. Neither of us spoke as I worked, my thoughts of Jamie as I recounted the hundreds of times I'd done the same for her.

Holly's thoughts were her own.

When I finished, she opened her eyes and studied my face in the mirror. "What was it that happened in there with Van?" Her tone was anything but accusatory, her anger gone, the question asked as if she were looking for confirmation to an answer she already knew.

"If I tell you," I said to her reflection, "I'm not sure you'll believe me."

"Please. I want to know. I want the truth."

I sat down next to her. She leaned against me like a lost child as I explained what Van had said and done to antagonize me.

She laid a hand on my knee. "I don't think you'd lie, Cage. Really, I don't. I told you that he was a friend, didn't I."

"I recall that you did. A 'bud' I think it was."

"Maybe I'm the one who lied. Just a little. The truth is, he scares me."

I put an arm around her bare shoulders—a reflexive action. "Then why invite him along to play house boy?"

The corners of little-girl eyes peeked out from under wet hair. "More truth? I didn't ask him to be here. My father sent him over."

So she'd told the judge of our date after all.

"It sort of . . . slipped out. He called to see how I was doing—did I want to come over for dinner? I said I couldn't— that I had a date. He asked who with, and I couldn't think fast enough." She dropped her chin. "I thought that if you knew, it would spoil everything."

"It's okay. Don't worry about it."

"He wanted to know why you were here. Why you'd come to the house in the first place. He told me that he thought you were married. I told him you weren't, and that you were in town on business and just wanted to say hi. Anyway, I told Van he could stay until we finished dinner—that we were going out to a movie. I didn't want him around all night." She took my hand and kissed it lightly.

"Holly, look, you are one of the most desirable creatures on earth. But—"

She pulled away abruptly, stood up and tightened her robe. "Don't say it. Please. I think you should go. I'll be okay. It'll all work out for me. I know it will. I'll be fine. You'll see."

I put my hands on her shoulders and kissed the top of her head. "I know you will."

She stepped back and stared at me, her eyes hardened and fierce. Something told me that I wanted to be as far away from Holly at that moment as possible. And fast.

Almost as if she'd read my thoughts, she shoved me away. "Go on, then!" She screamed. "Get the fuck out of here! Go home to your girlfriend. Just . . . go away!"

I nearly bolted for the door.

I grabbed my coat from the hall closet—checking to be sure the flash drives were in my pocket where I'd put them earlier—and walked swiftly to the rental car.

From the house, I heard the sound of something shatter, an angry cry of effort, another crash and considered going back to make sure she was alright but quickly thought better of it.

What help could I be? Holly was having a serious meltdown, courtesy of one Cage Royce—self-proclaimed sleuth, protector of women, gentleman, advocate to the underdog.

I drove away feeling so goddamned proud of myself that I could hardly stand my own company.

CHAPTER 15

WHEN I RETURNED to my hotel room, the message light on the bedside phone was flashing. I realized then that I'd had my cell phone turned off since the prior evening and had failed to fire it up again this morning. What was more probable was that the old subconscious had hung the *Do Not Disturb* sign on the room in my cranium marked, *Loyalty*.

I had three messages: The first, from Jamie calling to say goodnight, knowing I'd be in late and wanting to leave me a long distance tuck-in to find when I returned from prowling the clubs; the second from Jamie as well, calling to say good morning, and ask, how did it go?; the third, again from Jamie, this time telling me that an hour ago she'd received a call from Conklin, the Alabama attorney we'd hired to sit first chair on Robby's case. It was a matter of some importance. She'd given him my number. Had I gotten his message? Love ya, babe, and call me when you can.

As I listened to Jamie's voice, I felt just swell about the prior evening. Just great.

My call to Conklin's office was taken by his assistant who put me on hold, then broke in several times over several minutes to apologize and to say that her boss really needed to speak with me and would be with me momentarily. What gradually became a mild annoyance might on another morning, with a clearer head, have foreshadowed the urgent nature of his call:

Robby was dead.

"It happened in the early morning hours," Conklin said, "peacefully, and naturally for what it's worth. And, as I learned while I had you so rudely on hold for all that time, it was apparently a blessing. His system simply . . . shut down. Had he managed to stay alive, he might have lingered for who knows how long in a totally vegetative state."

"I'd hardly describe his death as being *natural*, Mr. Conklin. Or have you forgotten what the hell put him in the hospital in the first place?"

"My apologies, sir. I realize how upset you must be. What I meant to imply, Mr. Royce, was that no one slipped into his room and—"

"Forget it," I said. "It's not your fault—any of it. He was a good kid at heart. He never deserved this. This whole thing sucks."

"As concise a description as any," Conklin said. "If you'd like, I can begin with the arrangements for you. For his grandmother, really. It seems she's his only living relative."

"We'll handle the notification."

Conklin was silent for a moment, then said, "It doesn't look as if an autopsy is planned. The sheriff's office in Big Hope expressed their regrets, and released the body. It's as simple as that. Case closed."

The lilt in his voice led me to believe that there was more to be said. "Mr. Conklin, is there an 'and' or a 'but' in that last statement?"

"Yes, I suppose there is. It would seem that the fine Hamlet of Big Hope has skated again. Unless, of course. . . ."

"Unless we go after them for Robby's murder."

"We do have a witness to what occurred in the jail who at one point was an officer of the law, isn't that so?"

I considered it. "Good luck establishing credibility after the ruse we pulled. And I seriously doubt that the court is even close to impartial. It would be a game of 'who do you trust.' No, I'd say the legal avenue is pretty much closed. We'll have to go at this another way."

Conklin cleared his throat. "I, of course, did not hear that last comment, Mr. Royce. But the truth is, I did. Therefore, I trust you understand that following the tying up of loose ends my association with you and Mr. Carey needs to . . . conclude."

"I do. Thanks for being onboard to this point."

"You're quite welcome, sir," he said. I was about to hang up when he added, "Oh . . . and good luck—to all of you. Give 'em hell, Yank."

I pictured him standing erect—saluting the Confederate Flag.

After I hung up with Conklin, I called Jamie.

She was clearly upset at hearing the news of Robby's death.

"This whole thing is a mess," I said. "You were right. I should have stayed the hell out of it. Maybe none of this would have happened. Maybe Robby would still be alive."

"You aren't making sense," she said in her patient, calming voice. "You were only trying to help, remember? And from what you've learned about that awful place, what chance if any would he have had without you?"

"Yeah? And a lot of good it did. And what about Wes? How did I let him do it? Allow him to put himself in that kind of jeopardy? We don't even know where he is, or if he's alive."

"Be concerned, yes, but blame yourself . . .?" she said. "Last time I checked, he was a grown man who makes his own decisions. Why are you beating yourself up and tossing me in to boot over things you can't control? Why so angry? Is . . . everything *else* okay?"

"Just ducky."

She waited a beat before responding. "When will you be home?"

"Soon . . . a few days. I really can't say."

"Find Wes. Then we can talk about it, okay? It's not your personal war."

"It is for Luke," I said. "And that makes it my war, too."

I SHOWERED UNTIL STEAM fogged the small bathroom, put on clean clothes and went down to the lobby for coffee.

I grabbed the morning edition of the *Atlanta Daily Chronicle* from the convenience shop near the front desk and flopped down with it in a cushy chair by a gas log fireplace—a setting meant to evoke a safe and cozy "home-away-from-home" feeling for the lonely traveler. For me, it failed miserably.

My Blackberry chirped and vibrated in my pocket. It was Luke.

"Yeah," he said in response to the message I'd left him, "I heard."

"Where exactly are you?" I asked.

"Sittin' in my truck on the main drag and about two minutes from seriously fucking somebody up."

"I thought you were going to stay out of sight?"

"I can't do dick about finding Wesley if I'm ducking behind bushes, now can I," Luke said.

"Count to ten, partner."

"Right."

"And before you ask, yes I have the flash drives, and no I haven't looked at the contents yet—but I'll find somewhere to do that—and no, nothing happened."

"None of my bidness if it did. But I'm sure you feel better about it. Anything else?"

I told him about Van, about Holly's mood swings and the tantrum she threw.

"Girl's got an air leak."

"I hope her father has some understanding on that front," I said.

Silence.

"Luke, stay cool."

"Sure. You bet."

***

IN HIS OFFICE in Eufala, Russell Conklin—having finished his conversation with Cage Royce—set down the receiver, hesitated a moment, then picked it up again and punched in a series of numbers.

The Cain boy was dead. That should have been the end of it.

But it wouldn't be. Royce had made that very clear.

The connection went through.

"We have a problem," Conklin said into the phone.

A question was posed.

"No," he replied. "I believe we can handle it from here. I'll keep you advised."

CHAPTER 16

I FLIPPED THROUGH THE *Atlanta Daily Chronicle*, killing time until I'd be able to reach the judge's assistant and set another appointment with His Honor—not that I was looking forward to facing Holly's father; but Van's behavior had my interest in Zachary Rhetman on the rise.

The *Chronicle*'s headlines and sub heads were bold and brassy, the day's top local stories ranked by numbers of vehicles involved, amounts of blood shed, numbers of people killed, size of the fire. Moving on to foreign battlefields, terrorist activities, ecological disasters and economic collapse. All the news that makes you want to go out and have great day.

As I turned the final page on world destruction and human carnage, I came to the Regional Section—presented in snippets of wire copy, cut and pasted without bylines.

I was about to chuck the paper aside when my eye caught a stacked headline, and a single column of copy that read:

MURDER SUSPECT DEAD
Hangs Self In Cell

Eufaula, AL--- A man charged in the recent slaying of Raymond Lintz, a reporter with the Atlanta Daily *Chronicle*, died last night in a Eufaula hospital of complications resulting from an attempted suicide.

Robert R. "Robby" Cain, 28, of Panama City Beach, Fl, had been arrested following the discovery of a body lying in a ditch along Route 431 in the town of Big Hope, AL, later identified by Holly Rhetman of Buckhead, Georgia, and girlfriend of the deceased, as that of Mr. Lintz, 34, the victim of a single gun shot wound.

Cain was discovered hanging in his cell in a noose fashioned from a bed sheet. He was described by Big Hope police officials as "deeply despondent" at the time of his arrest.

I wondered why the *Chronicle* wouldn't have given it more prominent play. Another question for Gerard.

But a call to the judge's office came first.

ZACHARY RHETMAN WAS understandably a busy man; it came as no surprise that he had no time to see me.

"We can schedule no further appointments today." His assistant was polite, but firm. "His docket is full. Court recess is at four, and then I'm afraid he must head straight to—"

"It's important. Can you try again? All I need is five minutes," I pleaded.

"One moment." I was placed on hold. Whether she was checking with the judge, counting to ten, or filing a nail, I couldn't tell. "I'm sorry," she said as she came back on the line. "Have a good day."

"We'll see just how good it might be later," I said to the deadened phone..

That moved a meeting with Gerard to the head of the list.

I booked another night at the inn, then ducked back to my room to place a call to Jamie in private.

"I need your help."

"I've been telling you that for a few years."

"Cute," I said. "What I need is as much information on a few names as you can get. Work with LuAnn from the computers at the office—do some searches, Google up some leads."

"Rhetman?" she guessed.

"Zachary L. number three. Right. And Holly, too—for the hell of it. Also, try Gerard and Lintz. Key in anything you can think of—newspaper, reporter, circuit court judges, Big Hope, Muhammad Ali, John the Baptist, whatever."

"I get it. Anything in particular you're after?"

"Damned if I know," I said.

"We'll do our best. And, Cage . . .?"

"Yeah?"

"I love you," she said, not words she tossed around often, or lightly.

"I know you do. Why that is, I can't figure out."

"Among other reasons, Saturday mornings. You're one behind."

"I'm a lot behind."

***

GERARD'S OFFICE WAS empty when I arrived. His secretary said he was in the press room.

"Point the way," I said.

I made my way around intersecting hallways, through a dented metal door, up three flights of stairs and into a gymnasium-sized room alive with clattering noise.

It took a few seconds to find Gerard. He stood by a two-story whirring machine with newsprint that whizzed by in a blur like an endless ribbon. He was talking to an elderly man who sat hunch-backed on a stool with a visor on his head and garters on his sleeves. It was like walking into an old black and white movie; the only things missing were the newspaper that came spinning toward you on the screen with the world-changing headline, followed by the young boy on the busy street corner in a tweed cap yelling, "Extra . . . Extra! Read all about it!"

Gerard saw me. His shoulders dropped as he walked over. "So I guess I should count on the next time I go to take a shit, you'll be there?"

"You never know," I said.

"I don't have time for this, okay? This place runs on fucking WD-40. I got money and roller problems up the ass. We're printing the Metro and the Obits early on account of—"

I cut him off. "So why didn't you put the story in the local section? Or maybe on the front page?"

Gerard looked at me, confused. "What story? What front page?" he asked over the din of the presses.

"Robby Cain was charged with killing your reporter. Now they're both dead. That's not big enough news to run somewhere other than the bottom of the Regional Section? Not important enough for your own people to write it?"

He paled. "Cain is *dead*?"

"He died early this morning," I said.

Gerard took me by the arm and walked me through the door to the relative quiet of the stairwell. He looked confused. A bit lost. "I didn't know. Must have come in on the night wire. Didn't . . . didn't even know that it ran in our rag."

I studied him. "But, then, I never mentioned his name to you, did I."

"No, you didn't. But I . . . followed the story—you know, that he'd been locked up on the murder and figured he was your guy, right?"

"If you say so, Gerry."

Gerard frowned at me. "Look, Mr. Royce, I—"

"Cage," I corrected.

"Yeah, fine. Anyway, I'm done with this. Story over. Sorry about this friend of yours—client, whatever. Shit happens." He opened the door to the press room, stepped inside and closed it in my face before I could speak. He looked at me for a moment through the little window made of glass and chicken wire, like a man in lockup. "Go back to Florida. Forget this whole fucking business," he yelled over the noise, then turned on his heels and walked away.

I tried the door. It was locked.

CUT OFF FROM Gerard and with too much time on my hands before the judge climbed down from the bench, I drove around until I found one of those little stores in a strip mall where you can mail things, make copies, drop off FedEx packages or rent computer time.

I paid for the minimum thirty minutes, sat at my assigned computer and plugged the first of the two flash drives into a USB port. I clicked on the icon and opened it up. It was completely blank. No files of any kind.

The second flash drive left me royally pissed. Also blank. What had I expected? If not the answers to the secret of Stonehenge laid out in twelve point Times New Roman, at least a particle of insight on what Lintz had been writing.

Had Holly known all along that they were blank? Bet on it, Royce. She set you up like a freshman.

Lunch was a greasy hamburger and a flat soda fountain Coke at a pub in the same strip mall. Between bites that I choked down, I had an inspiration. I called the office to check on Jamie and LuAnn's progress, and to hand them another assignment.

"We're getting organized—got our list of keywords and phrases. If anything about any of our characters is in someone's server, we'll dig it out," LuAnn said.

"Do me another favor, would you? Go to the *Chronicle's* archives. Pull out and print anything you find that Lintz wrote while he was there. Maybe he ripped someone the wrong way and made a lethal enemy. Gerard says no, but he keeps flashing me mixed signals."

"I'll give that one to Jamie," LuAnn said. "I'll start on Lintz's background before the others. We'll put it all together and see what we have."

"Perfect," I said, wiping my chin. "Don't suppose you heard from Luke?"

"In fact, I did. He thinks . . . well, he thinks he found the place where Wes commandeered the tractor, and the phone he used to make his call. No other sign of him so far."

"He'll find him, LuAnn," I said. "If anyone can, it's Luke."

"What if the police find him first?" LuAnn said.

What if they already had? I thought to myself.

CHAPTER 17

EARLY THE PREVIOUS Saturday morning, Wes had hung up the payphone mounted to the faded wood siding of the abandoned corner store, then leaned against the building feeling faint, as though the call he'd made to Luke telling him of the attempt on his life had used up all the air in his lungs.

Wes calculated that the complex where he'd find the rental car would be to the southeast at a distance of six or so miles. He didn't know how long it would be before C.W. Vernon or one of his cronies showed up at the pot hole. When they did, the shit would fly on rapid wings and the roads would be infested with patrol cars.

The rush of adrenaline had worn off, the pain now unmasked. His back felt as though knives were carving notches in the muscle tissue with each breath he drew; he realized that he might be in deeper trouble than he'd first thought.

He pushed off the wall and stood swaying in place, light-headed. When he tried to move, it felt as though his feet had taken root in the packed earth.

As he forced the first labored steps back toward the tractor, a rusty pickup came to a skidding halt in the small parking lot. The doors were thrown open. Two black men who might have been in their late teens jumped out—one with a tire iron gripped in his fist.

Wes held up a hand. "Hold on, fellas," he croaked. "Ain't what it looks like. I've got only a few dollars, and I'm not drunk. I'm a police officer—used to be, anyway."

"You the kind of cop who goes stealin' a man's tractor?" the driver challenged.

"Who was it bloodied you up, nigger?" the other said, taking a step forward. "I oughta bust you up side a' the head where you stand."

"So that's it, is it? The tractor is yours? Hear me out. I got shot. They tried to run me down, tried to . . . kill me," Wes said with as much force as he could muster. "Cop named Becker. White guy name a' Coy. I needed wheels. Had . . . had to get away. That's the truth. I can . . . I . . . can . . . prove who I . . . ." And then his knees gave way and he sank to the ground, the light fading as he saw himself drifting downstream on a raft from his boyhood, the sky above the river steadily darkening until it turned completely black.

W ES CRACKED HIS eyes open in narrow slits. He lay on a bed, the objects around him dark and without definition.

He rolled his neck and moved his limbs as he dug into his memory, slowly putting the pieces in place until he'd completed a journey that took him from the truck stop to jail, jail to the road, from the car heading his way and the blast of the shotgun to the tractor, and the call to Luke—right up to the time the world had spun crazily and he'd tasted dirt.

As his sight adjusted to the dim light, he saw that he was in a small bedroom. On the opposite wall, gray morning light seeped in around the edges of a draped window.

He started to sit up but pain made him think better of it. His head dropped back on the pillow. Then he saw the old woman who sat in a rocker at his bedside. In the gloom, the furrowed lines in her black and weathered face looked like angry slashes.

"Those were bad boys you spoke of in the fever. Dead boys, now," she said, her voice crackling as though her vocal chords had been stretched and dried to the point of breaking. "You were wearin' the jail clothes. You a bad boy, too?"

Wes licked his lips, then clicked out a reply. "No, ma'am, I'm not. I . . .I got a wife and kids down home in Florida."

"Why you up here in trouble, shot full a' holes, then?"

His words came slowly, as if picked one at a time from a box and set in line in a sentence. "Tryin' to help a friend."

"And where's he?" the old women asked.

Wes cleared his parched throat. "Hospital, ma'am."

"He a good boy, too?"

"He is. Blamed for something he didn't do. They tried to kill him in the jail."

The woman considered Wes's answers—all of them, it seemed, for the time she took. "Was you who kilt the white trash?"

In his cloudy mind, Wes wasn't sure if she'd meant Becker and Coy, or Lintz. "Ma'am?"

"The po-lice-man and that red-neck."

He smiled to himself. "Lordy no, momma. I just got myself out of the way and the rest took care of itself."

The old woman nodded. "Happens that way sometimes. It surely do." She rocked forward and rested a hand rough as a rasp on Wes's forehead. "Cleaned you up good as I was able. You be fine in time. Back home to the missus and the children. But you gonna need doctorin'. And soon."

"Sure feels like I do," Wes said. "Best if I hightail it back home for that. I got transportation waitin'."

"Not unless you got you a driver, too," she said. "You pass out, somebody get kilt. Or the police catch you. They like roaches lookin' for food—crawlin' all over the roads. You safe n' fine here for now."

"Then you . . . you believe what I'm tellin' you."

The old woman breathed deeply. "God hisself don't always seem to know the truth. That's why we got bad boys walkin' around. But you call me momma and don't even think 'bout it cause you hurtin' and by yo'self. *I* know the truth, boy." She got slowly out of the rocker. "Now Momma go fix you somethin' to eat. Get your strength back up. Get more water in ya." She started to walk out of the room.

"Tell me, how'd I get here?" Wes asked.

"My grand boys hauled you up in the truck and brought you an' the tractor back. They're strong, too, but never seen nothin' the likes of you. They knew right off t'was you they heard talked about from the happenin's at the truckstop." She shook her head. "My grands, they hear too much. 'Somethin's going on, Nanna,' they say. 'Somethin' big gonna come down.'" She took another step toward the door, then stopped. "That's why you n' me's gonna talk some about it."

The light from the window shone on her face. Wes saw that her eyes were bright, and cast toward the heavens.

"Yes, sir," she said, "this time, I believe God has *seen* the truth and sent on His mighty dark angel to bear witness."

TWO

Why should there not be patient confidence in the ultimate justice of the people?

—Abraham Lincoln

CHAPTER 18

ICLICKED OFF WITH LuAnn, then tossed enough cash on the lunch counter to cover the unhealthy meal and leave a healthy tip.

The time for my unscheduled appointment with the judge was nearing. Before heading downtown to the courthouse, I had two more stops to make.

It's Jamie's belief that the boxy, mega-electronics stores and the digital fantasyland found within their walls marks the downfall of the family unit, and accounts for the increasing lack of creativity in otherwise imaginative young minds.

Maybe so, but there are other uses in the adult world for devices that run on processor chips.

I moved past the aisles of printers and computers, flat screen panels, digital readers and DVR's, studying the overhead signs as I walked, making a right turn at the one that included: *Personal Digital Recorders.*

If any information of value was to come out of the judge's mouth, I wanted it on record.

With my new, ultra-sensitive recorder in hand, I found a Home Depot where I bought a roll of duct tape and used it to secure the mini-device in the depression in my lower back, and the microphone to the center of my chest, both applications secreted under my sweater.

A T FOUR THAT afternoon, I positioned myself near the parking area of the Elbert P. Tuttle Building, activated the recorder and concealed myself behind a delivery truck.

At four-fifteen, Judge Zachary Rhetman and Van the Man emerged from the building and walked toward the judge's long black Cadillac. My pulse tripped; I was out of my element, about to digitize a conversation with a seated Circuit Court Judge without his knowledge, in all probability fatal to my law career if he found out.

With that calming thought, I set a line and pace that brought the three of us together at the rear fender of the judge's limo.

"Could I have a moment, Your Honor?"

The judge regarded me, his face expressionless.

Van produced a menacing scowl. "You. What you think—?"

Rhetman cut him off cold, then set his eyes on mine. "I would say that you've *had* your moment, Mr. Royce. I've spoken with my daughter. Your being here adds immeasurably to the insult. I should ask you to leave—now—before I— "

"Your daughter, Judge, is not a well person." I waited, but he said nothing, only looked at me with stone-cold eyes. "I was nearly seduced. That I allowed the opportunity to arise makes me less than honorable, I admit. But— "

"You got her drunk, Mr. Royce," the judge said. "Holly was inebriated and defenseless. You may have taken advantage of her without her knowledge or consent. Raped her, to be precise. She had to flee her own home while you slept. She called me for help. I sent Van to escort you out. You attacked him. When my daughter returned, thinking you had left, you assaulted her again in her bedroom. She fought you off. Her room is in shambles. I should have you arrested."

"Holly told you this?"

"Van was a witness to everything."

"Van is lying," I said, angered by the accusation. "He wasn't even there. Holly dismissed him after dinner. I dispatched him this morning. I'll ask you again. Is this what Holly told you?"

Rhetman looked around the lot. "Lower you voice. Better still, get in the car."

Van stepped between us and opened the rear door of the limousine.

"In the car, or leave," the judge commanded.

Van took hold of my arm. I shook it off. If there were anything more to be said, it would not be said in public. I pushed Van aside and got in.

The judge followed, taking the seat that faced me.

Rhetman smoothed his slacks and adjusted his tie in a show of composure and control. He pushed a button that raised an opaque partition that assured our privacy. "What Holly said, or didn't say, is of no consequence." His voice was calm, his tone, sure. "The facts, as I presented them to you, are."

"Lies, Judge."

"Leave me and my daughter alone, Mr. Royce." He leaned forward, forearms resting on his knees, hands clasped. "What happened between the two of you can remain your private business. But make no mistake, I will see you charged and arrested for rape if you continue to pursue my daughter any further in the matter of Mr. Lintz's death. I have a witness, I have evidence, and I have the power. You, on the other hand, have nothing."

"I have no intention of pursuing your daughter for *any* reason. No disrespect, but as you'll recall my telling you, I am spoken for—although that might seem a bit hollow at the moment."

He sat back and smiled. "So, then, let's leave it at that, shall we? Temptation befalls the strongest of us, Cage."

"Maybe that's best."

He nodded slowly. "And if Holly is a concern to you, she shouldn't be. One day she'll find happiness. She'll be fine." He took a deep breath. "Go home, son. All is forgotten."

As a confident Judge Rhetman reached for the button to lower the partition and end our meeting, I said, "No sir, all is *not* forgotten. Lintz was murdered, and because of it, my client is dead. I intend to find out why."

He lowered his hand slowly. "You are a fool, Mr. Royce."

"So I've been told," I said. "But, it seems I'm still here."

His eyes narrowed. "So it does."

"Tell me, Judge, what would you have done if I hadn't sought you out? You know I tried to make an appointment, but you weren't interested."

He smirked. "Only a dullard would need to ask, Mr. Royce. I knew you'd come, and that I would find out what I needed to know—that you won't go away. But you're not clever enough for this. Not nearly so."

I struggled to muster a reply, then let it go and got out of the limo.

CHAPTER 19

I DROVE BACK TO my home away from home, slipped into my room, removed the digital recorder and replayed my conversation with the judge three times—in each instance taking notes in order to identify the most important points.

I looked at the scribblings on my notepad: *One day/find happiness/will be fine.* It struck me that the words he'd used were nearly identical to what Holly had said in the moments before she'd gone into a violent rage. I'd also underlined: *to be left alone,* and: *not clever enough for this—not nearly so.* At least one thing was for certain: I had the judge's clear and undivided attention.

The judge had sent Van along to cook and to look. But what if Holly had agreed to his being there all along in order to set me up? But if Rhetman believed that I was stressing out his daughter by asking a few questions about Lintz, the inquiry she'd face in filing a rape complaint would blow her apart. He'd never put her through it. She'd never make it.

A bluff by the judge? Complicity on Holly's part? Now I didn't know what to believe.

It was after six; I determined that a martini would go a long way in helping oil the gears as I tried to decide where to turn next. So I grabbed a shower and ventured out to

The Blue Pointe Grill in Buckhead on the recommendation of the desk clerk.

I pushed through the big glass doors, then descended a set of curved stairs and made my way to the bar on the left, taking a seat halfway down, checking out the décor of the towering room, then the clientele as the bartender poured my first drink.

By the second round, the place was filling up. I found myself elbow to elbow with some of Atlanta's more stylish and upwardly mobile thirtysomethings. Twice, I gently rebuffed offers for cocktails and conversation from ladies of well-above average looks. I made a note to bring Jamie here on some special occasion so that I might fully enjoy the place as I finished the last of my Ketel One martini, up and dry.

I paid the tab, then turned to leave.

And, there she was. No, not Jamie.

"Hey there handsome," Holly said as she slid in next to me at the bar and kissed me on the cheek. "Thought you'd left town by now."

I was at a complete loss. "What are you doing here?"

The bartender approached and greeted her by name.

Holly ordered a Cosmopolitan for herself, then queried the bartender as to my drink of choice. "I live here, remember?" she said. "It's one of my hangouts. I should ask you the same question."

I glanced around the bar out of reflex.

"Don't sweat it. I'm by myself," she said.

"No boyfriend that you ditched in my favor?"

She laughed. "No. I meant Van."

The drinks came. We toasted to our health, sipped, then set our glasses on the bar.

"Look, I know you must think that I'm a total nutcase." She laid her hand lightly on the side of my face and tilted her head as she examined my cheek. "I'm sorry that I hit you."

"Forget it. It's okay."

"No, it's not," she said, then looked in the direction of the hostess stand. A quick smile came to her face. "C'mon, I've got a table."

Before I could turn her down, the bartender swept up our drinks and Holly was pulling me along through the crowd toward a booth, stopping to say hello to some friends, introducing me as 'my guy from Florida.'

She scooted in first; I followed. Holly moved back and sat uncomfortably close to me. "You saw the real Holly, the controlled me, at dinner, and then . . . well, you would have seen lots more if I hadn't passed out. I'm not the witch from this morning." She took a deep breath. "I take medication for these mood swings of mine. They started when I was seventeen—when Mom died. I miss a couple of doses like I did and I start to lose it. Add in my PMS, and you can forget it. Bad combo. You were the closest person, so I just sort of . . . unloaded on you."

I took a slow pull on my martini, smiling with my eyes, trying to cull out what might be fabrication, from what might pass for the truth. "I'm sorry to hear about your mother—about your troubles. It explains a lot."

"Thanks for being so understanding."

"I saw your father today—this afternoon," I said in a not so subtle switch of subjects.

Holly tilted her head and narrowed her eyes. "You did? Where?"

"At The Tuttle Building." I had no way of knowing what Holly might know about how he'd portrayed my encounter with her. So I just plunged ahead. "According to your dear dad, basically, if I don't run away he'll have me arrested for raping you—apparently with your confirmation."

She sat back in the booth as if she'd been shoved. "That's— I can't *believe* it! Why would he say something like that? Sure, he's protective, but— You must have misunderstood what he said. Or at least what he meant."

"No, Holly. I heard him correctly. And clearly. He said that you called him for help—that he sent Van over to kick me out."

She shook her head sharply. "It just isn't true. Yes, Van came over this morning without my asking, but he said it was on his own—that he just wanted to be sure everything was okay. I said, yep, way more than okay. He offered to cook us breakfast." She squeezed my hand. "Sweetie, it was so *totally* okay that I had to go and run off some energy or I was going to wake you up and rape *you*."

I wanted to believe what she said. Not about raping me, but about not knowing why Van had shown up in the morning.

But as with her father, I couldn't trust her. Not fully. So I asked a non-question that would give me the confidence to have faith that she was shooting straight with me. "Holly, when you came in here tonight, you looked surprised to see me. You even commented that you thought I'd left town. Maybe someone told you I had."

She looked at me hard, her mind at work. I was prepared for another slap across the face or to be splashed with a Cosmo. "Okay," she said, "I guess I deserved that. But, no, no one did." Her look softened. "It's a good thing I'm back on my medication, pal."

I studied her for a long moment. "Sorry. But I had to be—"

"You had to be sure. I understand that." She looked down. "The way I behaved, I thought you'd be halfway to Florida by now." A quick shake of the head. "No, the truth is you left because of . . . because of whoever she is. Anyway, it hurt. Then, when I walked in here and saw you at the bar, it hurt even more. I told myself to go right back out the door. But I don't give up easily. A girl can hope, can't she?" She lifted her eyes. "Can I tell you something?"

"Sure," I said. "Anything you want."

"Sometimes I stand in front of my mirror until I detach, so that it's somebody else staring back at me. I see this girl. She's got it all. But she never gets the guy.

"I'll look into her eyes until I'm inside her head. That's where the problem is. There's something happening in there that I don't understand—something I think I should know, but can't remember."

"Have you had counseling?" I asked.

"Oh, yeah. The real deal. When I was eighteen I even spent a month in a clinic. I don't recall most of it. I guess it made me better, but I just— I can't seem to get happy, you know? Maybe I should go see a shrink again."

"I think that's a really good idea. It might help."

She held my hand tightly. "Maybe."

"What about your father?" I asked. "What are you going to say to him?"

"Nothing. Unfortunately, it's his way. If he doesn't totally trust whomever I'm seeing, he's a real pain. This is a first, though. Maybe he's going off the deep end."

"Maybe he just doesn't like lawyers."

We ate and talked for the next half hour, a comfortable time of good mood and no further conversation about her father, or about us.

"So where are you off to from here?" she asked as we finished the last bites of seared tuna.

"Depends," I replied. "My client, he . . . ."

"Sorry. I read about that. I still have a subscription to the *Chronicle*. I'm gonna cancel it, though. It makes me feel creepy. You know, since Ray and all."

"I don't think you'll miss much."

"Me either." She sipped at her Pinot Grigio. "Back to Florida?"

"Eventually, yes."

She looked suddenly hopeful. "What's 'eventually' mean?"

"I still have work to do. My client didn't commit suicide," I said. "He was murdered."

It clearly surprised her. "Murdered? How can you be sure?"

"Someone saw it. And now he's . . . missing. Somewhere around Big Hope. So I guess that's my next stop."

The bill came, and I reached for it. But when I looked, the balance was zero. "Holly, I'd at least like to buy you drinks and dinner."

"*My* hangout. I told you. I don't play fair, remember?" She gathered up her purse. "Now, my gorgeous hunk, I'm going to go freshen up," she said bravely. "When I come back, I'm— I'm going to meet some friends at the bar, okay? It might be best if you're not here. Not if you don't want to be."

"I understand."

She slid out of the booth. "Bye, Cage. Be safe."

I sat there for a moment, watching her go. After a few steps she stopped and looked back at me over her shoulder with eyes that could stop your heart and blew me a kiss, her incredible beauty half-hidden by a sweep of shiny black hair.

CHAPTER 20

I WAS BACK AT my hotel by nine. I tried Jamie but there was no answer. So I checked with the staff at *The Hatch*, but no one had seen her all afternoon or evening.

Next, I called our law offices. LuAnn answered and handed the phone to Jamie. It had been an interesting project, she said.

By the time we finished talking an hour later, I had written on the pad in front of me a list of names and dates, and a collection of random comments laced with connecting threads—and somewhere among the jumble of notes and questions, perhaps the hidden answer as to why two young men with the biggest measure of their lives yet to be lived, had been murdered.

Lintz had been the first name on Jamie's list.

"I pulled him up on a Google search," she said. "But there wasn't much, just stuff on his being a reporter in Atlanta. No other history. So I cross-checked with the other hits on the name. Nothing fit. I gave that up and started to read his stuff from the *Chronicle's* archives. After a half-dozen columns, I *knew* I'd read his stuff somewhere else. What clued me was the style—the vocabulary, his pace, the cynical tone."

Jamie was a constant reader of big city Sunday papers— *The New York Times, The Washington Post, The Los Angeles Times, The St.Petersburg Times, The Boston Globe*—her mind a sponge for current events.

"Roger Lindman was the guy I'd read," she said. "I remember something about his quitting over a suspicion that he'd altered or embellished facts on an undercover story. It was never proven, but it was kind of a big deal at the time because he'd been touted as this big up-and-coming journalistic force. Anyway, I read some things he'd written as Lintz for comparison, and I'd bet my ass that it's the same guy—that Lintz and Lindman were the same person."

"So he changes his name and lands at the *Chronicle*— hardly a reputable publication, but still it's a job in a major city," I said. "The question is, did Gerard know who he really was when he hired him?"

THE SECOND NAME on Jamie's list was Gerard's. The search turned up information on everything from his having graduated from Syracuse University's School of Journalism to a listing of various jobs he'd held over his career, and an accounting of the awards he'd won.

"This guy is no slouch," Jamie said. "He's really into politics and history. He started as a beat reporter with the *Times* in New York and then headed to Albany where he ran the capital bureau for the *Times Union*.

"Seems he rode the butts of the Democrats up there pretty hard—too hard, and it cost him. They ran him off and he wound up taking a job at *THE ADVERTISER* in Montgomery as regional editor. That was eleven years ago. Only he didn't stay there very long. Looks like maybe thirteen months. Then he moved up to Atlanta and went to work as Editor for the

Chronicle. I got to thinking as I looked at his career path and made a connection: Montgomery is only a hundred or so miles from Big Hope. Gerard would have known if anything interesting happened there, or was reported in the local press that deserved coverage in Montgomery, wouldn't you think?"

"But he told me that Big Hope doesn't have a paper," I said.

"So I discovered. But *Eufaula* does—The *Eufaula Tribune.* And Eufaula's just up the road. As in, where they took Robby to the hospital?"

"Okay, so . . . . Wait a minute. Gerard told me I might want to check out the Eufaula paper's morgue for info about the murder suspects in Big Hope. The ones that never made it to trial. But he said it would probably be a waste of time."

"So tomorrow, I'll pay another visit to the *Tribune's* archives and see what I can come up with," Jamie said.

"You've been there already?"

"Oh, you betcha, sweet cheeks. I'll get to that in a minute. But first let me tell you what happened when I Googled up the name, 'Rhetman.' Juicy stuff. Grab a pencil and paper and I'll start with 'Old Zach the Original.'"

ZACHARY L. RHETMAN, a wealthy New England landowner, had come to Atlanta in 1866, not long after the Civil War ended. He saw opportunity in the ruined economy and the rebuilding of North Georgia following the pillaging that occurred as a result of Sherman's March to the Sea, and other Federal campaigns.

Confederate currency had been rendered worthless by the war; banks were basically non-existent. Southern farmers found it necessary to go into debt to those who could supply seed in order to plant a crop, only to hope that the harvest would be successful enough to repay their notes and start the cycle again. Often, it wasn't.

Rhetman built a chain of general stores throughout Georgia, stocking seed to loan on credit to the farmers, using the continuing profits of his New England farming enterprise for funding.

As farmers' debts mounted, Rhetman was able to direct what crops were to be planted by controlling what seed he would advance to the farmers, pushing cotton, bargaining for a substantial cut of the sizeable profits in the process—in some cases, calling in the notes instead and seizing the land for non-payment, combining parcels and creating huge plantations. In time, he amassed enormous wealth, and wielded considerable power.

Then, in 1881, Zachery Rhetman died of tuberculosis. In the years that followed, his son, Zachery Jr., increased the landholdings throughout the South in a series of shrewd acquisitions.

In 1929, Zachery Jr. retired and moved back north. *His* son, Zachery L. Rhetman, II, took over the business. And while the economy would struggle over the next decade, the Rhetman family found itself on the positive side of the imbalance in the distribution of wealth in the country that had helped bring on the depression. That, and the founding Rhetman's aversion to investing in stocks assured that their fortunes would only continue to grow.

"God only knows what Zach the Third is worth these days," Jamie said, "but it looks like Holly stands to inherit a bundle."

"Rich and unhappy."

"What?"

"Nothing," I said. "Just muttering."

"Pay attention here, pal. Questions?"

"Not so far."

"Okay, so you've got the basic outline; let me color in the history," Jamie said.

"There going to be a quiz?"

"You never know."

When Abraham Lincoln was assassinated, Jamie continued, it confused the slaves who'd been freed under The Emancipation Proclamation; they looked at the President and the Proclamation as being one and the same.

"So they thought their newly won freedom was kaput," I said.

"You got it. And Rhetman did zip to clarify the misunderstanding. He used it to build and control a large workforce of cheap labor that helped establish his cotton empire. He'd bribe the corrupt Federal overseers wherever and whenever necessary.

"Eventually, laws were passed and the blacks started to understand their rights and become a more viable force. So

Rhetman changes tactics and quietly starts giving chunks of money to the Democrats. He supports the party's radical arm—a bunch of vigilantes known by different names who were trying to hold the other whites from going over to the Republicans who had given the blacks the right to vote. If the black vote was cast at all, the Democratic Party wanted it to be for their ticket. Am I keeping you up?"

"No. Go on. I'm getting a tingling sensation."

"Okay, just checking. So by 1877, white members of the Democrats—friends of Rhetman—held office in nearly every state that had been in the Confederacy. By that time most of the blacks who worked in agriculture were penniless sharecroppers whose cut was never enough to get them out of debt. Essentially, Rhetman owned them. When he died in 1881, his son took over. Only he wasn't as coy as Daddy."

"Meaning?"

"Meaning that the son was an activist. He made no bones about his belief in segregation—that the color-line should be drawn in both public and private. He had black servants. He openly supported literacy tests and poll taxes designed to skirt the Fifteenth Amendment and prevent blacks from voting. I even found articles written back then that implied that he had an involvement with the Ku Klux Klan, although I couldn't find anything in the way of substantiating fact. But there *was* a photograph in one of the articles. It was a photo of the public hanging of a black man. Rhetman's identified as an onlooker in the caption."

"Jesus."

"And it doesn't stop there."

"The lynchings?"

"No. The bigotry."

Zachary Rhetman the Second wasn't interested in growing cotton, Jamie had learned. He'd seen the fortunes of the family rise and fall, and heard his father's stories about boll weevils and single-crop economies. Real wealth, he believed, was to be found in real estate.

"He was smart. He bet on the coming rebound in the economy after The Great Depression believing that Atlanta would eventually boom. So he set a plan to sell the majority of the family's landholdings, getting top buck for some parcels, putting others in trust for future sale and leasing out big tracts for farming.

"By the time Holly's father was born, Zach Two had finished the conversion of the land holdings. Now, here's the topper. Ready? He started in Georgia, but guess where he migrated some of the money?"

"Sam's Club?"

"No, you idiot, Alabama. *Eufaula*. He bought up a hunk of acreage along the lake—more in the surrounding country. After Rhetman, Jr, headed back north to Cape Cod, Rhetman II sold off everything but a hundred acres on the bluff where he built his new home. It was a private compound where he lived until he died. It seems that the lake was quite the social spot if you had bucks —drew a lot of hotsie totsie Atlantans there for the summer. The Rhetmans were front page. Here's a direct quote:

'There, he and his wife Florence recreated an era, stepped back to a time when slavery was in full blossom. Driving through the gates of the Windy Hill Plantation, where he loved nothing better than to drink Mint Juleps and regale his houseguests with stories of his father and grandfather, the Negroes, and how the Rhetman family had wielded its power and made its fortune, was in every aspect a true return to yesteryear.' Can you fucking *believe* it?"

"Wow. So, what happened to him?"

"Here's where it gets really interesting. Try this one: He killed his wife, then shot himself. There was a note predicting 'a great Negro uprising.' Another Civil War was coming—this one between blacks and whites."

"Holy shit. And Judge Rhetman and his wife, and later Holly, kept the compound, didn't they?" I asked, for confirmation.

"Up until Mrs. Rhetman died. Ten years ago. So, here's where it gets even more intriguing. Sort of sad, though."

Judging from her picture, Jamie said, Holly's mother had been dark-haired with fragile features, an elegant woman. When she died in a single car accident, she was only forty-nine.

It happened in July. She'd been at the wheel. Holly had been riding with her; it was a Friday evening. They were on their way to Eufaula. Judge Rhetman had gone down earlier that week to fish with friends.

The article speculated that Mrs. Rhetman had swerved to avoid hitting a deer and lost control of the car, slamming it into a tree. She was killed instantly. Her daughter had been ejected from the convertible and sustained a severe concussion.

The accident happened along a dangerous stretch of State Road 431 just north of Eufaula.

In the small town of Big Hope, Alabama.

CHAPTER 21

I TOOK MY PAD over to the desk and tore off the sheets of scribbled words I'd jotted down during my conversation with Jamie, then turned to a fresh page where I set up columns, each headed with a name: Gerard; H. Rhetman; J. Rhetman; Lintz; C.W. Vernon, et al.

I began culling through the cryptic notations I'd made during the call, selecting words and phrases that applied to each person and copying them under the proper heading.

Next, I laid out a chronology of events.

By four in the morning I had established the connections between people, places, and events. What was still missing, and what frustrated any further progress was a motive for the Lintz murder, and, of course, the name of his killer.

At six in the morning, I called Jamie back, waking her from a sound sleep.

"So what's the deal?" she asked, fighting to become fully conscious.

"I'm not sure," I said, sipping lousy coffee from the in-room, make-it-yourself pot. "Holly told me that she'd been hit hard by depression after her mother died. But she didn't say anything about it being an auto accident. A year later, she went into the hospital for treatment. She still takes anti-depressants. If she forgets to, she said she can get pretty nasty."

"That's a long time to be treated with medication. Unless her condition is chemically driven. Like if she's bi-polar, for instance. Is she still receiving therapy?"

"No. I don't think so."

Jamie was silent for a few seconds. "How does she speak of herself?"

"Not well."

"How about her father?"

"She says that he's protective. To a fault."

"Obviously, she wants to talk about it. She feels isolated, controlled."

"Why obviously?" I asked.

"Because, Slick, she's willing to open up details of her life to you, that's why. She must feel that she's gotten close enough to you to do that."

"What would possibly make her feel that way?"

"Her ex-boyfriend's murder. And Robby's. You're the central character in her mind. You are the one person trying to find out what happened. The white knight."

"I'm a little slow this morning."

"Slow? You're hopeless. What else did she say?"

"Let's see . . . . That one day she'll be happy—that the right person will come along. That she'll be fine. Pretty close to the exact words her father used when he spoke to me about her."

"Okay. She feels inferior. Daddy tries to bolster her confidence. Instead, she feels disconsolate. But she's hungry for a male figure in her life. Beware, boy. If she hasn't already, she's going to flip for you."

"Why do you say that?" I could have sworn my voice cracked.

"Because you're a specimen, and she's lonely and feeling unloved."

"Probably why she asked me to marry her, huh?" I said.

"Ha, ha."

"Okay," I said. "Enough of that. Here's another one. Holly feels her head isn't right. According to her, she should know or remember something important, but she can't pop the cork on it."

Jamie was quiet for so long that I finally asked, "You still there?"

"Yep. Just adding it all up. She went for in-house therapy after the accident—a year after, you said. If she was that bad, if she was suicidal or just an emotional basket case, they could have tried a number of things assuming that her pathology was okay. Shock therapy, for instance—something extreme to help erase the memory of the accident. It's possible that the severe concussion further compounded the memory loss.

"It can take years to heal, to even *begin* to cope with tragedy for some people. And you never know what might come along and push her over the edge. Another failed relationship could do it. Or someday when her father dies. I'd guess she leans on him for pretty much everything."

"I'd say you're right."

"Well, he isn't helping the situation. Neither is the medication, really. Not for the long haul. It's a mask."

A T SEVEN, I showered and packed. I checked out of the hotel, found a Starbuck's where I ordered a large coffee, then drove to the home of the *Atlanta Daily Chronicle* where I passed through the gate and parked.

No, the guard had said, Mr. Gerard was not yet in, but would be at his usual time of eight o'clock. And, yes, I could wait in the lot if I cared to.

I was more than worried about Wes; we'd last heard from him on Saturday morning. This was Wednesday. I wondered how much longer Luke could or should wait before confronting Sheriff Vernon. I'd be there later in the day; we'd decide then, or maybe—

A knock on my car window startled me. Gerard stood on the other side. I hit the button that lowered the glass. "Good morning," I said in a cheery tone.

"You're not coming in," he said. "I'm done—finished talking to you. I thought I made that clear." He started to walk away.

"So what happened in Montgomery, Gerry? Why'd you lose your job?"

It stopped him in his tracks. "What the fuck do you think you're doing spying on me," he growled.

"Googling is hardly spying. And unless I'm confused, I believe it was you who pointed me toward Alabama and the *Eufaula Tribune*?"

He stared at me in silence.

"For some reason, Ger, I think you lost your balls."

His jaw set. "You *always* get by on your fucking charisma? Alright. Five minutes. That's all you get." He turned and walked toward the building.

I was out of the car in a heartbeat and on my way once again to the nicotine pit that was Gerard's office.

CHAPTER 22

W HILE HOLLY HAD spent Monday planning a quiet dinner for the two of us and plotting her seduction, Wes had picked at his food, unable to find his appetite in the face of the pain he felt as he brought the fork to his mouth, finally consenting to having the old woman spoon feed him like a baby.

He'd slept away the remainder of Sunday, exhausted, weakened as he fought the infection and resulting fever from the buckshot lodged in his body; the wounds had begun to fester.

Mattie Franklin put down the fork and laid a hand on Wes's forehead. "I think it may be time that we see about some doctorin'. Your head feels like m'iron."

Wes listened to Mattie's words as if he were in a long corridor. When he spoke, his tongue felt thick. "What'er we gonna do? Can't go out to the hospital."

"You just rest a while. Mattie'll see to it."

"Sure. I . . . okay . . . ." he heard himself say as he slipped into unconsciousness.

Wes drifted up from a sleep filled with strange images and distortions—a place of too bright colors and too loud noises where the heat was unbearable, the air, stifling.

He was walking in wet sand; impossible because he was on a street chasing a white man, shooting at him with a pistol that weighed fifty pounds. He couldn't take aim.

Behind him, two men ran after him, firing shotguns. He felt the sting and impact of the hot pellets as they hit him, but he didn't go down.

A car came speeding toward him. Becker was at the wheel; Wes could see him through an enormous windshield, his mouth open wide in a scream that went on forever . . . .

Then Wes heard a male voice say, "That's the last of it. You'll be sore for awhile, but you'll heal. I drained the wounds and loaded you up with a shot of antibiotic. A couple of the pellets are too deep in the muscle for me to get, so you'll need to see about those in time. Meanwhile, Mattie has instructions on dressing those incisions and keeping you on pills. Couple days, you'll be good to travel—sooner, I suppose, if necessary. But I don't want you pulling on the stitches any more than you have to. I'd give you the, 'you were lucky' routine, but nothing was going to do you in other than a general infection if we'd waited a few more days. Questions?"

Wes opened his eyes. A heavyset black man with a salt and pepper beard cropped short stood over him. He held a glass of water to Wes's lips.

Wes drank before he spoke. "No, sir. I think I heard all of it, Doctor . . . ?"

"Jefferson. Lazarus Jefferson." A laugh rumbled deep in the man's chest. "Some name for a physician, right? My folks had a thing for the Bible and dead presidents."

Wes found that he was feeling much improved, the fever broken. "Thanks for whatever it is you did. I was pretty well out of it. Whatever I owe you for your services, if you'll just—"

"This was a favor for Mattie—and for you. She explained what took place on Saturday. There's lots of good folk around Big Hope. Black, *and* white. And then there's the likes of the Beckers and Coy Lodies. The way I see it, they got what they had coming. Good Lord's got his ways." Jefferson brought a chair over to the edge of the bed and sat down. "Miss Mattie's taken to putting her faith in you. That's her business. My business is keeping people healthy. Most of it depends on my medical skills, some of it has to do with giving out advice.

"Mattie's an old woman, Mr. Harland. She's had a tough go of it over the years. She's seen a goodly number of friends and family pass on. Two of her daughter Bess's youngest boys, twins they were, went missing a few years back. Bess didn't make it six months after that. Ask me, she died of a broken heart. The loss nearly drove Mattie insane.

"The reason I'm telling you all this, well . . . she's likely to bend your ear about evil doings going on around here. The devil's work, and such. I'll admit that some things have happened over time that you could look at one way or the other. But I believe most of the troubles come from being a poor backwater town. Big Hope isn't much more than a spit in the ocean."

"But, I know what I saw happening in the jail," Wes said. "Somebody strung Robby Cain up and called it an attempted suicide. Somebody also killed a man named Ray Lintz."

Jefferson leaned in closer. "You know, once in awhile I come up against the tough case. One I can't beat. It doesn't matter if I think it to be fair or not. It is what it is." He leaned back in his chair. "You got family back home from what Mattie says. You lucked out once. Go home. Forget this place. It won't do you any good to go prying into affairs that are none of your concern or worry. That's my advice."

Wes looked away. "I appreciate what y'all are sayin'. And I mean no offense. But let me ask you, Doc . . . if you came up on an injured man who you didn't know, would you just walk on by? Or would you stop to help."

The doctor shook his head slowly. "You know the answer," he said as he got to his feet. "But I've said my piece. What you do from here on out is your choice. Just don't be a fool about it. What you *should* be doing is figuring a way back to Florida. Call somebody to come and get you."

"No need to be callin'," Wes said. "I'd guess that somebody's already here, or on the way. Luke Carey. He's a lawyer, although he looks more like a lumberjack. Shaggy brown hair with gray streaks. The other one's Cage Royce. Lawyer, too. About six foot two, bit on the preppy side. Blond hair. I work for them. I would appreciate it greatly if you could get word to one or both if you see them hangin' around that I'm still on the correct side of the dirt."

"I'll keep an eye out."

Wes extended his hand. Jefferson took it. "You're a good man, Doc. Thanks. Maybe one day I can repay you in some way."

Jefferson walked to the door, then stopped and said, "Maybe so. But don't be doing it by bringing me any more work, okay?"

Mattie came into the room carrying a tray some time later. Whatever she'd loaded on board smelled mighty fine to Wes. He was famished.

She set the tray on the bed, then pulled the window blind closed against the dwindling daylight. "Doc says you'll be good as new in a week or so. Says you got friends maybe comin' to get ya."

"Maybe," Wes said.

Mattie helped him sit up; she propped the pillows carefully behind his back.

Wes cut a piece of pork chop and forked it into his mouth, the pain of his effort less than a third of what it had been, the taste worth every twinge.

She watched in silence as he ate, smiled at the sounds of enjoyment he made as he downed the chops and potatoes and gravy. In awhile she said, "Lazarus told you some things, I think. He's a good boy, too. But he tends to turn his cheek on trouble."

Wes shook his head. "Not much, really. Just, you know . . . we talked about my healin' and things."

The old woman scowled. "I know Lazarus thinks Mattie's a bit titched in the head. But it ain't so. People 'round here be accused a' killin' people. But there ain't no reason for it to happen. Then they get kilt before they can say, no, I ain't kilt nobody. An' my Bessie's twin boys just up an' disappear? No, I don't think so. I think they's here still. I can feel it. Lordy. This place, this Big Hope is the Devil's house."

Wes lifted the tray from his lap and set it aside. "You said, 'they got killed before they could say no.' You mean the people charged with murder? The ones—three of them, I think it was—that died before they had their trials?"

The old woman nearly swooned; she braced herself against the chair. "Lordy. How could you know? I swear you the Angel O' God."

He caught her elbow and helped her as she sat. "No, ma'am, I'm no angel. I'm just a man who's hopin' to set things right. That's all."

"You're His humble servant, alright." A tear rolled down the groove of a deep furrow in her leathery cheek. "Sometimes I think . . . maybe I been branded by Satan. But the Lord don't send an angel on to a lost sinner."

Wes took her hand, the skin wrinkled and dry, her nails thick with age.

The old woman began to cry, her head bowed, the drops falling on her arm like rain on parched earth. "They were just poor black folk who never hurt nobody. But they listen to Mattie talk about trouble, then go and say too much about it."

"So . . . you knew them?" Wes asked in a quiet voice.

Mattie nodded. "Church folk. We was all close to each other, and close to the Lord Jesus. We believed we might smite the evil in this place. I think that's why they was kilt."

"And the people they were accused of killing?"

"Same thing. They were all of them friends just 'sposed to have turned on each other. It made no sense." Mattie got slowly to her feet, shaking her head. "Ain't no truth to it. No truth a'tall." She took the tray from Wes's bed and shuffled toward the door. Then she stopped and turned toward Wes, much as the doctor had done. "Was God that brought you to this place. He gave you the power to crush your enemies an' deliver you from harm. Now, you do His work like He say."

She pulled the door closed behind her.

Wes lay back on his pillows, staring at the ceiling. He saw the faces of Tisha and his children, his brothers and sisters, his parents long since dead.

In time came the image of Robby, and the many faces of grief and tragedy collected over the years of police work, and held forever in his mind.

What if she's right? he thought. What if this old woman wasn't so crazy? What if I'm *supposed* to be here?

CHAPTER 23

I FOLLOWED GERARD UP the stairs and took my now-familiar seat in front of his desk.

He removed his coat and hung it roughly on the tree in the corner, then slammed the door. "Jesus-at-a-fucking-town-meeting. What do I have to do to—?"

"Cut it. Right now, Gerard." I'd risen half out of the chair and leaned on his desktop for emphasis. "People are dead and I think you might have a pretty good idea why. I'm done sparring, so grow some balls and talk to me."

Gerard loosened his tie, then rolled his sleeves up to his elbows. "For your information, I take offense with your reference to my testicles."

"You what . . .? Oh, for Christ's sake."

"I only got one, asshole, like it's any of your goddamn business. The other one didn't bother to make the trip down the fucking tube."

We glared at each other. Gerard's left eye twitched with anger. It was all I could do to keep a straight face.

"So?" I said.

"So the other one's a fake. I got a rubber nut in my sack, and it pisses me off. The fucker just hangs there—hot, cold, in the rack? Doesn't give a shit one way or the other.

Try explaining *that* in the shower and between the sheets all your fucking life."

"Do you and the missus have kids?"

The question seemed to confuse him. "Yeah. So?"

"How many?"

"Three. What the fuck difference does it make?"

"Boys? Girls?" I asked.

"Two boys. One girl."

"Interesting."

"Yeah? Why?"

I eased back down in my chair and sat there with a little grin on my face. "Because, Gerry, the left one makes the boys, and the right one makes girls. It's the X and Y chromosome thing."

He studied me hard through a long silence. "You sure about that?"

I smiled with satisfaction. "No, not really," I said.

Gerard tapped his fingers on his desk. "Asshole."

"I think you're bullshitting me about more than your balls, Gerry. And wasting my allotted time in the process. So I want credit put back on the clock."

"No chance. What else do you want?"

"For starters, the truth about Lintz—about Roger Lindman."

I could see the internal debate in his eyes. "I— Who the hell is Lindman?"

"Please. You're smarter than that. So am I. Maybe it was the publisher that didn't know Lintz was Lindman. Maybe he found out, and that was what your little 'come to Jesus meeting' was all about. I think Lintz had a story. A big one. Only I think he did more than threaten you with it for more space. Lindman was a big deal who got dirt on his shoes. If what he had was important enough, what would stop him from taking it across the street to the *Atlanta Journal Constitution*, and not just *threaten* to do it?"

"Yeah? And why would the AJC take a chance on him if they knew who he was?"

"Maybe they wouldn't. But you couldn't be sure. If you broke the big one with Lindman slash Lintz, all would be forgotten and you'd be a hero. If you lost the gamble, you'd be working in Fargo."

Gerard stayed silent.

"If I'm right, then two questions come to mind: What was the story all about? And who had the most to lose if it ever got published?"

Gerard shot forward in his chair. "Are you accusing me of popping Lindman? Are you out of your fucking skull?"

"Gee, Gerry. I thought you didn't know. Don't you mean Lintz? And, no, I don't think you popped him. But I do think you put him onto Holly Rhetman for some reason, and in some abstract way that led to his being murdered. What I'm not clear on is why you put me onto her father, and then backed off. But I can guess."

Gerard tried a smug look that failed. "Yeah? So, go ahead, Sherlock. Seems like you've got all the fucking answers anyway."

"Fine. So let's get back to your balls—both of them," I said. "The Rhetman family holds a lot of sway in Atlanta. Power and money do one of three things: corrupt, make good things happen, or control. My bet is that you pushed up against the judge or his family name and someone told you to stand down—maybe the judge himself, but I doubt it. I don't think you rate high enough. What did he say to your publisher, Gerry?" I gave him a hard look. "You wanted my help for some reason. I think you still do. It happened before, didn't it? Ten years ago. In Alabama. You were in Montgomery. The Rhetman family held land in Eufaula. They sold, you left and came here. What was the reason?"

Gerard lowered his eyes for a moment, then looked at me. "I was good once—really good. Now . . .?" He seemed to grow smaller as he spoke. "I'm a fighter, Mr. Royce, and a good fighter knows when to quit—when he's been beaten. No, I don't like the judge and I don't like the name. Once upon a time, I did. Christ, I wrote glowing columns about the bastard. I watched his career from the time I was in New York. He was a legal comer. Fine lawyer. Clerked for one of the Justices on the Supreme Court. I did a piece on him that I think helped him get the fucking appointment with the Eleventh Circuit. Then, something happened, and I got a glimpse into his guts. But all I got are suspicions. Not even sure of what I'm chasing exactly. Maybe ghosts. Maybe nothing. But I have a nose, and something stinks. So now I can keep digging, or I can keep my job." Gerard's eyes surveyed his cubicle. "It ain't much, but it's what I got. And you're right; fucking Fargo doesn't exactly give me a hardon."

"But you knew that *I* wouldn't quit, didn't you? Or at least hoped I wouldn't."

"Your choice," Gerard said. "But I promise you one thing. You come up with it, and you got proof? . . . we print it."

"That was Lintz's job."

Gerard shrugged.

"He got close, didn't he."

"I don't know what he got besides dead," he said. "What I know is, we had a deal. Lindman got a chance, I got a story—if there was one. Yeah, I knew who he was. But *only* me. Not the publisher. And, yeah, I threw him at Ms. Rhetman."

"With a purpose, I take it?"

"Why not work and have a little fun while you're digging away?"

I fought an urge to defend Holly. But Gerard spoke before I had the chance.

"But the dumb shit fell in love. He said he wouldn't push her. Some reporter, huh? Christ, he was on the inside of the family, and never even used his best source. And I fucking *handed* it to him."

Maybe he wasn't such a putz, I wanted to say. I let it go. "So it was your publisher that Judge Rhetman pressured?"

"That, I can't prove," Gerard said. "But, yeah, he thinks the judge walks on fucking Perrier. Everybody in this whole friggin' city figures him for office. I mean, look at the guy— he's got it all. Both sides of the aisle would fight over him like dogs in heat."

"He's got to be what—sixty?" I said.

"About. Not really that old anymore."

"But he hasn't made a bid, has he," I said. "You'd think a man like that would have an ego that needs constant feeding. So what's stopping him?"

Gerard got to his feet. "You tell me, Counselor. Find out, and bring me the proof."

"One last question," I said as Gerard opened the door.

He looked at his watch. "Thirty seconds."

"Why did you leave Montgomery?"

He thought about his answer, his hand lingering on the knob. "I started a piece on the Civil War—on the time *after* the war. I was writing it myself. It was good. I figured it would be interesting history from around the South. Something with journalistic merit, even, if you can fucking imagine that.

"I turn in a draft. The name 'Rhetman' appeared in the first installment. Some of the family history isn't so pretty. But it was what it was and the judge did all he could to distance himself—make amends, you might say.

"Anyway, the next thing I know, my publisher calls me in and tells me I should find something else to do. Tells me my job's getting the heave in another round of budget cuts. Oh yeah, and for some reason my piece wasn't gonna run. Right. And I got a ten inch dick. It was a con job. He was so fucking bad at it I wanted to laugh. My chain was bein' yanked. So I called him out on it. 'C'mon, Steve, that's crap and you know it. What gives?' I said.

"He looks at me like I'm the dumbest shit on the planet. All he says is, 'You're not from around here, are you.'"

CHAPTER 24

I SAT IN THE parking lot of the *Atlanta Daily Chronicle* searching for a phone number. When I found what I wanted, I punched the digits into my Blackberry but didn't hit SEND until I was heading south on the expressway, clear of heavy traffic and on my way to Big Hope, Alabama.

My call was taken by Conklin's assistant; I waited on hold.

"Counselor" he said as he came on the line, "good to hear from you—that is, as long as we're not about to walk around the obstacles known as State Statutes."

"No," I said. "But I could use your help on something."

"Oh?"

"The Civil War. You're a student—an expert, yes?"

Conklin cleared his throat. "You flatter me, sir. But, yes, I suppose I've collected a bit of wisdom on the subject over time. Anything in particular that interests you?"

"The reconstruction process."

"Process*es*, actually. It's rather a complex topic," he said, his voice and Southern accent seeming to deepen as he spoke about his passion. "To begin with, there was the rebuilding of the political infrastructure. Then, the physical reconstruction of whole towns and cities. Add to that the reversal of the ruination of the agricultural economy that occurred in the last stages of Federal occupation, and you have years of re—"

"I'm interested in what you might know about a man who built stores in Georgia and Alabama. Probably more places than that."

"If you could be more specific?"

"Rhetman," I said. "There's a judge in—"

"I know the name, sir. Why the interest?"

"Rhetman's daughter was seeing Ray Lintz. She identified the body."

Conklin went silent.

I thought maybe I'd lost the connection. "Mr. Conklin?"

"I didn't know. But I do know of the judge, and his daughter. And in general, the family's . . .background."

"You don't sound as if the Rhetman name particularly finds favor with you."

"Over history, the name did not sit well with many Southern Conservatives. Contrary to opinion that circulates even today, few Southerners were proponents of slavery, nor were they or are they proud of the years of segregation that followed its abolishment."

"I'm sure not—although I must say that I've seen evidence to the contrary. For instance, in Big Hope," I said.

"Prejudice and ignorance are social flaws that are as sure to go on as death and taxes, Mr. Royce. Racism, and the full-out arrogance that accompanies it are thought by some to be pathological traits."

"A pathological trait, say, like murdering your wife and then committing suicide?"

"That is the way the story is told, Mr. Royce."

"You have doubts about how the judge's parents died?" I asked, culling the question from the inflection in his voice.

"That doesn't much matter. The old man was a black eye on the face of a fine community, and frankly, not welcomed. It might well be that what was reported, was true."

"And that was it; the bigotry ended with the death of the judge's father?"

"Now it sounds as if it is you who has doubts."

"The judge is respected in Atlanta. And by the nature of how high he's risen in the ranks of the law, you'd have to assume that he's . . .socially adept—that he's fair."

"That is a proper assumption, Mr. Royce," Conklin said. "He has apologized in every way possible for his family's history—for his father's actions. He is to be admired for his courage."

I didn't care for the judge—not after my last encounter. And I didn't trust him. "Completely without prejudice, Mr. Conklin?"

"Is any man, beyond the Lord, totally and completely without bias, Mr. Royce? But yes, I find him, and his personal record, to be unblemished."

CHAPTER 25

WHILE I DIDN'T buy the idea that bigotry could be passed along from one generation to the next like eye color, I'd thought that Rhetman's father's beliefs might have had some negative impact on the judge growing up. I tried to conjure up a connection and envision how it might have played into the breakup of Lintz and Holly, and even into Lintz's death.

Desperate men reason in the extreme; and I was feeling just that.

At Phenix City, as I turned south toward Eufaula, and Big Hope, Alabama, my Blackberry played its loud tune signaling an incoming call.

Luke had at last located Wes.

That was the good news.

The problem was, how to get him out alive.

WHEN HE'D REACHED Big Hope on Monday afternoon, Luke had spent an hour driving around, noting the location of specific buildings, such as the courthouse with the county jail situated in the basement.

But mostly, he took his time and learned the roads—where they went, at what points they intersected, how they looked, how they *felt*. "Every game's got two basic elements," he'd once told me, "Players, and a board. When the situation dictates that you need to haul ass in a hurry in enemy territory, you best be able to hustle your piece around the game board faster an' better than your opponent."

On one of his repeat circuits, Luke found the scene of the accident that had nearly cost Wes his life. Then out on Highway 431, he located what he believed to be the white markers that Robby had spoken about in ethereal terms. The center cross with which he had collided was laying on the ground as Robby had described, raising the hairs on his neck, Luke would later admit. Finally, and as he'd told LuAnn, he'd visited the abandoned corner store out in the countryside where Wesley had made his call, the phone's receiver still coated in dried blood.

When he felt he could draw a map of the area from memory, Luke went on a search for a secure place to stay.

He located his base camp in Eufaula, in an out-of-the-way area of the lake, a place where blue collar Southerners might head for a low budget weekend with a favorite girl, or a summer vacation on the water with the family; where a sign that read, "Closed for the Season" didn't apply if you had cash to pay. A place like *Katie's Kabins*.

"I wouldn't be doin' this for just anybody," Katie said as she turned the key in the lock and let Luke into Kabin #7. "You're the only guest I got and I don't plan on takin' in more before the season starts up. But I understand what it is to be down and out on your luck. And the way it sounds to me, that woman a' yours got no heart whatsoever. She tosses you out on your butt, and now she's got her *boy*friend a lookin' for you on account of you took back the truck you been lettin' her use? Kick her square in her business is what you shoulda done." She handed Luke the key, then held out her hand. "That's two hundert an' a half in advance through Thursdee noon. This here's a smokin' unit like y'asked for and if y'all chew use a cup or do it outside and spit in the bushes to the back there and not in the kitchen sink where it'll stain. Sheets n' towels'er clean but the place's been closed up so they might could smell a bit musty. Baseboard heat works good but turn it way down before ya go lights out so's not to burn the damn place to the ground. Tanks'er off so what hot water ya'll need ya'll can boil up on the stove That's it. Have a good stay and ya'll come back and see us."

Katie pulled the door shut behind her.

Luke tossed his gym bag on the dresser in the single bedroom, then did a quick turn around the pine-paneled cabin. The bathroom was cramped, the kitchen more a closet with a half refrigerator and a two burner propane stove. But the main room was spacious, large enough for a pullout couch, a good sized television, a table and four chairs and a recliner that left no doubt that it had apparently reclined once too often.

The window looked out back over a common barbecue area with picnic tables set beneath widely-spaced pine trees. Beyond that, he could see Lake Eufaula and the boat dock and ramp advertised on the sign out front that also promised free HBO. The place would do just fine, he thought. He'd holed up in a lot worse in his time, and probably would see far worse yet.

* * *

IT WAS NEARLY six in the evening by the time he was settled. With the lack of communication from Wes gnawing at his head and a need for food gnawing at his stomach, Luke decided to kill two snakes with one shovel and shake it up from the get go; so he got into his pickup and headed to the truck stop for an early supper, and a little fun.

He parked between two dusty dump trucks in the lot out front and went inside, taking a seat at the far end of the counter where he lifted a menu from the stack jammed between the napkin holder and ketchup bottle in front of him. Clipped to the inside was a listing of the week's specials. Monday was Brunswick Stew and corn bread.

Tammy's mother came through the swinging door that led to the kitchen a minute later carrying a fully loaded tray raised up on one shoulder, and an expression on her face that said she was not in a good mood.

She made her way to a table at the rear of the restaurant where four men sat in conversation that stopped as she banged the tray down and distributed the plates of food as a sloppy dealer might a deck of cards.

"Evenin'," Luke said as she came back to the counter. "What's in the stew?"

"Everything that was a special on the menu last week, plus some pork and gravy from the noon hour and the rest of the hash from breakfast," she said as she stared at him. "Probably some of the barbecue you and your buddy ate last time you was in here."

"See, that's the thing I love best about Brunswick Stew," Luke said. "No two cooks ever make it the same, and that means it's always an adventure. I'd go a big bowl with corn bread and coffee on the side, if you'd be so kind. Pie later— peach, unless you got somethin' special in the kitchen you'd recommend in its place."

Doris was the name on her plastic badge. Doris said, "What I got special in the kitchen is no damn help, so I hope you ain't in no big hurry." She filled a mug with coffee and set it before him; the place mat and silverware followed. "Where's blondie?" she asked.

"Sorry. Who?"

"You know, the big tipper—the one that was with you in the booth over yonder the other day when that coon got his head busted. Tammy near creamed her jeans over that one."

Luke pursed his lips in thought. "Creamed over which, ma'am? The colored, or the towhead?"

Doris smiled in spite of herself. "Bit a' both, I 'spose. That ape'd a' scared the paint off a house and I'd bed that stud blond horse myself if'n I was twent—if'n I was ten years younger."

"Speakin' of which," Luke said, "where *is* that Tammy?"

The smile on her face turned cold. "What's it to you, mister?"

"Name's Luke. And, nothin' in particular. Just that you said you lacked help in the kitchen and I didn't see her's all. Just . . . makin' conversation."

"She's . . . she's pretty busted up right now. Boyfriend trouble. You know . . . with what happened and all."

Luke made a show of searching his memory, then smacked his palm on the counter. "A'course! Deputy Becker. Tammy told me about him when we were chattin' about the ruckus. He's the fella what was killed in that road accident. She must a' had her heart broke in two."

"Now, how in the world would a stranger from Florida know 'bout that?"

"Don't believe I mentioned to you where I was from, Doris."

"Why, Tammy . . . she—"

"Nope, can't recall that I mentioned it to her, either," Luke said. "Not that it's important, mind you. Could be you heard it from Deputy Becker. He was kind enough to point out to me that my driver's license had expired."

"Guess that's it. Yeah. It is. I remember it was because that colored boy was from there, too. Randy. Yeah. He mentioned it to me."

Luke nodded in thought. "Okay. Anyway, I sure would like to get on to that stew, Doris. My gut's growlin' like a pack a' wolves."

She wiped her hands on her apron. "You bet." Then she was off to the kitchen, and, Luke guessed, to the phone.

Luke had half expected to see the sheriff or one of his deputies come through the door sometime during the meal;

but dinner was consumed and paid for without a uniform to be seen anywhere.

He finished the last of his coffee, then stepped out into the poorly lit parking lot, fished a cigarette from the soft pack in his shirt pocket and walked casual-as-you-like over to his pickup. He stopped before opening the driver's side door to snap open his Zippo and strike the flint. The flame gave off enough light so that in the side view mirror, he could make out the reflection of the lower legs and booted feet of a man stretched out flat in the truck bed.

Not here, he thought. No sir. There'll be no witnesses, and no unexpected help.

The roads that spurred off the main highway were pitch black. Luke drove just below the speed limit, the radio tuned to a country music station, a cigarette tucked in the corner of his mouth—all the signs that he suspected nothing out of the ordinary if his uninvited passenger cared to venture a peek through the rear cab window.

At the intersection he'd chosen with a purpose in mind, Luke suddenly swung the truck violently to the right, then whipped the wheel back to the left and flew through the turn. He felt the impact right through his seat as his mystery rider slammed hard into the wheel well on one side, then rebounded and collided with the other. He punched the accelerator of the big V-8 into passing gear. The truck shot forward; when it reached seventy miles an hour, Luke smashed his boot down onto the break pedal, sending his passenger flying into the back of the extended cab. This, he thought, is why you don't let kids or dogs ride in the bed of a fucking pickup truck.

He settled in at fifty miles an hour and drove the final half-mile to the bottom of the hill where a pot hole remained unfilled and a tree bore the fresh scars of an auto accident.

Once there, he pulled onto the narrow shoulder and flipped on the bed light, then got out and walked to the back of the truck where he lowered the tailgate.

His would-be assailant was a young man with a mullet haircut wet with fresh blood. He lay on his side, semi-conscious; Luke yanked him like a log from the truck, letting him fall to the ground in a loud explosion of exhaled breath.

The man lay there gasping for air while Luke searched him for weapons, coming away with a sap and a nine inch switchblade knife. Finally, the lad coughed life back into his lungs and started to struggle.

Luke stood, towering above him. "Sit up," he commanded.

The young man groaned.

Luke encouraged him with a tap of the sap he'd taken, hitting him on the side of his head just above the ear. "There a yard sale on these things around here?" he said, administering another light blow, this one to the forehead above his nose, splitting the skin so that blood ran down his face, getting across the point that sitting up would be a good idea. "Pull off your boots. And your socks, too, if you're wearin' em. Do it, or the next swing goes to your nose and I can't be held responsible for where the bone ends up."

Mullet-head seemed to latch onto the idea that Luke wasn't in good humor, and complied with the order.

Luke collected the boots, then scooped up a handful of pebbles from the ground and dropped half in each. "Put 'em back on—without the socks."

The man looked at him blankly. "Why the fuck should I do that?"

Luke held up the knife and the sap. "I don't imagine you were fixin' on carvin' turkey or crackin' pecans with these little dandies, were ya? I got a missin' buddy loaded up with buckshot courtesy of you and your fucking friends. So don't give me any more reason to get madder than I already am, son. Just do it!"

Mullet man slowly righted himself and struggled into his boots. He climbed up into the truck bed with considerable effort at Luke's instructions.

"Stand up full. Now, jump off. Right here. Right onto the pavement."

"Jesus, man that's gonna—"

Luke sprung the catch on the switchblade and jabbed at the reluctant leaper's leg. "Now, partner. Ain't gonna repeat myself."

"Fuck!" he yelled as he went airborne. When he landed, the bones in the soles of his feet were badly bruised, a few broken by the impact. His breath came in little yelps as he fell to his knees. "I'll kill your ass for this, you motherfucker," he managed, squeezing out the words through clenched teeth.

"I have good reason to believe that you already had a hand in more than one killin'. Maybe I oughta flip your switch right here." Luke crouched down so they were eye to eye. "But, there'll be time for that later, if need be. We can talk about it then. For now, what you are, sonny boy, is my personal message board. You can tell good old C.W. and the rest a' the boys that time's up. Fun's over. I was them, I'd up and disappear faster and further than a fart in space."

The young tough wiped blood from his eyes, then spit more into the dirt. "I was you, I'd collect what's left of that nigger boy a' yours from whatever swamp he's in and get the fuck away from here while you still can. This is *our* town."

Luke looked him straight in the eye. "You know," he said calmly, as if addressing a misbehaving child, "the truly sad thing is, I can see that you believe that to be the truth. I'm not sure why you carry around that conviction, but I'll accept it. So, if it comes to it, I'll take your life simply to end your goddamn ignorance. And I'll sleep easy on it."

The man with the broken feet rose, cried out in pain and barely kept his balance.

Luke closed the tailgate then walked down the side of the truck and opened his door. Before he got in, he looked back at the man who now sat grimacing, holding his feet, his boots tossed aside. "Y'all tell the sheriff that we're clear on one thing." He lit a cigarette, inhaled deeply and blew out a long stream of smoke toward the night sky. "Far as I'm concerned, this is war. Some kinda holdover from history that for some reason miserable folks like you and your kind won't let rest. And trust me on this, partner, now that you've brought us into it, we won't be leavin' 'til it's settled."

CHAPTER 26

L UKE TOOK A two mile walk the next morning to knock the edge off his tightly-wound nerves, then bathed in the icy waters of Lake Eufaula before driving to Big Hope for breakfast.

He cruised by three possible eateries, then returned to the first, selecting it by the goodly number of vehicles angle parked at the curb out front.

The forty-five minutes it took to order, eat, peruse the *Eufaula Tribune* and drink a quart of coffee went by without incident. He'd collected a fair number of glances, but no one among the mix of patrons seemed to take a special interest.

He lit up the first cigarette of the morning as he left the café, then dug in his pocket for his keys, paying no attention to the man reading a folded newspaper who approached from his left—not until the man ran into him.

"My fault. Sorry," the man said to Luke. "Wasn't watching one bit where I was going."

He was black as ink with a closely cropped salt and pepper beard, his head bald and shiny in the morning sun.

Luke's muscles tensed, but he saw nothing threatening in the man's eyes, or in his body language. "No harm done, partner."

"Good day to you then," the black man said, extending a hand to Luke who took it, and the folded business card that was pressed into his palm.

Luke closed his fist around the rectangular piece of heavy stock without shifting his eyes from the man's face. "Good day to you as well," he said, then moved to his pickup as the other man walked away, his eyes again on the morning paper.

Luke drove back out to Route 431 and headed north for a mile or so on the open road, checking for any sign of a tail. Satisfied that he hadn't been followed, he pulled onto the shoulder where he stopped to inspect the card that he'd shoved in his pocket.

Printed in raised letters on the front was the name, Lazarus Jefferson, M.D., together with a phone number and address, and the doctor's office hours; on the back was written, *15 minutes. Park behind office. Use the back door.*

L AZARUS JEFFERSON OPENED the rear door to his office on the second knock.

Luke said, "My friend. What's his name, Doc?"

"Mr. Harland. Wesley."

"And, who might I be?"

"Well, according to his description, either Paul Bunyan, or an attorney—one of two lawyers that employs him. I'd venture that you're Luke Carey."

"Good enough." Luke moved inside and took a seat in one of the two chairs in front of the doctor's desk. "What's his status, Doc?"

"He'll be fine. But it isn't safe for him here," Jefferson said as he sat in his high-backed chair. He provided Luke a quick rundown on Wes's condition, and an idea of where he was.

"We owe you," Luke said. "And you're right. It idn't safe. For any of us." He gave Jefferson a summary of what had happened the previous night with the man hidden in the bed of his truck.

"Donny Becker," Jefferson said. "The late Deputy's brother."

Luke whistled softly. "You don't say. He got any more of 'em?"

"Two. Both older, and just as mean. They're part of a group of men that folks around here tend to avoid—especially black folks. They keep pretty much to themselves if they're left alone. The sheriff seems to keep them in line most of the time. But it's just a show. They can do pretty much what they please. Frankly, most of us just let it go—accept it for what it is. It isn't going to change on our account."

Luke chuckled lightly. "I'm not laughin' at the situation, Doc, so don't take offense. But it seems to me like you were impartin' a bit a' advice just then."

Jefferson smiled. "Guilty. I tried with your friend as well."

"No harm in tryin', as they say, but you should know that what you said about not changin' is an echo of what Donny Becker spit at me last evenin'."

Jefferson was slow in responding, his words measured when he did. "I could take that as an insult. But I won't. Point made. Only, you don't live here, and so you don't know the history of the—"

"History's what helps set out the future. And a part of it we're dealin' with here stretches way beyond this little burg a' yours."

The doctor shrugged. "Agreed. But that doesn't give you the right to come to Big Hope and use the town as a staging ground for some particular battle aimed at correcting the evil and inequity in the world, Mr. Carey. People will get hurt. It will only get worse, not better."

Luke worked to keep any anger out of his voice. "I'd ask kindly that you not accuse me of carryin' on a crusade. This town stepped up and shit in *my* lap, not the other way around."

Jefferson cleared his throat. "And what's the cure, Mr. Carey?"

Luke let the tension drain from his words. "Damned if I know. Anyway, I should be thankin' you, not goin' off on ya like I did. Sorry 'bout that."

Jefferson nodded, a reflective smile etched on his lips. "Second opinions are sometimes called for. Unlike many in my profession, I encourage it. But it seldom alters the diagnosis."

The doctor stood. "I trust you can find Mattie's house from the directions I've written out. She doesn't have a phone. I'll stop by and let her know you'll be out to get Mr. Harland sometime after dark. I'll check him over, but I'm sure he's fine to travel."

Luke took the sheet of paper that Jefferson held out to him, folded it with great care and slipped it into his shirt pocket. "Before I go, is there anything else I should know—any of that history you referred to that might help?"

Jefferson took his time in answering. "I came here from Birmingham five years ago to help out an elderly physician. I bought the practice from his estate. He was the only black doctor in town and his patients had nowhere else to go. He'd been here for years and shared a number of stories with me over his checker board. I've heard stories from several of my patients as well. In any event, what I understand of the past is predicated on second and third hand accounts—sometimes conflicting stories. It would be unfair of me to indict others based on hazy recollection, or speculation."

Luke studied Jefferson closely. "I don't doubt that, just like the rest of the country, Big Hope has more good folks than bad. But I'd give odds that the underbelly of its history runs down closer to the flames than most. And it appears that there are those around here doin' their best to see that it doesn't flicker out."

Jefferson focused sharply on Luke. "You've seen it yourself. It becomes vicious." Jefferson returned to his desk, indicating to Luke that he should again sit. "I haven't seen it written anywhere, nor taken the time to try and confirm it, but as I understand it from my collection of local historians, the root of this . . . this bitterness and conceit is found in deeper soil. It's the name, Mr. Carey, as strange as that may sound, the name of the town itself that stands as a symbol of the underlying riff.

"You see, Big Hope sits on land that was owned as part of a larger plantation by a decent family. When the hope of freedom became a reality, they deeded the parcel where the town was eventually built to their former slaves. They felt sincerely that those they had enslaved should benefit from the years of sweat and labor. The former slaves in turn proclaimed to the family— or so the story goes—that their act of generosity had given them 'big hope for the future.'

"Soon after, the family sold the remainder of their land and moved on. The freemen began to build a modest community, but as was the fate of most freed slaves, they had been cast into an unfamiliar role. They weren't skilled in business. They ran short of seed to plant their crops, and the money to buy it. Like many, they turned to the white merchants who could provide what they needed, generously *allowing* them to buy on credit.

"Within two years," Jefferson continued, "they'd lost it all. Some factions just drifted off, but others remained to work the land they'd lost to the whites in the credit swindle.

In time, the plantation was shut down and the land sold off in smaller parcels for farms, and the town eventually grew into what it is today."

"It must feel damn near like a mockery to the blacks who're the descendants of those who got fleeced," Luke said.

Jefferson rose from his chair and walked slowly to the door. "More than damn near," he said as he saw Luke out. "It is."

CHAPTER 27

L UKE SAT IN the cab of his truck memorizing the directions Lazarus Jefferson had given him, then swung the pickup out of the driveway and headed southwest, passing the courthouse with its flag flying at half-staff in honor of Deputy Randy Becker who would be buried at one in the afternoon.

The approach to Mattie's house was from the east, taking Luke past the abandoned store, turning him right on a gravel road two miles further on, then having him travel another quarter mile, the truck tires kicking up a dust storm in his wake. He wouldn't risk stopping in daylight; but he didn't want his first visit to an unfamiliar place to be in the dark, either.

The house sat a hundred feet back from the road—a one-story dwelling with peeling paint, the tin roof streaked with rust, a pickup parked parallel to the front porch where an old woman sat on an equally old sofa looking with some interest at Luke as he drove by without slowing down.

It was another half-mile before Luke came to the next farmhouse, a near-twin of Mattie's. A mile more, and the narrow gravel road ended at a T intersection.

As he slowed to a stop, he saw a patrol car in his rearview mirror a hundred yards behind him, a vehicle that had been obscured by the pickup's trailing dust. Luke made his turn; twenty seconds later, the police car followed.

He drove just above the forty mile per hour speed limit; the officer mimicked the pace and followed him for nearly thirty minutes, matching him turn for turn. Law enforcement knew Luke was in town because he'd *wanted* them to know. But this angered him—not that he was being tailed, but that he'd been careless enough to allow himself to be followed before he'd wanted to warrant such close attention. In his mind's eye he saw the deputy who had been standing in the parking lot of the courthouse when he'd passed by, the trunk of his cruiser open. That had to have been it. But not everything was lost: At least he'd been alert enough not to stop, or even slow down as he'd driven by Mattie's house.

Okay, then, no harm done. Well, what the hell: if the local authorities wanted to chew up the county's gas dogging him, he'd be happy to oblige; if they wanted to see what it was that he found to be of interest, he'd give them plenty to consider.

Luke drove the county roads, slowing several times as he went by houses and mobile homes, hitting the brake lights here and there. At one point, he stopped and got out, spread a road map across the hood of his truck and peered at it closely for several minutes, making nonsense notations with a pencil.

He got back in the truck and continued on, then stopped at a stand of pine trees where he sat in the shade, lowered his window, and had a cigarette. When he finished, it was back on the road and on with the show.

After an hour, Luke figured that he'd provided the deputy with plenty of possible locations where Pickett might be holed up. It was time for a break.

Luke pulled into the truck stop just before noon. Doris was behind the counter serving a scraggly-looking man in coveralls and a baseball cap turned backward on his head, his stringy hair looking as though it had been washed in fish oil.

As he took a seat several stools down, Luke heard the squeak of the entry door opening behind him. Doris looked up, then disappeared into the kitchen without acknowledging Luke with so much as a furtive glance.

The deputy sheriff who'd been Becker's partner took the stool next to Luke. He removed his hat and sunglasses and set them on the counter. "Nice morning for a drive," he said.

Luke didn't respond, opening a menu instead and making a great study of the choices.

The deputy swiveled his stool sideways. "You always this rude?"

Luke put down the menu and met his eyes. "Sorry, you say somethin', Officer?"

"You know goddamn well I did. I seen you out driving all over hell and back. Looked to me like you was scouting around for a place to rob. You're a stranger, and I get paid to watch out for your kind. Now, you want to tell me what you're up to?"

"Doin' your job. Good for you. Looks like if I buy a few acres around here, I'll be well protected. Makes a fella feel all safe inside. Yep, that it does. All warm and fuzzy."

"That's a load a' crap, mister."

Luke smiled at the deputy. "And why is that?"

"First, there ain't nothing around here for sale. And two, you didn't say shit about no land deal the other day."

"Well, I thought about it and decided Big Hope was just too friendly a place not to be. A man could live and die right here without a care—long as he's the right color, if you catch my drift." He looked at his watch. "Say, that reminds me . . . you got yourself a funeral in a few minutes. Don't want you to up and forget, now, do we?"

The deputy jumped up. "Alright! That's it! Let me see some identification." He tried to inject some authority into his words. "And I mean right now."

Luke rose, looming over the young officer who seemed suddenly to pale a shade or two, as though Luke had cast a shadow over his confidence. "Out in my truck, son. Be right back." He pushed past him and started for the door, the deputy quickly at his heels.

Luke opened the door of his truck and got in, slamming it behind him.

The deputy pounded on the window. "What the hell do you think you're doing? Out of the truck. Now!" he shouted through the glass.

Luke lowered the window. "Got things to do, and you're wastin' my time."

The deputy reached through the window and made a grab for the keys in the ignition.

Luke caught his fingers in a twisted grip and pulled the deputy tight against the door so that he was unable to reach across his body for his service revolver. "Okay, Barney. You most certainly know who I am, and, maybe why I'm here," he said. "What you don't know is who *else* knows it—who else might be here or on the way. To boot, you got no idea what we've learned about this shit dump town a' yours. Most likely, a fella in your position's without a clue as to the truth of it." He tightened his grip.

The deputy swallowed hard, his Adam's apple clicking in his throat. "You're assaulting an officer of the—"

Luke snapped the deputy's right index and middle fingers with a sharp turn of his wrist. The cop's jaw clamped shut, stifling a scream. "Now, you go back inside and wait 'til I'm good and gone, and nothin' more'll happen to you. As it is, a few weeks in a splint and you'll be right back pickin' your nose."

The deputy pulled his right hand free of Luke's grasp and back through the window, immediately cradling it in his left. He made no comment nor attempt to engage Luke further.

A LITTLE BEFORE ONE that afternoon, Luke pulled his truck to the curb on the side of the public square opposite a grouping of white chairs that sat in semi-circular rows on the lawn in front of a gazebo where a lectern and microphone had been set in place. He lowered his window, and lit up.

Precisely on the hour, Sheriff Vernon approached the microphone and spoke to the gathering of uniformed officers and townspeople—all white—his words reaching Luke's ears in echo.

When he'd finished, Becker's partner—his hand now bandaged—spoke for several minutes about his friend and hero.

Next, it was a man Luke hadn't seen before, but assumed by his constant reference to "my bro" to be one of the other brothers Doc Jefferson had mentioned. He was followed immediately by Mullet Man who limped to the podium and read a few halting lines from a crumpled paper he'd pulled from his shirt pocket.

The last speaker was the waitress, Tammy, who lasted fifteen or so seconds before she began blubbering and had to be helped back to her seat by the fallen deputy's partner who promptly placed his left arm around her and began to rub her back with his good hand. Luke guessed that it wouldn't be long before he got up the nerve to try rubbing more than that, and not long thereafter, sweet young Tammy would stop protesting and start to warm to his touch.

The service ended at two with a long-winded prayer delivered by an aging pastor who promised the gathered faithful that Randy Becker had served his fellow man with selfless sacrifice and would be welcomed into The Kingdom of Heaven by a host of angels. There, he would live a life eternal in blessed peace. Can I get an 'Amen.'

Luke had serious doubts that Old Saint Peter would find a reason to open up the Pearly Gates to a man like Deputy Becker.

After a final hymn, Becker's coffin was carefully and slowly loaded into a white hearse and led by police escort to a small cemetery a mile south of town.

Luke followed at a distance as the caravan wound through the countryside, then pulled over and parked on the shoulder of the road just beyond the entrance to the graveyard.

From there, he watched through the pine trees as the casket was removed from the hearse and placed gently atop supports that spanned the open grave; the mourners gathered beneath a green tent, and the interment service began.

He could see Becker's partner—his arm once more around Tammy's shoulders—standing near the head of the bronze casket. Next to them stood Becker's two brothers. C.W. Vernon, however, was nowhere in sight.

Luke leaned against the pickup's fender, his back to the service, and waited.

Sheriff Vernon pulled his unmarked unit in behind Luke's truck a few minutes later. When he got out of the car, Luke noticed that he'd changed from the formal uniform he'd worn at the funeral; despite the cool day, the sheriff was now dressed in everyday khakis, his shirt, short sleeved, his head, hatless, his eyes covered by sunglasses. "Bum a smoke?" he asked as he walked toward Luke.

Luke pulled the pack from his shirt pocket and handed it to Vernon. The sheriff tapped out a cigarette and accepted a light.

"Keep 'em," Luke said as Vernon held the pack between them. "Pack'll no doubt give up a good set of prints."

Vernon smiled as he handed the pack of cigarettes back to Luke. "Thanks anyway."

"Doris wear a badge, does she?"

"Nope. Don't take no women on the force. Goddamn pussy problems'd drive me crazy."

"Too bad about Becker," Luke said.

"Kid was an idiot. Couldn't write a jaywalker without fuckin' it up." The sheriff searched Luke's face. "So, my friend, how y'all see this thing workin' out, anyway?"

Luke blew out twin jet streams of white smoke through his nose. "Tough one, idn't it. Seems as though we're both in pretty deep."

Vernon considered it. "Idiot or not, I got one in the ground already. The way you go about it, I'd say they'll be more before it's over. You? You got one on the run. Hounds made him for a spell, then lost him. Picked him up again at the phone, then lost him again. He's still around, or you wouldn't be. And you got more assets here, or in the know. I understand that. It's why you're still suckin' air. You're right. It *is* tough."

"You forgot one, Sheriff. Critical oversight."

The sheriff narrowed his eyes as he looked squarely at Luke. "That there was not my call."

"Result's the same," Luke said. "The Cain boy's still dead."

Vernon let his cigarette fall to the ground where it lay like a smoking fuse. "So call it even. Gather up your nigra and be on your way. Time's runnin' out."

"Then what? You wipe it clean on all counts? Everybody's happy? All in, all said?"

"One time offer. Turn it down, and no way I can let that colored boy or you or anyone else walk off. I'm willin' to gamble that you can't sell this shit you got in your head to anyone on the outside. Randy's partner can shoot with the other hand. His brother with the busted feet's ready to jack you any way he can. Not so much the bones, as the humiliation. You're good, but you can't win."

"Maybe if Cain had made it, we coulda bargained. But he didn't, and I have no compromise available unless you'd care to pursue the Lintz killin' in the proper manner."

"Case closed."

"Figured as much."

The sheriff shook his head. "I guess that's it, then. I could take you in now. Assault on an officer. Use you for bait. Pull your plug. You name it. What do you think I should do?"

Luke chuckled. "If it was that simple, you'd 'a done it already—or at least tried harder than you did with that stunt you pulled with Becker's brother layin' wait in my truck."

"I boxed his fuckin' ears half off his goddamned head for that. He was on his own. It was me 'stead of you? . . . I'd 'a kilt him on the spot."

"Trust me. I thought about it."

"I'll bet you did. But you haven't answered my question."

"You're fishin'. We both know it. You'll not get an answer. But I'll give y'all a freebie, Sheriff: The Honorable Judge Zachary Rhetman."

Vernon paled. "I wish I hadn't heard that. Truly I do."

The two men stood three feet apart, measuring one another, their eyes unblinking. Finally, Luke flipped his cigarette butt to the dirt, then crushed it under his heel. "It's on, then?"

Vernon sighed deeply, then said, "It is."

"You have a change of heart, or need a meet, you call my cell." Luke handed the sheriff a piece of paper. "I'll set it up so you go down easy as possible."

"Goddamn, you're a hard-ass," Vernon said as he walked to his car. "Jesus fuckin' Christ. They're not nearly worth all this shit." He got in and slammed his door. "None of 'em are."

Luke looked at him through the open window.

The sheriff held his eyes. "So, you're gonna try and bring it down around our ears, ain't ya. Well, you're a goddamned fool is what you are. Yes sir." He started the engine, then slipped the gearshift into reverse.

"And why is that, Sheriff?"

Vernon smiled, but without any pleasure as far as Luke could see. "You're not from around here, are ya."

"Not originally," Luke said. "But I am now."

CHAPTER 28

M Y LONG PHONE conversation with Luke brought me within a half hour of Big Hope. When I drove past the town thirty minutes later, I'd half expected to be stopped in a roadblock.

The directions Luke had given me were simple enough, and I pulled in to *Katie's Kabins* late Wednesday afternoon; Luke's truck wasn't in sight. I knocked on the door of Number 7. There was no answer.

"Bang, you're dead," Luke's voice came from behind me causing my heart to suddenly pound in my chest.

"If you're trying to make a grown man piss his pants, you nearly succeeded," I said as I turned around.

"Get used to it." He unlocked the door of the small cabin. We stepped inside. "Base camp," Luke remarked. "Not much to it, but we'll tough it out. Hope you're partial to cold showers."

The table and counter were stacked with grocery bags. "At least we'll eat," I said.

"Restaurants are no longer an option."

"Where's your truck?" I asked.

"Observant, aren't ya. It's at the apartment complex. The rental's outside."

I cracked open the door. "Oh. Yeah. How could I have missed it?"

I took the next few minutes to fill in the blanks on Holly, her father, Gerard, and the history given me by Jamie and embellished by Russell Conklin—adding chapters to what Luke had gleaned from Lazarus Jefferson.

"We get Wesley clear, we can get into it full bore," Luke said. "I'll be one surprised sonofabitch if for whatever reason Vernon hasn't contacted the judge by now. I thought he'd crap watermelons when I brought up the name Rhetman."

Near dusk, we drove a loop of roads that brought us past the back of Mattie Franklin's property, the house and outbuildings visible in the distance across a dusty field.

"We'll go in this way," Luke said, "after dark."

"Why not get it over with now?" I said. "We haven't seen a cop anywhere."

"*You* haven't." Luke grinned in the failing light. "Son, you missed the rental car in front of the friggin' cabin door. How'd you expect to pick up on the three cruisers we've gone by— one in the woods a mile back; one behind the corner store; the last one in the tall grass off your right shoulder fifty feet in at that last intersection. Vernon might be a hick town cop, but I'd guess he's got other history. He's fair competition."

"What if one of them saw us?" I said.

"Well now, they *obviously* saw us."

"I mean—if they . . . ."

"Made us? Noted the vehicle maybe, but won't put anything together 'less they see it again. But they won't."

***

W E WAITED UNTIL dark, plus a few hours, before returning, approaching from the opposite direction we'd come from earlier. Luke killed the lights and pulled the car into the woods a half-mile from Mattie's house.

He took the .38 revolver from the duffel bag in the trunk, handed it to me, then stuffed a switchblade knife and a sap in his pocket.

"What am I supposed to do with this?" I asked.

"It ain't for stirrin' spaghetti, partner. Use it if you have to."

I stopped in my tracks. "You're serious."

"I guarantee *they* are."

My mouth was dry. "I don't know if I could."

"Christ-a-Mighty. Your feet need booties, then wait in the car."

I'd never heard him sound so cold. This was the Luke that lurked in dark shadows—the Luke that worried Jamie. I took a deep breath, collecting myself.

"If we run into a problem," Luke said, "don't think. React. They'll kill you as soon as cut a fart."

The adrenaline hit. My heart raced and I began to shake. "I'll be okay."

"Alright then," he said. "Keep focused. Now . . .let's get to it. Wesley's waitin'. "

* * *

W E STAYED IN the tree line until the lights of the house flickered into view across the field.

The moon was obscured by a heavy cloud cover; our dark clothing made us all but invisible as we started across the open stretch of ground, the newly-plowed earth soft underfoot.

Halfway to the house, Luke suddenly stopped. "Pen light," he whispered. "Two o'clock."

At first, I couldn't see it. Then, my eye caught the thin beam.

"He's walkin' toward the back of that outbuildin' to the right," Luke said. "You go the long way 'round to the left of the house. I'll head straight on in and see what's up. You wait 'til you see two sets of three flashes each. That'll tell ya I'm clear. Then, come to my position. Stay low and stay loose. We only get the one chance at surprise."

"Okay. Okay." I started walking away.

"And take that heater outta your goddamn belt and keep it at the ready," he said.

It took five minutes to reach the house.

I crouched twenty feet away behind a stack of tractor tires, the .38 gripped tightly in a sweaty hand. The lights inside were on, but the perimeter was dark. Out front, I could make out the hulk of a pickup truck; a second vehicle—a car—was parked beside it, but I couldn't tell exactly what it was.

The minutes dragged. Finally, I saw the patterned flashes of light coming from Luke's position. I retraced my steps back to the field, then cut an angle toward him. He was squatting over a body, the sap dangling from his fingers. We moved away in silence.

"Becker's brother," he said. "I rattled his pan but good. "

"They know Wes is here."

"Vernon's crafty. He knew from the blood that Wesley was shot. Musta kept an eye on Doc Jefferson and had him followed yesterday. I shoulda figured it."

"There's a car out front," I said.

"Somebody else'll be inside. Prob'ly Donley. Becker's partner."

"Now what?"

Luke considered it. "Chaos. You through the front. Me in from the back. Lots a' noise. You hit the door, fire a couple rounds into the ceiling. Yell it up. But keep your eyes and your brain on what's in front of you. You'll only get a second of advantage. Use it. Whichever of us gets the best chance takes him down."

"What if there's more than one?"

"Small house," Luke said. "Front door'll open on the main room. That's where I'm bettin' they'll be. Back'll give onto the kitchen. I'll come in fast and quiet, and take out whichever one you don't."

"And this is going to work?"

"Far as I know."

"Comforting."

We checked our watches. Thirty seconds to get in place, get ready, and go in. No time to think about what I was doing.

I stood in the shadows to the right of the house. Three steps up to the porch; ten feet to the door; fifteen seconds to a situation I'd never encountered.

What the hell. There's a first time for everything, right? That's the thought I held on to as I ran up the stairs and across the porch.

The door splintered off its hinges as the full weight of my body crashed against it. I tumbled into the room and came up yelling. "Don't fucking move!" I fired a shot toward the ceiling, the sound deafening in the confined space.

The uniformed deputy I recognized as Becker's partner sat in the middle of the room playing solitaire. His eyes went wide. I flipped the card table in his face; he went over backward.

Luke came through the backdoor. "Clear!" he shouted as he came into the room.

The doors to the bedrooms and the bathroom were open, the rooms empty.

Donley lay on his back, my foot pressing hard on his chest, the pistol pointed at his head. "Where is he?" I demanded.

He looked up at me, red-faced, gasping for air. "He's not here."

Luke stepped in and yanked him to his feet, throwing him against the wall. Donley sank to the floor, stunned. "He . . . I . . . ."

Luke stood him up. "One word at a time, Bucky boy. And make sense."

"They's, ah . . . they's both gone."

"*Who* both? Where?" Luke thundered.

"I told ya. The sheriff took'em. Pickett and the old lady."

Luke rocked him into the wall. "Took 'em where?"

"Stop. Please. You'll bust somethin' inside, okay? I'm supposed to give you a message. A number. In my pocket."

I jammed my hand in his pants pocket and turned it inside out. A piece of paper fell to the floor. Scribbled on it was a phone number.

"Y'all suppose to call him. That's all I know. I swear it."

Luke took Donley by the throat; in seconds, the deputy lay unconscious on the floor. "Wait here," he said to me.

Thirty seconds later, Luke came back into the house with Becker's sapped brother slung over his shoulder. He dropped him on top of Donley. "Now there's a certified shit pile if ever I saw one." He took the handcuffs and keys from the deputy's belt and snapped one side of the cuffs around Donley's thin ankle, the other on Becker's brother's wrist.

"Fuck's goin' down?" Two young black men appeared from nowhere and stood just inside the doorway, a shotgun leveled at us by the one on the right.

"You kin to Mattie?" Luke asked, his voice dead calm.

"Who the fuck wants to know?" the man with the shotgun snapped.

"Vernon and his boys took her and a shot-up black name a' Wesley Harland." Luke said in answer.

The one without the gun took a step forward and looked at the men on the floor as if to verify what Luke had said. "Goddamn," he exclaimed. "It's fuckin' Dipshit Donley and Donny Becker." He turned to Luke. "You Harland's buds, ain't you."

Luke stood. "We are."

"What's gonna happen to Grandma?"

"Nothin'. Not yet. We got a number. We could speak with her to be certain, but I'm a' no mind to make a call. I'd like to keep 'em guessin' if you'll agree."

The two men glanced at each other. "What? You askin' for our okay?" the one with the shotgun said.

"It's you holdin' the blower, son."

"Name's Isaiah," the black man said as he lowered the shotgun. "This is my brother Zeke. We picked your friend up at the store—brought him here."

"What're we gonna do?" Zeke asked.

"Find 'em both, if we can. Vernon's gonna keep 'em out of sight," Luke said. "Question is, where? And we're much obliged for what you did for Wesley Harland."

Isaiah nodded, then narrowed his eyes in thought. "There's a place we ain't 'spose to know about. No nigger is," he said. "And no brother with a brain is gonna' get near it. Disphit, Becker, C.W. and a few other fucked-in-the-head white retards hang out there."

"Worth a shot," Luke said. "You boys up for it? Gonna need help on this one. There's some serious shit about to fly into the picture. And we don't have a handle on it yet."

Isaiah flopped down on the couch, nudging Donny Becker's head with a boot in the process. "His kind have had their day. There's things Grandma says happened over time around this place that ain't right."

"We know some of the history," I said.

"I'm talkin' about what's gettin' people shot *now*."

"There's a tie," Luke said. "It's got to do with a judge from Atlanta—Rhetman—a powerful name after the Civil War."

"Yeah, I know," Isaiah said. "Grandma says it's the name a' those who stole up the plantation and sent the free niggers packin.' But like I say, that shit's got dust on it."

"What else have you heard about the Rhetmans?" I asked.

It was Zeke who answered. "Well, some white chick with the same name put her ride into the trees a few years ago, if that's what you're referrin' to—drunk on her ass. Killed her own momma. That's it. Ain't been nothin' else since then."

I looked at Zeke. "You got it wrong, son. Her mother lost control of the car and hit the trees. Her daughter was thrown clear," I said. "It was in the paper."

"You say *what*? No sir. What I know is what I saw."

"The accident? You *saw* it happen?" I asked.

"No, man. But just after. We were maybe fifteen at the time. Cops went screamin' out to the highway. We jump in Cueball's truck and head out after 'em to see the fuss. I did, anyway. Isaiah

214 Murder In Big Hope

was off someplace. Anyways, we get there and the sheriff's got it all blocked off. Can't get near the spot. The lights are flashin' and I see a tarp on the ground. Cool. Somebody's dead. Kid's way of thinkin', ya know? So I go around into the trees and come on it that way. It's a rag top. All bashed in and fucked up. Couldn't see the tarp or anything else from there. Just the girl in the driver's seat. Figured she was dead from the blood on her head. She wasn't a momma, though. That's for damn sure."

"And you're positive about this?" I asked.

"Better believe it. Cops clear everybody out. Cueball an' them take off all hangin' out the back a' the truck. I stay where I am an' watch the show. Wind's blowin' my way. I can smell the booze, man. Jack, maybe. Sweet. Ambulance comes. They pull her out a' the car and do all that doctor shit. Off she goes. Then Vernon starts walkin' around talkin' on his radio. Then the meat truck comes an' they load a body. Hook truck, too. Then off *they* go. Sheriff sends everybody else away, but he stays. He starts kickin' dirt around like he's lookin' for somethin'. He starts comin' in the woods near me, then he stops and squats— takes his hat off and stares right in my direction. But he doesn't see me. Shit, I ain't gonna get caught, so when he turns and goes the other way, I sneak off and come out down the road."

I looked at Luke. "Different story, huh?"

He reached for a cigarette.

"Not in the house, man," Isaiah said.

Luke put the pack back in his pocket. "Any idea what he was lookin' for, Zeke?"

"Nope. Only, as I'm leavin' to walk back to town, this slick dick in a Caddy comes blastin' past me headin' north. He screeches it dead where the sheriff's at. I wait to see what's happenin' but all they're doin' is talkin'. So off I go."

"Slick dick?" I said.

"White dude. Greased up hair all slicked back."

SHERIFF VERNON HAD stepped back quickly as the Cadillac came to a skidding stop at the side of the road, showering his shoes with gravel. His mouth was dry; his stomach roiled.

The driver got out. "You did right to call. How bad is it?"

"It's bad," Vernon said. "The wife's dead. Girl's all busted up to hell. She was liquored up to boot."

"Goddamn. This could cost him the appointment—cost *us* everything. Have you talked to him?"

"Not yet. Figured we'd go see him at the plantation."

The other man thought for a moment. "Alright, then. Here's how we play it."

The sheriff listened, then said, "What about the medics?"

"I'll take care of it. Don't concern yourself about that. Let's—"

Vernon cut him off. "There's a complication." He led the other man to where a tarp lay in the brush. He lifted the edge so the other man could see what the sheriff had covered up.

The man stooped down to have a closer look. "Anyone else see this?"

"No," Vernon replied. "I figured that would not be a good idea."

"That's fine thinking. This goes unreported. It has to. This little matter would end it for good. And, he'll be in our eternal debt." The man stood. "Shovels, Sheriff. We need shovels."

"YOU EVER TELL anybody about all this?" Luke asked Zeke when he'd finished.

"I wasn't never 'spose to be out with that crew. Grandma'd have my ass. So, no, not then. But later, yeah, I told her. She'd seen it in the paper, same story as you dug back up. I set her straight on it. She swore me on Jesus, I don't say nothin' to nobody. *Nobody*, she says. Get us in trouble with the whites and the cops and we get nothin' but grief from then on. So, I don't. Just Issy . . . Isaiah."

Becker and Donley began to stir. We dragged them outside to a shed and trussed them up to a post in a sitting position with a length of rope.

I turned on a garden hose and sprayed water in their faces. Donley came alive, sputtering; Becker bobbed his head, but that was it.

Luke squatted down close to Donley's face. "Where they at, Dipshit?"

"I do not know, man."

"Get some air in your head. Where are they? I'm not fixin' to ask again."

"I still don't know. I swear it." Donley repeated. "I'm not shit to C.W. I'm not on the in, if you know what I'm sayin'. He just gave me the number and told us to wait. You'd show, he says. Don't do nothin' but tell you to call, he says. Then we split. That's the truth. I got nothin'else."

I could see it in Luke's eyes; he knew Donley was telling the truth.

"What was Donny doin' skulkin' 'round out back, then?" Luke asked.

"Went to take a piss. Wouldn't do it in no coon crapper, he says."

"Oh, really," Zeke said as he stepped over and straddled an unconscious Donny Becker, and unzipped his fly.

Luke and I turned away and walked outside with Isaiah.

CHAPTER 29

W E DROVE MATTIE'S pickup back to the rental car. Zeke and Isaiah slid into the back, the shotgun between them; Luke sat quietly, blowing smoke out through his cracked window while I followed Isaiah's directions to the cabin in the sparsely populated southwest corner of Big Hope County where we suspected Wes and Mattie had been taken.

I dug out my Blackberry and scrolled down through the phone numbers in my directory.

Luke shot me a questioning glance.

"Gerard." I found his home number and hit SEND.

"Have you got a clue as to what time it is, and how much I do not fucking want to talk to you?" Gerard said when he answered.

"There was an accident ten years ago. You were scared for your job—maybe a lot more than that. I can see why."

"You don't know what the hell you're talking about."

"I have an eyewitness that puts Holly behind the wheel, Gerry. She killed her mother under the influence. Headlines. Maybe even jail time. Rhetman got it covered up somehow—got the story switched. You wanted his ass for it. I think you were waiting to blow him up if he ran for office, but he never did. You put Lintz on it. Then me. And I'm tired of doing your dirty work. Maybe you know who killed Lintz, too. What else is there, Gerry? Don't you hold out on me. We've got people jammed up in a bad way."

Gerard spoke after a long silence. "No, I don't know who killed him. I could guess, but it would be one-in-three at best. Yeah, I knew about the accident. The info came out of one of the EMT's over a six pack of beer. Next day, he quits and moves away. I couldn't track him for shit. His partner says I'm fucking brain dead, it was the old lady behind the wheel. I try the Big Hope Sheriff's office. I might as well be the plague, but they fax me the accident report anyway. It's bullshit, but it's official. End of story."

"You've got to come forward on this."

"Why? You already got a witness."

"He was a kid," I said. "A black kid. What weight do you think he'd swing?"

"I got nothing but corroboration from an A.W.O.L. EMT. Good luck."

"I see your point. But you're letting him get away with it."

Gerard laughed. "Power can make anything go away."

"He'd go so far as to kill for this?" I said.

"Who says he did?"

"But he at least knows about it—and probably who did it. He's still guilty."

"That's a formula for blackmail," Gerard said.

"You think they'd take him on?"

"He pulled off the cover-up for his daughter. That had to cost him. Pay once, you keep on paying."

"I don't know. He's too cocky. I've thought about it, but it seems too thin."

"People do crazy shit over a lot less," Gerard said. "And he's crazy about Holly."

"Maybe that's it. Maybe not. I'll ask you again, what else are we chasing here?"

"It's gone too far. There's nothing more I can do. You're on your own. I'm . . . Goodnight, counselor."

Dial tone.

We pulled the rented Chevy into the woods a half-mile from the lane that led to the cabin. The gate was closed and padlocked, but fresh tire tracks marked the dirt.

"When we get on the other side," Luke said, "spread apart twenty yards to either side of the path. There's no rush, so don't go trippin' up. We get the cabin in sight and see a vehicle— lights, anything—stop dead and we'll re-group. Cage, up and over first. Go with Isaiah to the left. Zeke, you and I have the right flank."

We moved ahead slowly in the darkness. Ten minutes later, we saw light filtering through the trees.

Luke recognized the sheriff's unmarked car as we approached the cabin, stopping thirty yards short where we huddled. "Vernon. Maybe one more. Two at the most," he said. "We'll wait 'em out. When they get no call from us, they'll get itchy—maybe they already are. Somebody's bound to go and check Mattie's place. When Vernon comes out, I'll—"

The Blackberry in the pocket of my jacket went off. In the quiet of the woods, it might as well have been a fire horn. I dug it out and killed it, but it had taken me at least five seconds to silence it.

We froze in place and waited.

In seconds, the lantern inside was extinguished. The door creaked open and the shadowed figures of two men emerged and disappeared around the back of the cabin. The door was closed behind them.

"Goddamnit. I didn't—"

"No time," Luke snapped in a harsh whisper. "It's done. They'll split up and come from both directions. We try n' make a run, the noise'll do us in. We gotta outflank 'em. Cage and Isaiah, wide right. Big loop. Twenty yards between ya. Same for Zeke and me on the left. Try like hell to get the jump on 'em, and keep the noise down. No firearms unless it's the only way. Now go!"

We moved rapidly away on a straight line for a hundred long strides, then traced the sweep of a second hand that would go from three o'clock down to six and bring us back to the same position in front of the cabin, but a football field away. Halfway through the arc, we heard someone, sounding heavy and clumsy as he trounced through the woods.

Isaiah and I split wider apart, then crouched and waited; from the sound, he'd pass between us. But then his approach changed, shifting so that I was nearly in his direct path.

I gripped the pistol around the cylinder, intending to use the force of a blunt object to the head to bring him down. He was steps away now. I held my breath, tensed the muscles in my thighs and readied myself to spring up and smash the .38 into his temple.

Then, he stopped. I heard a slight rustle of dried grass, then a raspy sound, like air being blown through a hose. Someone fell to the ground.

"Cage? Where you at?" It was Isaiah.

I reached him in ten paces. A body lay at his feet. A long, thin knife was in Issy's hand. His eyes were wide and he was shaking violently. "Oh, man! What the fuck'd I do?"

"You didn't have a choice," I said. "I might have blown it. Come on, let's go find Zeke and my partner."

We looped back the way we'd come. Luke and Isaiah's brother were waiting. "Everybody whole?" Luke asked.

"Pretty shook. But, yeah. You?" I said.

"We're good. I took care of it. Now the prize."

We dropped back and stationed ourselves along a line at twenty yard intervals—the brothers at forty-five degree angles off the corners of the cabin while I took up a position directly in front of the door, now about forty yards away.

Luke made his way in a crawl to the sheriff's car.

I checked my watch. Thirty seconds to go. Twenty. Ten.

I fired two shots from the .38 into the cabin roof.

Luke hustled to Vernon's cruiser.

The headlights of the unmarked unit came on, illuminating the cabin like a sound stage at curtain call. Then the strobes concealed behind the front grill began to pepper the windows with rapid explosions of red and blue.

Another shot into the roof while Luke scrambled away.

I took out my offending Blackberry and punched in the number given us by Dipshit Donley.

"Ollie, Ollie in free," I said when the sheriff answered.

"Give me Carey," he said.

Luke came down the dirt track. "No sense of humor whatsoever," I said, handing him the Blackberry with a shaky hand.

"Your move," Luke said into the phone. He listened for several seconds, then said, "Can't do that. Uh huh. No, I understand. We'll consider it. I'll call ya back in one." He hit END, then said, "He wants a meet. It can only go one of two ways from here."

"Sounded like he asked for something else," I said.

"A swap, and a two-way deal. Can't do the first. He's really fucked with us findin' him. So we can float the second."

"You trust him?"

"I did. Not now. But we got a three-man advantage. He'll figure it at one."

Luke sent Zeke and Isaiah to opposite sides of the cabin, just out of reach of the headlights.

Vernon had offered to come out—unarmed—and stand in the light in front of the cruiser. No tricks. No games. One of us would hold a gun on him while the other went in and got Wes and Mattie. We'd agree to leave Big Hope that night with no hassle. Mattie's life would serve as the guarantee for our perpetual silence.

Luke called him back and said we had a deal. He'd lied, of course.

But then, so had the sheriff.

Vernon came out of the cabin and stood on the front porch in the glaring wash of the headlights, hands held at shoulder height, the red and blue flash of the strobes lending a surreal quality to the scene.

"Down on the dirt. Walk to the car," Luke called out.

The sheriff descended the stairs, a gap of a few yards now separating him from the porch at his back.

I could see the two brothers move quickly to the cabin where they pressed themselves against opposing side walls.

Luke and I split up and approached him, the gun extended in my hand and pointing at the center of his chest.

"Who's goin' in?" Vernon asked, shielding his eyes from the glare of the headlights with one hand in an attempt to see us. His other fell to his belt line.

"That'd be me," Luke said.

At the sound of Luke's voice, Vernon dropped down out of sight behind the hood. His first shot went blindly in Luke's direction; with the second and third, he took out the headlights that lit him up. The fourth whined through the air over my head.

I hit the ground. In the flashes of red and blue, I saw Zeke and Isaiah rush the sheriff's position, unseen by Vernon.

"Don't kill him!" Luke roared, reinforcing his prior order.

I went to the driver's side and switched off the strobe lights. Zeke dragged Vernon to his feet, hands locked behind him in his own cuffs.

"Get your goddamn hands off a' me, boy." Vernon pulled loose. "It's not done," he said to Luke.

"Inside." Luke took the sheriff's arm and marched him into the cabin.

Wes and Mattie were bound hand and foot to straight backed chairs, tape stretched across their mouths.

Mattie's grandsons freed her; Luke did the same for Wes. Both appeared unharmed.

"This is Satan's house," Mattie said, eyes fixed on Wes. "Dark angel o'God called y'all here so we might be saved."

"Mighty impressive," Luke said to Wes.

"Ain't it, though?"

"Good to see you alive and well, partner. You too, ma'am"

I'd turned up the kerosene lantern. We'd stepped back in time. The interior of the cabin was just as Isaiah had described it from a frightened childhood memory when he and his brother had stumbled across it while hunting. I studied the photographs on the walls; my eyes settled on the rack of white garments hanging on hooks like deflated ghosts.

"Stop gawkin'," Vernon said. "Live your own life."

"I can't help myself," I said. "I've never been inside a shithole before. Always wondered what it might look like."

"None a' this is gonna help the situation," Luke said. "Best if we all keep our feelins' in check and put our minds on the problem."

"And just what is it you intend on doin' about it?" Vernon asked.

"Who're the two dead outside?"

"Crackers," Vernon answered. "Nobody anybody's gonna miss. I can handle it easy enough."

"And what about Donny Becker? Dipshit Donley?" Luke asked.

"Donley's a fuckin' retard. But Becker's crew are gonna come lookin' for their buddy soon enough when he doesn't . . . . Ah, shit, now there's a freebie for ya'll."

Luke nodded. "Had it figured anyway. Don't let it throw you. Just tell me how long 'til they might show, and how many you think's comin'."

"Why should I tell you anything else?"

"Good point. You're goin' down anyway." Luke turned to me. "You and Zeke grab a handful a' those sheets and hoods. Get everybody dressed. Wesley? . . . you and Isaiah un-cuff the sheriff and get one of those shit sacks on him, then lock his hands up in front. Let's get it done. Time's a wastin'."

We went to the row of hooks and began collecting costumes. Zeke's hand stopped in mid air. He was looking at one of the framed pictures. "Slick dick," he said. "How 'bout that?"

"What?"

"Yeah. The one burnin' up blacktop the night that white girl took on the tree."

I looked at the picture. "Which one?"

"Right here. This one."

He stood in a deep green robe at the center of the picture, surrounded by several others dressed in white, cradling a pointed hood under one arm and smiling with pride. I added a few years to his craggy features, a bit more gray to his hair.

The inscription on the mat bordering the photograph referred to him not by name, but by title.

Grand Dragon of the Big Hope Klavern of the Ku Klux Klan.

To me, he was Russell Conklin, Esquire—attorney at law, Civil War historian, and quite possibly the last person to see Robby Cain alive.

CHAPTER 30

"WELL I'LL BE goddamned," Luke said as he fitted a hood on his head.

"Your language," Mattie admonished. "You'll be goin' to hell, you take His name so."

Luke checked his anger. "My mistake, Mizz Mattie."

"Would y'all just look at me?" Wes said. "At this solemn moment in history, my dear momma's doing a three-sixty in her grave for certain."

We were all in costume. KKK garb. We had to bring whoever showed up in close before they caught on.

To make each of us less of a target of choice, Luke had the sheriff put on a gown that was clearly not his own—too long at the ankles, too tight in the chest.

C.W. looked like a chubby transvestite in a prom dress a size too small.

The fractured sweep of headlights penetrated the trees. A vehicle had entered the gate and was curving its way slowly toward the cabin.

"Show time," Luke said. "Everybody out. Isaiah behind the sheriff."

We assembled in a group on the porch.

The vehicle came around the final bend, its headlights and the beams from the floods on the roof bar now fully on us. The driver gave a friendly toot on the horn, then stopped, the mud-caked SUV dipping on its front shocks and oversized tires. Doors began to open.

"Stay inside and kill the lights!" Luke shouted from behind his white veil. "Sheriff's got a blade set on his heart."

The driver complied. We were cast again in semi-darkness.

"Weapons come out first," Luke ordered. "Then step out. All a' ya."

One by one, pistols and a rifle hit the ground. Then the doors opened fully. The interior was illuminated by the overhead light. Four men. None in uniform. One I thought I recognized from the truck stop.

"Three of y'all on the ground face down, spread eagle. There's a shotgun trained on your heads. Driver? . . . turn it around and leave it runnin'. Then git on back out and over with the others. One chance is all you got. Make the best of it."

When the SUV was pointed in the opposite direction, Luke sent Zeke behind the wheel and had him back it up to the foot of the porch.

Issy walked the sheriff down the steps.

"Not a word to anyone—inside or out—'til you hear from me," Vernon shouted at the men. "And that's an order!"

I gathered up the weapons and tossed them into the rear cargo bay.

Wes helped Mattie into the front, then got in next to her.

I climbed in the third row seat with Issy; Vernon sat in the middle row.

Luke went over to the sheriff's unmarked car, slashed all four tires and ripped the microphone and cord out of the radio. Then he stood over each of the four men and patted them down, coming away with two cell phones. He walked back to the SUV and asked me for the rifle. "Listen up, you sorry sacks a' shit," he said to the prostrate men. "Y'all lay there with your dicks in the dirt and think about dyin'. I'm gonna walk this wagon on out 'til I can't see you. Might take awhile, if I lag behind. I see a hair twitch? Bang." He waited ten quiet seconds, then for emphasis fired a round into the earth a foot to the right of one of their heads.

"The fuck!" the man bleated as his body appeared to levitate several inches off the ground and thud back down.

Luke walked alongside the SUV for a few yards as we started back toward the gate, then opened the door and got in next to me. "That went well, don't y'all think?"

"What I think," Wes said, "is it's a goddamn good thing my friends are basically fucking insane."

"Angels ain't supposed to have the mouths of those who drive the garbage trucks," Mattie said.

Zeke drove us back to the stashed rental car.

From there, we disabled and ditched the commandeered SUV deep in the woods, split up and took different routes, then rendezvoused at Mattie's truck.

"Y'all gonna nced a place 'til this blows on by," Luke said to Isaiah as we stood together in the moonlight of a clearing sky, the vestiges of the Klan having been removed and stuffed in the trunk of the rental.

"Ain't gonna blow by ever—not in this town, it ain't" Issy said.

"I might agree," Luke said, "if our intent was to hightail it back down to the Sunshine State and leave y'all to cope."

Issy laid studied eyes on Luke. "What're you sayin', man?"

"What I'm sayin' is, A, you helped Wesley, and that was no small thing, and two, far as this whole bidness has come, we've got no option but to put the Cherry Bomb in the pumpkin and see what blows."

Isaiah and Zeke exchanged glances, then looked at their grandmother.

"He speaks the truth." She fixed her eyes on Luke. In the moonlight, her cheeks glistened with tears. "The Dark Angel was sent so's you'd follow. You're a troubled soul. You got the darkness. Different from evil, but with a power as strong— maybe stronger." Mattie reached up and laid a weathered hand against Luke's cheek. "Luke traveled with the Apostle Paul. Done it for Jesus Himself after the Resurrection. Spread the word o' God. A part of that word was, 'An eye for an eye.' Now, you go spread the word so's it brings down the house of the Devil."

Luke touched her hand. "World's full to the brim with evil. What we got here's a drop, but we'll do our part to see it fall. That I promise."

Mattie shuffled off toward her truck.

Isaiah stepped over to Luke. "Don't know that she's got her head on right—about why y'all are here—but what y'all doin' means somethin'. 'Preciate y'all, man."

Luke nodded, then said, "Afraid the farm's out a' bounds. Might be we got time to cruise it and collect what we can."

"Nothin' but a leasehold," Issy said. "Rent by the month. Don't turn much from the land. Zeke and me got a camp. But they'll know where that is, too."

Luke and Zeke took Mattie to the farm; Issy and I went to the camp and gathered up some clothes and personal items.

We met up again thirty minutes later south of town.

"Won't be long before they hike out from the cabin," Luke said. "Don't know how long they'll wait to hear from the sheriff before they make a fuss. We need to get on the road."

I PULLED THE RENTAL into *Katie's Kabins* a few minutes after midnight.

Mattie, Zeke, and Isaiah parked their truck next to us in front of #7.

Wes waited while Luke extracted Sheriff Vernon from the back seat, then took him inside.

Luke started off toward the motel's darkened office. Before he'd made it ten feet, the lights came on and a short woman in a checkered bathrobe with her hair in curlers came out into the parking lot. "Evenin', Mizz Katie," Luke said as she approached.

Katie came to a stop in front of us, hands on hips, then looked around Luke as if he were a tree trunk and glared at the rest of our little group. "I said I'd take in the one a' ya, not the whole damn shelter."

"Not to worry," Luke said. "We're fixin' to pay a goodly sum for the accommodations."

"I ain't openin' up no more a these—"

"Need three at two hundred each per night. Figure a three night minimum, although I doubt it'll be that long. That's—"

"Eighteen hundy. I *know* how to add. So add in two more to round it off. Same rules as you got."

"Two more on top, "Luke said, "if you'd be kind enough to throw the breakers on the water heaters."

Katie considered it. "Two more on top a' that—that'll make it twenty-four, the way I got it totaled—and I'll take a pass on all the questions I got runnin' around in my head."

Luke smiled. "Katie, next time I need a truck? . . . you'll handle the deal. Sold."

"Credit gonna cost another two. So that makes it . . . ."

He dug out his wallet and began counting out bills into Katie's palm. "Let's make it an even three thou."

"What's with that?" Katie asked as she gladly accepted the additional bills.

"Call it a good faith gesture."

She glared at Luke. "You ain't got a screw backin' out on y'all, do ya?"

"It's entirely possible," Luke said.

"Thought so." Katie stuffed the cash in her bathrobe pocket, then padded off toward the office, mumbling to herself. She returned in a minute with keys for Kabins #4, #5, and #6. "Best a' what I got. Water'll take awhile to heat, but it's on its way. Whatever y'all're up to, I don't want to know. Only that it ain't whorin'."

"No, ma'am," Luke said. "Nothin' bad as that."

We put Mattie and Zeke in #6, sandwiched between Wes and Isaiah in #5, and me—along with the sheriff—in #7. Luke moved to #4, a studio unit and the one closest to the road. Each of us, C.W. excluded, was armed. Even Mattie.

I took the bedroom; Vernon was shackled to the foldout couch in the small living room.

The water was tepid when I tried the shower; I stretched out on the bed to wait for it to heat up. That's when I remembered that my Blackberry had gone off outside the cabin and nearly brought the house down on our heads. I turned it on and checked for messages.

One. From Jamie. "Cage. When you get this, call me. It doesn't matter what time. It's Holly, Hon. She tried to kill herself."

CHAPTER 31

ITHREW ON JEANS and a sweatshirt and went out to the parking lot where I'd be out of Vernon's earshot.

I'd expected to find Jamie asleep at one in the morning, but she was wide awake. And wired.

"How did you hear about it?" I asked with the kind of concern for the judge's daughter that you might show for a close cousin, or an old girlfriend you still cared about.

"First, tell me you're alright. Wes called Tisha. She called me. Thank God he's in one piece. She said you and Luke—"

"I'm fine, Jamie. Everything's okay."

"Okay? You call what happened, *okay*? You might have been hurt. Worse. You—"

"We'll talk about it when I get home."

"So I shouldn't worry. Is that it?"

"No. You should. You will. But it's not going to change anything. Now, tell me about Holly."

Jamie took a deep breath. "Okay. Let me focus here for a sec." A long pause, then, "She called me. You, really. She took an overdose—marginal, it turns out. A cry for help. Not the real thing."

"She said that?"

"No. No, it's my professional take. It happens. Her head's a scrambled mess. It has to do with the accident where her mother died—and her treatment. Some hack set her off without taking the time to read the first chapter. He tried to put her under to—"

"I can't listen this fast, babe."

"Sorry. Okay. Holly went to see this guy today. He does stop smoking, don't chew your nails, stop overeating kind of stuff. Hypnosis. Really dangerous in the wrong hands.

"She tells him what's going on, and he says, fine, I can get to the bottom of it with you.

"She's been doubling up on her medication the last two days, so she was easy. He started to probe and must have lost control of the session and it came flooding back way too fast. He rushed her out of it, but the damage was done. Bottom line, she's convinced that she was the one driving, not her mother."

"She was, Jamie. She was behind the wheel."

A long silence. "Oh, my god. This girl is in for a rough go."

"That's only one of her problems—*our* problems."

"Wes said the attorney you got for Robby was—is—what, a *Klansman*?"

"Authentic as they come. And when I asked Conklin about the judge, he all but took the witness stand as a character reference in his defense. If there's a link, then I believe the judge has some serious dirt on his hands."

"Holly's in a bad way already. No telling what this might do to her."

"Where is she?" I asked.

"Home. She admitted herself to the hospital. Said the overdose was an honest mistake. Thought she had a handful of vitamins. She's an adult. They pumped her stomach and let her out."

"She's not a bad person," I said.

"No, I don't think she is either. Just confused. And lonely. And . . . well, she said she tried—hard—but you turned her down."

It stopped me like a punch. "That doesn't count for much right now—not with what's in front of us."

"It does to me," Jamie said.

"So, you know I'm faithful."

"It's not so much that."

"No? What then?"

"If you didn't love me—if I couldn't have you for my own? . . . I'd want you as my friend when things got tough."

CHAPTER 32

VERNON STUDIED ME as I walked back into the cabin. "Problem?" he asked. "Looked like someone stuck a hot poker up your ass the way you went flyin' outta here."

I turned a straight-back chair around and sat down to face him. "You're dirty, Sheriff. A bigot, and a disgrace to straight cops everywhere. Maybe even a murderer."

Vernon shook his head. "You don't know jack about who I am. This idn't your town. Not even a part a' your world. No sir, you come from a place where your mommy and daddy wiped your nose for ya all your life. Country clubs. Summer camps. A college boy. Lawyer. You ever work labor all day under a scorchin' sun? Spend a night sweatin' in a single-wide while your daddy gets drunk and whips on your ma? You got any idea what it's like to watch your kid sister quit school at sixteen and start pumpin' out babies without knowin' how to read or write worth a damn? Does any a' this ring a *fuckin'* bell in your head?"

"Don't give me your sob story."

"It's not mine. It belongs to the warped-out nutballs that I get paid to keep in line. On *both* sides of the law. Poor and dumb with no way out's a losin' combo. Things don't go right sometimes. No one sets out to make it that way. Your partner understands that. He might not approve a' what he sees, but he's got manners—respect. What the hell's your problem, sonny?"

"Among other things? Robby Cain."

The sheriff shook his head slowly. "Like I told your partner. That was not my call."

"No? Then whose was it?"

"Go fish."

"How about Ray Lintz?"

"Throw in another line."

"What did Judge Rhetman have to pay to get you to cover up the facts of the accident, Sheriff?"

His eyes shifted. He tried to cover his surprise, but it failed.

There was a witness—right in your own backyard, and you never knew it."

Vernon looked away. "Get Carey in here."

"Why?"

"Because you still don't get it, " Vernon said.

"What's there to get?"

His look was one of exasperation. "Ever been in a war? Fought a battle? Shot people and watched 'em die?"

I rolled my shoulders, a reflex action I instantly regretted.

"Didn't think so. Now go on and get Carey before you fuck this up all the way to the top floor."

V ERNON AND LUKE exchanged nods.
"Your lieutenant's got a ways to go," Vernon said.

Luke sat in the chair I'd been in, the handoff complete. "So, where are we?"

I took a second chair from the table and sat off to one side.

"I think we need to negotiate," Vernon said.

"There's too much equity been spent, Sheriff."

"Gotta get by it, Cap."

"It's personal."

"Talk to me," Vernon said.

"The boy, Robby. I need a name. Rest of it's your bidness."

"You got a guess?"

"I've got to hear it," Luke said.

"What's my get back?"

"We'll work on that later. As it stands, you're at zero. You need to build credibility here. The more the better. Trust me on this."

Vernon locked eyes with Luke. "Conklin."

"Go any deeper?"

Vernon hesitated. "I suspect you know it does."

Luke nodded. "But, what the hell was the need?"

The sheriff leveled his eyes at Luke. "Before I start, I'm askin' you to believe that I did the best I could under the circumstances, though the facts are gonna be of little comfort."

LINTZ HAD BEEN to Big Hope more than once, the sheriff said; the night he was killed was his unlucky third visit and just plain bad timing for Robby: Conklin was in town. He'd come up from Eufaula for a meeting.

"Rhetman had a watch put on Lintz in Atlanta. Part of it had to do with his daughter. But his real concern was for what that boy was after down here, and when he might come snoopin' again."

The judge's man watched late that afternoon as Lintz threw a small suitcase in his car, then tailed him as he left his apartment and headed south on GA400.

He stayed with him through the city and past the airport exit until he was certain of where he was headed. He calculated time and distance, then called ahead to Vernon as instructed.

Deputy Becker pulled the BMW over just inside the Big Hope County Line. He shined his flashlight through the glass into Lintz's eyes.

Ray lowered his window, shielding his face from the light with one hand. "What's the problem, officer?"

"License and insurance card, sir."

Lintz produced the documents and handed them to Becker.

Becker studied the license, making sure he had the right man. "Step outta the car, Mr. Lintz. Hands where I can see 'em."

"What did I—?"

"Now!"

Lintz complied. Becker shoved him roughly against the side of the car, kicked his legs apart and frisked him, then pulled his arms behind his back and snapped handcuffs onto his wrists.

"What's this all about?" Lintz protested. "I haven't done anything!"

Becker took him by the arm and led him to the patrol car. He opened the rear door. His brother, Donny, climbed out. The Deputy pushed Lintz's head down and shoved him into the cruiser, slamming the door behind him. "Stash his car," he said to his brother. "Don't fuck around, either, and don't get any smart ideas. Just get it out of sight until we're told different."

Donny started toward the BMW.

"I'm tellin' ya, Donny, do not screw this up."

"Yeah, yeah. Sure. But, shit, I kin smell the friggin' leather from here."

Deputy Becker would answer none of Lintz's increasingly frantic questions as they drove. He did his best to tune him out. Finally, he'd had enough. "Shut the fuck up!"

It stopped Lintz cold. Finally he said, "This has to do with Judge Rhetman, doesn't it." Lintz 's voice was a now a mix of fear and resignation.

"Bingo wingo."

"What's going to happen?"

"Beats me," Becker said. "But if I was you, I'd wish myself someplace else."

"Conklin wanted him delivered to the Klav—to the hunt camp," Vernon continued. "That's all I knew about it. What happened there was . . . . Ya gotta understand that everything else—the ones that got too nosy from time to time—Conklin had it handled outside the club. My hands weren't on it." Vernon shifted his eyes to me. "You can think what you will, but Klan violence belongs to the past. Suppose to, anyway. Doesn't mean we're not firm on the rights of White Supremacy and what's happenin' to the country, but it's different now. There's respect to it. It's a belief like anybody's."

"Not quite," I said.

"Not worth my air to argue with you. Anyhow, Conklin went over the top. No one said it, but I think his aim was to draw us tight around him. He's got a mean streak, keeps talkin' about how we've wussed up, how we need to rebuild our strength and go back to the old practices. He'd brought some of his armed crazies. No one had the balls to try and stop him. Me included, 'though I finally put an end to it."

BECKER DELIVERED LINTZ to the hunt camp. He locked the gate behind him, then drove the cruiser up the path toward the cabin. As he came into the clearing, his headlights fell on the large cross that had been erected to the left of the porch. "The man's gonna *preach* tonight!" he said in a tone of awe and reverence.

The twenty men that formed the heart and power structure of the Klavern stood in their white robes and hoods, their faces concealed behind lowered veils. They'd gathered in a circle around a bonfire, facing out, their arms crossed on their chests.

As Becker brought Lintz toward the members, the Klanvocation parted, and a figure in a dark green robe stepped forward.

"Leave him, Deputy."

Becker retreated to the cabin to dress in his costume. When he returned to join the group, Lintz had been stripped of his clothes. He stood completely naked before the hooded men, shaking, his hands bound behind him.

"Bring forth the light to the teachings of the Maker," ordered the man in the dark robe.

A torch was drawn from the bonfire and touched to the ten-foot cross. In seconds, it was fully engulfed in flames, the heat driving the men to widen the circle.

"Let the fire signify the word of God who made first and in purity the Aryan Race, casting sin and imperfection on the dogs of the earth, directing them to breed only among themselves, and to serve in humility and with gratitude, those of the White Supremacy.

"Before us stands one who would see us fail in our glorious mission to carry forth His word, to defend the honor of The United States of America against the filth of the growing minorities—heathens who would spread lies and see us discredited and defeated through deceit and defamation." He turned to Lintz. "Raymond Lintz, liar, threat to all that is pure and right, you are hereby condemned by the very Word of God and sent to hell for your sins!"

Two men stepped forward. A rope with a noose on the end was tossed over the low limb of a Live Oak.

Lintz was in shock. He was shaking so badly that he could no longer stand on his own. His bladder let go; he was reduced to begging and blubbering in words that no one could understand.

"We all thought that was it—that Conklin had broken him and that'd be enough," Vernon said. "We'd never talked about anythin' like this. Then, before it really sank in—what Conklin's real intent was—they hung him." He looked down at his hands. "Poor bastard kicked and swung on the end of that rope, his eyes and his tongue bulgin' out his head. Some a' the men puked. Couple ran off into the woods. What was in my head, I don't know. Maybe they'd a' hung me as a traitor if I'd tried to stop it. I just don't know. Conklin and a few others had gone crazy. I just needed to help that kid—to do *some*thin'." The sheriff choked up, and couldn't speak. He dropped his head in his hands, his shoulders heaving.

"So, you shot him," Luke said quietly. "Put him out of his sufferin'."

Vernon nodded, collecting himself. "Everybody wandered off after that. Conklin patted me on the back for addin' to the show. Congratulated me. Jesus Christ. Anyway, he left it to me to figure out what to do. He hadn't thought that far.

"I cut Lintz down and hid the body. The kid was a reporter. Havin' him just disappear mighta left too many questions open. I was up the creek on how to take care of it. Then, the night deputy came in with Cain's pistol, and it all sorta fell into place."

"What happened to Robby in his cell?" Luke's words were sad, yet sharp enough to cut steel.

"Don't know, exactly. Same two that did Lintz, I guess. I never saw their faces. I was told to leave the yard door unlocked."

We sat in silence for a time.

"Gonna need your help, now, Sheriff," Luke said.

Vernon looked at him for a long moment. "You gotta make it work for me. You don't, I got nothin' to give. Not sure how exactly I'll clean up the rest of it, but you gotta understand. It's my life we're dealin' with here. Conklin will show no mercy, and you know it."

I watched Luke's eyes closely. His cold stare confirmed his understanding.

"Alright, then," Vernon said. "Your word? You'll make it work?"

Luke clenched his jaw as he weighed the sheriff's offer. "Agreed."

Vernon relaxed his shoulders then, and breathed slowly. "I may be a Judas who will burn in hell for this, but . . . go ahead and tell me what you need."

CHAPTER 33

I AWOKE AT FIRST light, made coffee, then went out into the face of the cold morning air where I found Luke and Wes sitting at a picnic table behind the cabins.

"Vernon?" Luke asked.

"Snoring his ass off, like he doesn't have a care in the world." I sat next to Wes. "How are you feeling?"

"Better than you, I think."

"Get it off your chest, Cage," Luke said.

"Fine. So you're just going to let him skate? That's it?"

Luke studied a thumb nail. "No, that's not it. Trouble is, you'd like it both ways—Vernon *and* Conklin. Rhetman, too, if he's part of it. Not gonna happen, Cage."

"Do you mind explaining to me just why the hell not?"

It was Wes who answered. "We left two dead in the woods, and kidnapped the sheriff. Got witnesses waitin' to move on Vernon's lead. It would come down something like this: We had it in for the Klan. We tried to break up their happy little family. It turned nasty. Any evidence to the contrary is already history. We got Issy and Mattie and Zeke. Oh yeah, and me. An escaped inmate. So where Vernon's concerned, we either buy him off the way he wants and get Conklin, or we take Vernon in someplace and with luck, someone believes us and we get outta jail free. But then, so does Conklin."

"And what guarantee do we have that Vernon won't turn on us after we nail Abe Lincoln?" I asked.

"That's assumin' we do," Luke said. "Vernon's gonna need to see it with his own eyes. Don't think for one minute that he's rolled over. He's buyin' time. He'll play it off whatever happens. We get Conklin, he'll spill Vernon all over the stage before he goes down. Vernon knows it. Hell, he'll be on the Left Coast or up in Idaho before the sun sets. We don't get Conklin? . . . who knows."

"So," I said, "from where we sit, we're nowhere?"

Luke shrugged. "First things first. Let's go roust the sheriff and get a phone to his ear."

"USE YOUR CELL," Luke instructed the sheriff who'd come fully awake at the first nudge. "Conklin'll have caller ID and it better look right. Don't get cute. I got a second sense about such things, and I'm not in a good mood."

"Russ, it's C.W.," Vernon said when the call went through. He locked eyes with Luke as he spoke. "We got problems. I got the nigger back in irons out to the camp, but his buddies are raisin' hell." He listened. "Nope. That ain't gonna do it. Don't know how, but they got somethin' on the accident." More silence. "Yeah, a blond guy and some fuckin' rock pile. They got old Mattie's gran'nigs with 'em." Vernon shook his head. "Nope. Don't know where. I did, we wouldn't have a problem, now would we. We need to meet on this. Tonight, at the—" Conklin cut him off with a protest loud enough to bleed through the ear piece. "I gotta tell ya . . . your goddamn clients don't mean shit right now." Another break while Vernon listened. "Okay, good. Eight, then. I'll get word to 'em somehow to come get their spook." A beat. "I'll handle it, no problem." Vernon listened a final time. "Yeah. See ya tonight." He clicked off.

"That was just fine," Luke said.

Vernon studied the closed phone as it rested in the palm of his hand. "Man's been good to me."

"Man's your ticket, now, Sheriff."

I called Gerard at nine. "It's confirmed."

"How much you got?"

"The accident."

"And Lintz?"

"It's not pretty."

"You kept your word. I'm impressed," Gerard said.

"I don't know how much you're going to get on Conklin—how much you'll be able to print."

"Conklin? Wait a fucking minute, here! It's Rhetman I'm talking about. I think he's a. . . . . You and I had an understand—"

"He's what?" I said.

"Forget it."

"Okay fine. So he's a Rotarian. Anyway, I just wanted you to know that if whatever there is goes anywhere, it goes to you."

"Are you fucking with me, Counselor?"

"Gee, Gerry, why would I do that?"

"Where are you?"

"No chance," I said.

"Why? What the hell you think I'm gonna do?"

"How do you know Russell Conklin?" I asked. "And his connection to the Klan?"

"What fucking crystal ball makes you think I even know him?"

"You're a newspaper hump, remember? I think you know more than you can print right now—that you've known whatever it is for a long time."

"Power, Counselor. It can also kill."

"I kept my promise. Now you do the same for me. Not a word anywhere until I call you again."

"How long?"

"I don't know. Tomorrow. Soon." I waited. "Gerry?"

"Yeah, yeah. But it's gonna give me fucking hemorrhoids, the waiting."

"You'll live."

Jamie called an hour later. I answered her questions with grunts and half-sentences and as little detail about what was happening as possible.

"I talked to Holly again," she said when she'd given up probing. "She called this morning. She's not great, Cage. Her world's crashed in around her. She feels she needs to confront her father, but she's afraid of what will happen if she does. He's all she has, and right now, she hates him."

"Where is she?"

"Home. In bed. She's too depressed to move. I'm really afraid of what she might do. I'm about to leave for the airport. I'll be at her house by one this afternoon."

"That's good," I said.

"I really don't know how much help I can be, but I can make tea, you know?"

"You'll do a lot more than that."

"We'll see. Stay safe, babe. Don't get hurt. I want you home."

AT SIX THAT evening, we left Mattie at the motel and headed for the Klan's cabin.

Luke rode with Wes and Vernon. Issy, Zeke and I followed in the truck. We turned north on State road 431 and headed toward Big Hope about the same time, I would later learn, that Van was driving the judge across the Chattahoochee River from Georgia into Alabama.

He wasn't alone; Rhetman had company.

CHAPTER 34

JAMIE SWUNG HER rental car into Holly's driveway at one-fifteen.

She rang the bell, and waited. When the door finally opened, Jamie's heart was nearly broken.

Holly's eyes were reddened and distant, her dark hair chopped and hacked into a headdress of short spikes. Coffee stains marked her robe. She looked nearly deranged.

"Holly?"

Judge Rhetman's daughter blinked her eyes rapidly at the sound of her name, then fell against Jamie, collapsing at her feet.

Jamie sank to her knees and gathered Holly in her arms. "It's okay, hon. Everything is okay."

"It's all . . . it's all come back. Everything. I just want to die. That's all. Please, God . . . please . . . ."

HOLLY AND HER mother had left Atlanta in heavy traffic, the top down, a two-quart jug of Mint Juleps set on the seat behind them.

It was hot. Charlene sat next to her daughter sipping a cool drink—her third since they'd left Buckhead, her fifth since they'd begun loading the car in the early afternoon.

"Better slow down, Mom. We've still got a long way to go."

"How 'bout you catch up instead, sweetheart? One or two won't hurt." Holly's mom retrieved the jug and filled a plastic tumbler for her daughter, adding a fresh sprig of mint.

Holly took the tumbler and nestled it between her bare thighs below the hem of her mini skirt. "Dad would kill me if he knew."

Her mother smiled. "Knew what, baby? That you wrap those long legs of yours around that boy John Chisholm's neck every chance you get?"

"Mother! Please!" Holly hated it when Charlene got drunk. It happened often, more easily with each passing year, and always led to the same subject. "Let's not."

"No, no, no. Let's. There's nothing to be ashamed of, you know. That powerful little love pocket in your crotch will get you whatever it is you want in life."

"I'd like to think it'll be me."

Charlene laughed. "I'm sure you would. I mean, look at you. Your daddy and I humped up a piece of fine art. There's no doubt about it, my gorgeous little girl."

Holly couldn't conceal her disgust. "You're gross."

"Just being honest, kitten. You really think some boy's going to take the time to find out what's inside your head—what you read, what charities you support—before he tries to slip it to you? No way. Not unless you make it a condition of entry, he won't."

"I'm not . . . easy, Mom. For God's sake."

Charlene sipped her drink. "Tell me then, sugar . . . what exactly did you make little Johnny give up before you let him in?"

"What? *Nothing.* I mean, why should he? I like him. We're serious about each other. Besides, we haven't been, you know . . . ."

"Oh, stop. Of course you have."

Holly took one hand off the wheel and retrieved the plastic glass. She took a long pull on the sweet liquid, fighting to control her temper. "Look, let's try another subject, okay?"

Charlene tossed back the remainder of her drink and poured another before she responded. "Such as?"

"Such as . . . why don't I have a brother. Or a sister? Why didn't you and Daddy ever have another child?"

"I've explained all that, dear."

"No, Mom, you haven't. Anymore than you've told me why you and Daddy don't sleep together."

Charlene turned fully toward her daughter. "I beg your pardon, young lady! How dare you—"

"It's true. You can't hide something like that. I hear the arguments—the fights. I see it in his eyes. The way you look at him. The way you avoid each other. Jesus, the house feels like a freezer some nights."

They rode in silence for several miles.

"That was very hurtful, Holly," her mother eventually said.

"I'm sorry. I didn't mean it to be. I'd like to see you guys happy, that's all. Maybe . . . well, maybe if you wouldn't drink so much, you know?"

A smirk came to Charlene's lips, her words slurred as she spoke. "Maybe if your poppa could keep his rod out of the African bush country, I wouldn't."

Holly glanced at her mother. "What are you saying?"

"I thought you knew everything about your father and me, Miss Smarty."

"I said I was sorry, okay? Now, what do you mean?"

Charlene reached in back for the jug. She overfilled her tumbler. "Shit, now look at what you made me do. Looks like I peed my shorts." That made her laugh. She was getting deeply soused. "Anyway, so you really don't know, do you."

"No. I really don't. The truth is, I don't even know what you're talking about."

Charlene took a long, sloppy hit of her booze, then wiped her mouth with the back of her hand. "Gone fishing, my ass."

"What?"

"Your father. The only fishing he's done at the plantation this week is in bed. Blow fish. Black grouper. It's those bubble-ass, tight-butted little *negresses* he's so fond of."

Holly cut fiery eyes toward her mother. "What are you saying? You're drunk out of your mind. Daddy would never—"

"Ask him yourself. It started after your grandfather and grandmother were . . . . I'm supposed to accept it. Like it's a family tradition. Right. He's a bastard. I hate him for it."

Holly's head was spinning. "Then— If it's true, why do you stay with him?"

"Why do you think? Money. Position. All the things I worked my little twat sore to get."

Holly took the drink from between her thighs and downed it in one long gulp, then asked her mother to refill it. "I don't believe this," she said.

"Of course you do, Holly. You think I'd tell you that I've been thrown over for a Mamba queen if it wasn't true?"

They traveled in silence. Charlene drank until she nearly passed out. Holly finished what remained in the jug. She felt woozy, and sad. Her mother had destroyed the image she held of her father. What would she say to him? How could she look at him the same way again?

By the time they reached the Alabama border, it had grown dark. Holly's head began to bob as she fought fatigue, the alcohol, and the depressed feeling that gripped her heart.

Charlene dozed, her mouth hanging open. She came awake when the road began to twist and turn, the ride becoming bumpy. "Where're we?" she asked her daughter.

Holly snapped her head up and blinked her eyes clear. "Ah . . . almost there. About at Big Hope, I think. Twenty minutes, maybe."

"I don't feel so good, hon. Can you slow— Oh crap, I'm gonna be sick, Holly. Quick. Pull over."

Holly slowed, but it was too late.

Charlene dropped her head between her knees and began to throw up on the floor. Her body was wracked by the intense convulsions. She began to cough, then choke.

Holly's eyes left the road and trained on her mother. The right front tire left the pavement, jolting the car and spinning the steering wheel in her hand as the tire caught on the sharp brim.

The car veered wildly. Holly slammed on the brakes as she looked in panic through the windshield at the woods that rushed toward her. A scream escaped her. "Oh my God!" She slammed her eyes shut as she felt two distinct thumps as the weight of the car crushed the small bodies.

In the next second, the vehicle impacted the trees and jolted to a dead stop. Charlene flew from the car.

Holly's chest was compressed against the steering wheel; her head whiplashed and smashed against the windshield. She sank into a dark hole, the image of the children's faces frozen in terror hanging before her like a horrible photograph.

WHEN HOLLY STEPPED from the shower, Jamie was there to offer her support. She wrapped her in a towel and guided her to the makeup table where she eased her onto the bench.

She'd prepared tea, and handed a mug to Holly as she took a comb and began working on the snarls of odd-length hair. "You know, I think we can make something out of this," Jamie said when she'd worked out all the knots and taken the scissors from the table. These were the first words either had spoken since Holly had broken down, then responding to Jamie's calming voice, had haltingly recounted the story of the accident.

"Does it matter?" Holly asked quietly. "Does any of it matter?"

"It may not seem like it right now, kiddo, but . . . yeah, it matters. You've had a real shock. No one would have reacted any differently—not the hair necessarily," Jamie said with a laugh intended to lighten the mood. She began to snip at the uneven ends. "But something just as symbolic."

"Something meant to be self-destructive, you mean."

With Holly's impromptu haircut styled, her makeup on and her figure accented by tailored slacks and a close-fitting sweater, outwardly she looked like a different person.

"It'll take time," Jamie said as they sat together. "And hard work. But you can do it—not alone, but with the right kind of help."

"What about my father? I hate what he did—god, what *I* did. I don't know where to start with that. Those . . . oh my God, those little kids. I . . . ."

"It was an accident. Not something you set out to do. As for your father, honey, I could write a book. Believe me. When it's right, you'll talk to him—listen to his side of things. Then, well . . . only you can decide where it goes from there. He didn't want to see you hurt—didn't want you to suffer."

"Great. Look how everything turned—"

The door bell rang.

Holly's eyes widened with anxiety.

"Are you expecting anyone?" Jamie asked.

"No. Who—?"

"I'll see who it is—tell them you're sleeping."

Jamie closed the bedroom door behind her and went into the foyer. Through the peephole she saw a short man with a bald pate standing with his back to the door. She depressed the TALK button on the intercom. "Can I help you?"

He turned around. Through the fisheye lens, his face appeared to be ninety percent nose. "Friend of Holly's," he said through the tinny speaker. "Can I have a word?"

"She's sleeping. She doesn't feel well."

"Maybe I can cheer her up."

"I don't think it's a good idea right now," Jamie insisted. "Come back later."

"Give me a break, huh?" He scratched his chin, then pushed the button again. "Look, tell her . . . tell her that her guy from Florida's here. Wants to ask her a few questions, that's all."

At first, Jamie was nonplussed. "Who?"

"Guy she's been seeing. You know. We're kinda an item. Look, lady, just open up, okay? I'm short on time here."

Jamie began to steam, although she hid the fact. "From Florida? Could I have your name please?"

"Yeah, sure. It's . . . Cage. Cage Royce."

Jamie took a deep breath, then opened the door.

Gerard stepped forward.

She timed it perfectly. The cartilage of his nose gave way under the heel of her hand as the short, sharp blow struck home—just as Luke had taught her.

Gerard fell backward, landing on his ass. He drew his hand away from his face, looking at the blood in his palm as if it belonged to someone else. "Jesus fuckin' A. Who the hell?"

Jamie straddled him. "Gerard, isn't it? You stupid little man. What did you think you were going to accomplish?"

Gerard craned his neck upward. "Where'd you come from?"

"The bitch factory. On a bad day."

"Hey, look. I'm only trying to help," he said.

"Right. And I'm just trying to express myself."

"Wait a minute here . . . . Oh Christ. Gotta be it. You're what's-her-name. The girlfriend. Look. He called me. That's the truth."

"That much, I believe." Jamie said.

"So now what?" Gerard asked.

"It depends. Why are you here?"

"My fucking tires need air. Why the *hell* do you think I'm here? Among other things, her old man's a fuckin' Klan junkie. I was sorta curious to know how she felt about that, you know?"

"What are you talking about?" Jamie asked.

Gerard struggled to his feet. "Ooo . . . somebody didn't share."

Jamie blocked the door. "You're not seeing Holly. Clear?"

Gerard backed away a step and held up his non-bloodied hand. "I got it, I got it."

"Now, why don't you go crawl back into your hole."

"Why don't you ease up? What have I done to you?"

"You do it to Cage, you do it to me. And in this case, Holly."

Gerard wiped his nose on his shirt sleeve. "How about a Kleenex, here."

"You were just leaving, remember?"

"Does she know about the accident?" Gerard asked.

Jamie was silent.

"Okay, okay, I'm sorry," Gerard said. "It's just that I've been after her old man for a long time, and it's close—really close."

"*You* have been?"

Gerard absorbed the verbal blow. "I tried. Twice. All it got me was trouble. Honest, I tried to tell Ray that he was crazy to keep after it. But he wouldn't listen. Ego. Career. This was his salvation."

"But you didn't try and stop Cage, did you."

Gerard looked at Jamie. "Do you think it would have made a difference?"

Jamie offered no answer.

"Alright, then. How about a truce? So I goofed up here. I shoulda waited like he asked."

"So why didn't you?"

Gerard averted his eyes. "Because . . . well, lady, because when it's over, who knows if your guy'll be around to tell the story?"

A knot formed in Jamie's stomach.

Gerard waited a beat. "Can I come in now and clean up at least?"

"You going to behave yourself? She's in a fragile place. Try to get to her and I will seriously kick your ass."

"No problem. Mum's the word."

Jamie considered it, then stepped aside. "Alright. But only for a minute."

Gerard went into the powder room; Jamie went to Holly's bedroom to tell her that someone from the paper had come by to talk about Ray's benefits.

But she never got the chance to tell Holly the lie.

ZACHARY RHETMAN SAT in chambers staring at the phone on his desk. Conklin had sounded stressed. Understandable, he supposed, given that he'd nearly blown everything.

But now, the circle was closing nicely, and all the loose ends were about to be tied up in knots—literally.

Gerard would be an easy afterthought. This was Atlanta, for God's sake. City of sin. Decidedly black, savage. People got mugged. Killed. It happened daily. What would you expect from these people? The day would come, however. There was a grand design.

So why shouldn't Conklin be kicking up his heels? Then again, maybe he was. Maybe the judge was reading too much into it. Still, it was prudent to be cautious. He trusted Conklin to a point, but too much knowledge in the wrong hands could one day turn against him. The more he thought about it, the more concerned he became. No harm in checking, was there?

Rhetman reached for the phone. He punched in the numbers. His call was answered on the second ring. "Zachary Rhetman, calling. How are you? Good. Good. Is he in, please? Yes, I'll hold"

A minute passed. It never failed. It annoyed him no end. But we all have our quirks—a little something that makes us feel important. Without conscious thought, he retrieved the golf ball from its holder and began the ritual game of toss and catch, toss and catch.

Finally, Conklin came on the line. "Good afternoon, Your Honor," he said, "how is the great city of Atlanta?"

"Fine, Russell. Same as it was when we spoke earlier. However, it isn't Atlanta that concerns me right now."

"Oh?"

"It's you, my friend."

"Sir? In what regard?" Conklin asked, sounding dumfounded by the question.

"Have you spoken with Sheriff Vernon today?"

Conklin hesitated before answering. "No, not since last evening. I've been in court, and in conference on other issues. I can call him, if it would ease your mind. However, the situation is fluid and I hesitate to reach him at an awkward moment."

"No, that's alright. I suspect this is all in my head. Do you trust him, Russell?"

"Vernon? Why, yes. Completely. I believe he's proven himself."

"That reminds me, Counselor, I failed to thank you for your assistance on that Cain situation."

"I was glad to have lent a hand, so to speak, although I found the whole affair regrettable."

"Yes, in a way, I suppose it was."

"Is there anything else, Your Honor?"

Rhetman let out his breath. "No, Russell, but thanks. You've always given me good counsel. There will be a place for you when I reach the Court. That I promise."

"We'll see it become a reality, Zachary."

"And I'll see you this evening, Russell."

With his confidence restored, Rhetman felt certain that everything would go as planned. God—his god—the god of White Supremacy would not let it be otherwise.

The judge looked at his watch, then called the garage for his car and driver. He'd seen Holly's number registered on his caller I.D. earlier. But she hadn't left a message, and there'd been no answer when he'd tried to reach her. This whole affair with Lintz had her deeply upset.

There was still time, he decided, to see Holly before he headed south. His baby, the love of his life. In time, she would be fine. Happiness waited for her. He was sure of it.

In fact, for a misguided moment when the blond, fair-skinned Aryan, Cage, had entered his chambers, he thought perhaps *he* was the perfect one—the perfect man for his daughter. A man, Rhetman now considered, who if given time and opportunity would have, among other things, made a whore out of his beloved little girl, and done great if not irreparable damage to the cause.

Indeed, sheep's clothing came in many styles and cuts.

CHAPTER 35

THE LIMO TRAVELED north on the Interstate en route to the house the judge had bought for Holly four years earlier—a place where he'd always be welcomed, the guarantor of his daughter's happiness and security.

Rhetman planned to surprise her, as he most often did. It was one way of protecting her from the clutches of anyone other than a suitor who had been thoroughly vetted and questioned and met with his approval. He'd dropped in on all the young men who'd approached his precious little girl, using servants of the minority races like Van, and others before him without Holly's knowledge to intimidate and drive off those not worthy of her affection.

As usual, the judge used the delivery entrance, avoiding the scrutiny of Holly's direct neighbors and giving him the excuse of not realizing she had company, should the moment prove to be inopportune.

Van pulled the limo next to the garages. He opened the door for the judge and accompanied him to the house.

Jamie tapped on the bedroom door. Behind her, she heard Gerard in the powder room, spitting and coughing.

Holly opened the door to her bedroom and stood to one side.

Over Holly's shoulder, through the glass of the sliders that gave onto the back yard, Jamie saw the gleaming black stretch limousine and the two men who walked toward the back of the house.

Holly followed Jamie's eyes. "My God. It's my father," she said, her voice unsteady. "I don't want Daddy to see me like this. Upset, you know? He freaks over it."

"Does he have a key?"

"Yes. And he doesn't knock."

"Shit! Gerard's in the bathroom," Jamie blurted.

Holly looked confused. And scared. "What?"

"Stay calm. Let me figure this out. Okay, I'm . . . a neighbor. Sue Brown. Just introduce me, and I'll say that I have to go. That I have to pick up the kids and that I'll come back later. Right now, I've got to get Gerard out of here. Go to the door. Stall them!"

Jamie ran for the powder room.

Holly froze.

Gerard came around the corner, his nostrils stuffed with tissue.

The back door opened.

It was too late.

"MY APOLOGIES FOR binding your hands," the judge said to Jamie, "but from the looks of Mr. Gerard's nose, it seems that you and Van might have attended the same classes of instruction in the Martial Arts."

Jamie sat opposite Judge Rhetman, facing the rear of the limousine. Gerard was next to her, bound hand and foot. Holly was slumped on the seat next to her father, her eyes dazed, the heavy dose of lithium taking effect.

"Eighteen hundred milligrams given in two equal doses several hours apart is the max," she said to the judge. "You've put your daughter at risk."

"So then, not only an expert in self-defense, but a doctor as well are we?"

"Neither. But I *am* a licensed psychologist. What you don't know is that your daughter overdosed on the same drug two days ago. Its effects can be dangerously cumulative, depending on the rate of renal discharge. One reason it's not even the drug of choice today. Whoever prescribed it for her needs—"

"Overdosed?"

"That's what I said."

"I— She'll be fine. I want her calm. It's for her own good. She's not well. I've been involved in her therapy for some time now. I know what I'm doing."

"Sure you do. Look. Her hands are shaking. She's lethargic, disoriented. She's suffering from lithium intoxication. She should be in a hospital. It's a good possibility that she's going to need to have her cardiovascular and respiratory functions supported until her system clears. If not, she could fall into a coma. She could die."

"You are bluffing. And not very well. She'll be fine, " the judge snapped.

"You're a fool," Jamie said.

Rhetman reached out and slapped Jamie sharply on the cheek. "How dare you speak to me that way?"

Jamie tasted blood in her mouth.

"The fuck!" Gerard said. "Now you hit women, you prick? How about you—"

Rhetman flicked a finger hard against the bridge of Gerard's broken nose.

Gerard shrieked at the pain. Blood began to trickle from his nostrils.

"I suggest you keep your comments to yourself, or I'll have Van spend a little private time with you when we arrive."

"I'm okay, Gerry," Jamie said. "Just keep your cool."

"Good advice," the judge said.

"Care to tell us where we're going?" Jamie asked the judge.

"To a party, my dear," Rhetman answered, "where you and Mr. Gerard are among the guests of honor."

CHAPTER 36

WE TOOK THE robes, hoods, and weapons and proceeded on foot.

The sheriff's unmarked unit still rested on its slashed tires in front of the cabin.

"Place makes my skin crawl," Wes said.

"Can't imagine why," Luke said. "It's really kinda quaint."

"Funny man, you are."

We went in and hung the outfits back on the rack.

Issy and Zeke searched the woods, reporting upon their return that the bodies were gone.

Vernon sat down on the top step of the porch and placed his arms around a support post as instructed. "There's more."

Luke eased back on his haunches, studying Vernon's face. "Let's have it."

"Conklin told me the boss is comin'."

"The boss," I repeated, as if to confirm the statement. "And just who would that . . . . ? Of course. Gerard had it right."

"What does it change?" Luke asked Vernon, his eyes narrowed.

"Conklin's gonna want to put on a show for him."

Luke nodded.

"He's gonna expect that I'd a' gotten the boys together and been here early to take care of it. There's wood and tools and a gas can out back. It's got to look right. You got to get a cross up. Then, soak it."

"Issy, you and Zeke mind a bit 'a carpentry?" Luke asked.

"We'll handle it," Isaiah said.

"Far as assemblin' the multitudes, Sheriff," Luke said, "you, Cage, Wesley and me 'er gonna have to do as stand-ins."

"He'll be lookin' for maybe twenty men. I'd dress the pair of black boys, too."

"They'll be busy," Luke said. "Anyway, it'll be dark, and we shouldn't need but a minute or two."

"There needs to be a bonfire goin'. He's a careful man," the sheriff said.

"Well now, that makes us a pair, then, dudn't it."

MATTIE LOOKED OUT the window of Kabin #6, past the picnic tables to the lake beyond.

The last of the evening light reflected off the dark water like Devil's Fire. Her bones ached as though they were turning to stone. In her mind, she saw the face of the Dark Angel. He called to her, and her blood ran cold.

She struggled into her sweater and went to find Katie.

ISSY AND ZEKE carried the large wooden cross they'd nailed together to the side of the cabin where Vernon said we'd find a hole already dug.

We soaked the cross with kerosene, then set it in the ground. I used dirt from the charred earth around the site to support it. When I was done, I leaned on the handle of the shovel and looked up at the trees, wondering for a moment which limb had carried Lintz's weight in the last seconds of his life.

The brothers went to set a pyre of deadwood for the fire.

Luke and Wes came around the corner of the cabin. "Hour to go, gents. Time to set it up," Luke said.

Issy and Zeke each took a rifle; they headed off to their posts in the woods near the entrance of the rutted drive. They'd wait for Conklin to show, then fall in at a safe distance behind his vehicle.

Wes, Luke, and I donned white tunics, setting the hoods aside for later. We went back out onto the porch.

"The robe. That's a damned desecration," Vernon said, looking at Wes. "Goddamn sacrilegious, is what it is."

"Yeah?" Wes said, "Well, if it makes you feel any better, I'm planning on wiping my ass on it when this is over."

Vernon shook his head. "What'd I ever do to you?"

"You've got to be fucking kidding me," Wes said.

Luke unlocked Vernon's hands. "Need you to suit up."

Vernon stood up, rubbing his wrists. "Can't," he said.

"Oh?"

The sheriff nodded toward Wes.

"Well now, I'll be goddamned," Luke said. "Wesley, why don't you pick out another one—give the sheriff here back his party dress."

IN MATTERS INVOLVING the judge, Conklin had always been cautious. It bothered him now that his mentor felt even a twinge of doubt about Vernon's loyalty; he had no such doubts of his own. But as often happened, the judge's concerns slowly but surely took hold of him.

So Conklin had his assistant connect him with the Big Hope County Jail where he asked to speak to the sheriff. The officer on the evening desk said that he hadn't been in since yesterday, but that he'd left a message on the night machine. He was taking a day or two off to go fishing.

No, he hadn't. Vernon *hated* fishing. It was a warning.

Van opened the partition that separated him from the passenger compartment. "Call for you, Judge."

Rhetman lifted the handset from the walnut case affixed to the armrest next to him. "Yes?"

"You were right to be concerned," Conklin said. "Not about Vernon's loyalty, but something isn't right. He's not where he should be."

"I see. I appreciate the information." Rhetman smiled to himself as he ended the call and entered numbers for another. "It appears as though the militia is planning a campaign of their own," he said to no one in particular as he waited for his party to come on the line. "Rhetman here. I need ten good men. And supplies. I'm twenty minutes out. Move." He looked at Jamie and smiled as he returned the phone into its cradle. "Luckily for us, we've captured the queen."

Next to him, Holly's shaking was becoming more pronounced.

"She's getting worse," Jamie said. "She needs help. She needs it *now*."

"I will tend to my daughter when this business is finished. She will be *fine* until then!"

ISAIAH SAW THE approaching lights, and signaled his brother.

A stretch limo rounded the bend and pulled onto the shoulder short of the entrance. Two other vehicles followed.

Doors were opened. Men gathered. Issy couldn't count their number in the fading light, but one thing was for damned sure: There were too many.

Issy and Zeke beat feet, sprinting to the cabin. "Somethin' bad's up," Isaiah said, his hands on his knees, gasping for air. "They comin'. Bunch of 'em."

Luke whipped his head around and glared at the sheriff.

"No way I could've undone it, Cap. I would have if I could have."

"You got a message out. A fail safe," Luke said.

Vernon nodded.

"Why didn't you say somethin' about it?"

"Honest to Christ, I forgot. That's on my own ma. I swear to Jesus."

Luke actually grinned at Vernon, then turned to us. "Spread out like before—you and Zeke. Into the woods. It gets bad, don't think. Just do what y'all need to. We'll talk it out later." Luke fired the order, then turned to me. "You and Wes get your weapons and wait by the cruiser."

Vernon looked at Luke. "They mean to finish it, Cap. No prisoners."

"Inside, Sheriff," Luke said, then opened the screen door and pushed him through. He came back out after a moment holding a wooden chair and a robe. He smashed the chair on the porch floor, shredded a tunic and wrapped strips of cloth around the end of one of the broken legs, then doused the rags with kerosene.

Conklin led his band proudly through the woods, the Grand Dragon now in full regalia, his men marching behind him in white robes and conical hats, their faces obscured.

Jamie struggled for calm as she was propelled forward in the middle of the group, her hands tied behind her, each arm in the grasp of a hooded escort. Next to her, Gerard stumbled his way along.

Inside the cabin, Vernon paced nervously. If he took the gamble and it all went wrong, he understood that he was a dead man. Luke wouldn't hesitate; but at least it would be quick. It had been there in the parting look. As their eyes locked for no more than an instant, something deep within Luke Carey had spoken his intent more clearly than any words could have.

Conklin, on the other hand, was a certified madman, and would show no mercy.

But, too many had died already. It had to stop.

Luke held the burning torch in one hand, a pistol in the other. "Best I can tell y'all is to follow my lead. If it turns to shit, Cage, you start poppin' from the left on in. Wes, the middle on out. I'll shoot from the right. Zeke and Issy'll cover the flanks. Now, off with the robes. Change a' plans. Don't want anybody to get mixed up. Okay? Let's go."

We used the disabled cruiser as partial cover. Luke came down the steps and set off the bonfire, then returned and stood on the side of the porch closest to the cross. My pulse pounded in my ears.

The beams of their flashlights appeared first. Then the group of robed men rounded the curve and came into the clearing where they stopped abruptly.

As the fire grew, the night was painted with an orange glow.

A figure in dark garb stepped forward. The light of the fire caught its green color, and shone on his unmasked face. "Lay down your weapons," he said, "and accept the wrath of the Creator for your sins."

"Let's try it the other way," Luke answered. He stepped closer to the cabin door and held the torch at the opening "Out a' those aprons and hit the ground face down. Vernon's trussed up inside. It's splashed in kerosene. Do it, or he sizzles."

Vernon shouted from within. "Christ, he'll do it, Russ. He ain't kiddin'."

Conklin raised his hand.

The group behind him parted.

Jamie stood in the center of the half-circle.

My heart stopped.

Zachary Rhetman stood behind her, his arm around her neck.

CHAPTER 37

K ATIE THOUGHT THE old woman was off her rocker. "Borrow ma car? I bet y'all can't even drive. Ain't about t'see y'all kill yerself."

"Mattie been drivin' the truck and the tractor many years, woman. I need to go quick. Nothin's gonnna happen to the car. Do this for me, God will smile on you. Say no, you help the Devil."

"I don't know what bee flew into yer hat, grandma, but, don't be tryin' that voodoo crap on me."

"Ain't voodoo, Miz Katie."

"Then, just what might it be?"

" Afraid Mattie cain't say."

"Well, then, afraid Katie can't help y'all."

"Just call me a taxi, then. Please."

R HETMAN PRESSED THE muzzle of his pistol into the hollow of Jamie's throat. "Weapons on the ground, gentlemen. I shouldn't have to ask more than once."

I was lightheaded, unable to think clearly but knew the only thing that mattered in that instant was to keep Jamie alive. I tossed my pistol into the dirt.

"Cage," Luke said quietly. "Nothin' rash. She can handle it. We'll come up with somethin'."

I had to believe it, or I would get us all killed on the spot.

Wes's revolver hit the ground; Luke's followed.

"The torch, as well. Mr. Carey, is it?"

"No problem, Your Honor," Luke said as he sent the flames spinning through the air off the side of the porch.

The torch landed at the base of the cross; flames began to lick the wood.

Rhetman tensed, but didn't move. Behind him, the Klansmen stirred and exchanged muffled words.

"I admire your stubbornness, sir," Rhetman said above the steady roar of the growing fire, "but I'm afraid your cause is lost."

M ATTIE HANDED THE cab driver a crumpled wad of bills, then moved across the small lot as fast as her feeble legs would allow and pounded on the back door.

The cab drove off as the outside light came on, and the door opened.

"You the only hope we got," she said to the man who answered.

W E STOOD AS a group with our backs to the bonfire, facing the hooded figures to either side of Conklin and the judge, our hands bound behind us.

Jamie leaned against me; I could feel the tremors of the terror that passed from her body to mine.

Gerard positioned himself between Wes and Luke, looking, perhaps, for protection, or to find comfort within the boundaries of their combined bulk.

I was nearly numbed by the scene: Several yards behind the semi-circle of robed ghosts that flanked the Grand Dragon and Rhetman, a hangman's rope dangled from the thick branch of a live oak.

It was Conklin who spoke.

"The Whites who stand before us have banded with the African and abandoned the dignity and grace of the Aryan race to co-mingle and co-conspire against the rightful rise of their own people, and the glorious resurrection of The Ku Klux Klan to its rightful place of power and leadership.

"We tread on the soil of the Great State of Alabama where Klansmen were once revered for their benevolent stance in support of those progressive measures that would see our White children educated in proper fashion, and our White economy thrive.

"We held the State's highest office, and shall do so again in honor of the great Bibb Graves. We sat on the Supreme Court of the United States of America, and shall do so again in the fashion of the Honorable Justice Hugo Black.

"At no time in our nation's history has there been a greater need for the rule and the role of the White Supremacist. We shall begin here, tonight, to root out the traitors and the minority dogs that suckle greedily at the teat of this great country.

"We shall send out the message from east to west, north to south that on this night, in the greatest state in the Union, The Ku Klux Klan has begun to write the third and greatest chapter in its long and prideful history!"

ISAIAH HEARD THE sound of dried twigs breaking under the weight of footsteps behind him.

His pulse quickened as he crouched down and pivoted slowly, straining to pick up the dark shape of motion among the pines. Now the sound was to his left; now his right. There was more than one.

He stood and brought the rifle to his shoulder, sweeping it back and forth quickly in a steady arc.

"Keep it down," he heard a man—a *black* man—whisper. He knew the voice, but it couldn't be.

"Keep it down yourself," another answered.

"Dwight? Bobo?" Issy said softly. "What y'all doin' here?"

The two men converged on Issy. "Hopin' to save your sorry nigger ass. Your grandma's got things whipped up good this time. What's the scene?"

Issy said, "It's bad, man. Really bad."

CONKLIN WAS IN full sweat by the time he'd finished his oratory.

This was it. This was his moment. Tonight, he would solidify his position as Imperial Wizard—the unquestioned potentate of what was to be the most powerful incarnation of the KKK that the country would ever witness.

He wanted to hang them all, but it would take too long. The African would have to do. It was symbol enough; the pictures would tell the story. The others, he'd have shot. On their knees. An execution. The woman first.

"HOW MANY YOU got?" Issy asked Dwight. "Six. Total," Bobo said. "Us, an' four comin' up the other side."

"Zeke's out that way. They'll meet up with him, if he don't shoot 'em first."

"How many *they* got?" Bobo asked.

"More than us," Isaiah said

"It'll have to do, then."

"Let's get around to the others," Issy said. "Best if we're together."

They started to move out. "I do not fuckin' believe this shit." Dwight said.

"Then get religion, my man. We're all gonna' need it."

"COME FORWARD," CONKLIN commanded of Wes. Wes smiled at us, then stepped in front of Conklin. The back of his shirt was soaked in blood from the strains he'd put on his stitches trying to free his hands. I wondered at his calm, at his control. I hoped that Issy and Zeke would have the courage to take down a few of the Klansmen. I suppose Wes did, too.

Two men hoisted Wes onto a plank set between saw horses. The noose was placed around his neck.

"You shall be hanged for the sins of your kind," cried Conklin. "Speak your repentance, or burn in hell."

Wes peered down at Conklin. Their eyes locked. "Fuck you."

Judge Rhetman stepped forward and held up his hand, quieting the restlessness in the assembled Klansmen. "Your courage is commendable, sir. And I truly regret the seeming brutality of what must take place here this evening." He looked at Conklin with hidden contempt— at the fire in his eyes, the hate on his face, then turned back to Wes and spoke again. "What began as a quiet movement in defense of our great nation and its founders has, I'm afraid, taken on a life of its own—beyond what I had foreseen.

"But dampening the rising will of the people is a daunting task. Those gathered here, and thousands like them are the people who understand the need to bring change to the laws of the land through proper interpretation of the words of our White Forefathers. In time, a rational and well executed strategy will see our goals accomplished. Our borders will be closed, illegal immigrants expelled. Our White Children will receive the education they deserve. Other races will again assume their separate status in the business and social arenas of our nation."

"And just how are you, one man—no, make that one sick racist—gonna make that happen?" Wes challenged.

Rhetman smiled and slowly shook his head. "Sir, I am not a racist. I am a *realist.* I speak of survival. Here in the South, it is the Klan. In other parts of the country, we are referred to as Minutemen, or the Militia. No matter the name attached, we are all patriots.

"Never have I envisioned the elimination of any ethnic or religious faction of this land—only the regulation and realignment of society, so that society and government might co-exist and best serve each other."

"That so?" Wes huffed. "Then explain this rope around my neck. And tell us what you plan to do with my friends, motherfucker."

"Your language, sir, seems to emphasize my point." Rhetman quipped. "Nonetheless, in regard to your question, no true freedom has ever been won without sacrifice. Your actions and those of . . . your friends . . . have been to destroy me, to damage our campaign. You asked how I might affect the changes necessary for the survival of this country. It will take time, sir. My nomination and appointment to the Supreme Court of the United States is all but assured after the coming election. The country will soon inaugurate a president who understands the mission.

"As those on the Court grow old, they lose their way. Visionaries will be appointed in their place as they step down voluntarily, or are . . . removed. The alliance between the Executive and Judicial branches of government will, in time, bring about sweeping changes, and the citizens of this great land will rejoice.

"You, Mr. Harland, and your friends, will participate through your deaths. While you are unable to see it now—cannot imagine the glory of what I describe as a better Union—you will thank me from above on behalf of your children. How foolish it is for you to try and stop what is right."

VERNON PEERED OUT of the cabin window. It had somehow all gone wrong. Rhetman was a levelheaded man. A *judge*, for chrissake. But he'd fed on the violence and given Conklin his way. And it was Conklin who would be the undoing of all Rhetman hoped for. Couldn't the man *see* that? Had he lost sight of . . . ?

Then, as the sheriff saw the judge through the window nod to Conklin, he knew what had to be done.

ON THE JUDGE'S nod, Conklin signaled the hooded men to either side of Wes; they ripped the board from beneath his feet; the rope drew tight.

At that instant, I heard a loud report issue from the direction of the cabin.

Conklin was blown off his feet.

I knocked Jamie to the ground, then bolted to the tree and slipped my head between Wes's legs, stood up and took his weight on my shoulders.

Rhetman spun toward me and raised his pistol.

I saw Luke's body fly off the ground, his feet at shoulder height. Judge Rhetman was propelled in the opposite direction by Luke's powerful kick; his pistol was knocked from his grasp and into the dirt.

Gerard pitched himself on top of Jamie, covering her torso.

Then, in the light of the bonfire, I saw men—black men—running toward us from the trees, guns raised and aimed at the white robed figures who'd frozen in place as the round blew a hole in Conklin's chest and spattered their tunics with his blood.

CHAPTER 38

L AZARUS JEFFERSON CAME into the clearing, a shotgun pressed to his shoulder and trained on Judge Rhetman who had struggled to his feet. "Stand where you are! All of you!"

The Klansmen were encircled by the other men; Jefferson lowered his weapon and ran to the tree. He threw the plank back on the saw horses and climbed up to loosen the noose that was cinched around Wes's neck.

Once lowered to the ground and his hands unbound, Wes rolled onto his back and sucked raspy gulps of air deeply into his lungs.

Jefferson freed my hands. I went to Jamie, rolled Gerard aside and took her in my arms. "It's alright. Everything's okay."

I undid the rope on her wrists. She threw her arms around my neck.

"Wes. Is he going to—?"

"He'll be fine."

Gerard lay motionless on his side. I rolled him over. He opened his eyes and looked up at me. "Jesus in fuckin' Jerusalem. We done yet?"

"Yeah, we are," I said. "In under five minutes, at that."

The doctor freed Luke's hands, then stooped down to examine Conklin's body. He drew the Grand Dragon's robe over his face.

"Damn lawyers," Luke said from where he stood over my shoulder. "Can't trust a one of 'em."

Isaiah, Zeke, and the other men who had come to our defense stood with guns trained on the Klansmen.

Luke and I joined them.

"Much obliged," Luke said to the group of young blacks.

"What happens now?" Isaiah asked.

"Send your buddies back to their homes," Luke said. "Not sure how the whole thing'll play out, but they weren't here. We'll shoulder what flack there might be. Now, leave the way y'all came. You're good soldiers, everyone a' ya. Issy, Zeke? Keep the Klanners here occupied while we gather up the weapons and sort some things out."

The others drifted off into the woods—men who were no more than boys. Boys who had saved our lives.

"Which one do you think shot Conklin?" I asked Luke.

He looked at me, eyes knowing, but said nothing.

Jamie ran toward Jefferson on the other side of the clearing where he was standing guard over the judge. She said something to him. Jefferson pushed the judge in the direction of Izzy and Zeke, then took off with Jamie. I caught up with them as they jogged quickly along the dirt track toward the main road.

"Holly," Jamie said. "She's in trouble, Cage. She might not make it."

"What—?"

Suddenly, she stopped short. "Oh, shit! Van. He drove us."

"I'll take care it," I said, then broke into a full run ahead of them.

I reached the limo. Van was nowhere in sight.

Holly lay across the back seat, her limbs jerking in spasm. Her breathing was labored. "Hold on," I said. "Just hold on."

I thought I heard Jamie and Jefferson approaching, but the sound came from the wrong direction. I left Holly and went around the back of the limo.

Van was on the side of the road, hog tied and gagged. I freed him just as Jamie and the doctor got to Holly.

"What the fuck's going on?" he said, his eyes frightened. "I heard a shot!"

I dragged him a few yards away from the limo. "What happened to the accent?"

"Don't start with me, okay? I just want to get out of here!"

"How much do you know? Lie to me, you're fucked big time."

"I don't know nothing about nothing. What is this place? All I do is what the judge says. I don't ask about his business. I get a paycheck. That's it. I swear."

I ran a quick mental assessment. Fear speaks the truth. "So, now you're fired."

"Fine by me."

"You got money?"

"Yeah. Sure. You want it?"

"No, asshole. You need the money to make it back to Atlanta. And then somewhere else."

"No problem."

"You have a record, Van? Been in trouble with the cops?"

"Small stuff. But I don't need any more on my sheet."

"Okay, here's the deal. You drive these people to the nearest hospital. Leave the limo with them, and disappear. Got it?"

"You see," he said with a wink, "Van drive good for people. Like for Judge. Chop chop!"

BY THE TIME I made it back to the clearing, the Klansmen's hands were bound together; they were joined in a human chain that ended at the tree where Wes had nearly died.

Judge Rhetman sat in the dirt at Wes's feet like a sullen child.

Isaiah and Zeke were nowhere to be seen.

Sheriff Vernon stood alone, leaning a hip against the rear fender of his cruiser.

I walked over to him. "It was you, wasn't it?" I said.

He crossed his arms over his chest and looked away. "It was me, what?"

"You shot Conklin. But . . . how? Why?"

Luke drifted over to us. "I don't imagine the sheriff feels much like talkin' right now, Cage."

I looked at Luke. "You gave him a weapon. He could have—"

"What matters, is that he didn't." Luke turned from me and spoke to Vernon. "You want any help with this?"

"I'll handle it. Best if y'all just be on your way."

Luke took the pack of cigarettes from his shirt pocket. He offered one to Sheriff Vernon, took one himself, then lit both. "Coulda been worse."

"Coulda been."

"What now?" Luke said.

Vernon drew smoke deep into his lungs. "It went bad, but there's still some logic to it, you know."

"Is there, now? We might could battle on that one another day. You'd lose. In the long run, you will anyway."

Vernon extended a hand to Luke, who gripped it. "I'll take my boys now, and be on my way. The judge stays with you. Do what y'all need to. He's finished either way. Consider it a fair trade. Lock up when y'all 'er done, and leave the key under the mat, hear?" He broke the grip. "And stay outta Dodge, Cap. I got troubles enough." Vernon started to walk away, then stopped and locked eyes with Luke. "I'm sorry about the boy, Robby. Deeply sorry."

Luke nodded. "I'm sorry about a lot a' things. Enough to fill a lifetime."

C.W. Vernon, Sheriff of Big Hope, Alabama—town and county of the same name—collected his men who hoisted Conklin's body on their shoulders, and disappeared into the dark.

We gathered up the saw horses and the wooden plank, the vestments of the outlaw bigots who would have seen us dead, the hangman's rope, the weapons, and tossed everything into the cabin.

Luke sloshed kerosene around the front porch, then disappeared inside where he emptied the can onto the walls and floor—then tossed it into a corner and came back outside.

He'd fashioned another torch—dark green strips wrapped tight as a fist around a branch. With a flick of his fingers, he struck the flint of his Zippo and touched the lighter to the cloth.

The flame grew until it was a ball of fire that sent a glow up into the canopy of the live oak that stood like a centuries old sentry against the dead black sky.

Luke drew back his arm, ready to send the fire on the way to its mark.

"No!" Rhetman roared as he sprang to his feet and broke for the small building in a dead run. "No! The roster. The records. So much work!" He bound up the stairs, tripped on the edge of the porch and was sent sprawling through the door, screeching in pain as he disappeared inside.

I started after him.

Luke grabbed my arm, stopping me in my tracks.

The diminished flames of the burning cross suddenly flared as the cruciform crashed to the ground, sending fiery embers onto the floorboards of the front porch, quickly setting the cabin aflame.

From the hole where the cross had stood came a glow; smoke rose from the spot in shapes that formed images of whatever the mind cared to imagine—apparitions that were born in one moment, then faded in the next as the cabin became an inferno and the heat of the fire set the ghostly images adrift, and into the freedom of the night.

EPILOGUE

MARCH HAD BEEN a mild month in the Southeast. The dogwoods and azaleas that dotted the sprawling lawns and graced the long, winding drive of the sanitarium on that clear April morning were in full bloom.

The air was pure and smelled of spring—of freshly mown grass and new beginnings.

We waited together on a glider on the veranda of the white clapboard building, the Victorian latticework at the corners of the roofline and the rails as intricate as the web of a spider, the gray paint on the wood plank flooring beneath our feet glistening in the angled sunlight that spilled across our laps like a warm blanket.

"I'm not sure what to expect, what to say."

Jamie held my hand. "Don't expect anything, hon. I told you, it's a long process. But the fact that she's ready to have visitors—that she asked to see us is pretty encouraging."

"She wouldn't have made it without you," I said.

"Or without you. You gave her the spark of hope she needed."

I shook my head. "So you've said. But I don't see how, or why."

"I know you don't."

Holly stepped through the screen door and onto the veranda. She shielded her eyes from the sun as she looked out across the lawn, scanning the chairs and benches set along the crushed stone pathways.

Her hair had grown and touched her neck just below the line of her jaw. She'd draped a white sweater across her shoulders and drew it more tightly around her as it billowed slightly in the cooling breeze.

"Holly," Jamie said as we stood up to greet her.

Holly turned toward us, her eyes bright and full of life. Her face glowed, and a smile beamed on her lips as she rushed to embrace Jamie. "It is *so* good to see you."

"How are you?" Jamie asked as they parted.

"On the mend. Lots of baggage, but the people here are great. Thanks for setting it up. I couldn't have found a Starbuck's, the shape I was in." Holly turned her eyes to me, but still spoke to Jamie. "Did I ever tell you that you have the sweetest, most handsome man on the planet in your life?"

Jamie nodded to Holly. "Go ahead, honey, it's perfectly okay."

Holly stood on tiptoe and put her arms around my neck. She lifted her eyes and kissed me lightly on the mouth, then hugged me for long time. When she stepped back, tears threatened, but the smile was still there. "I love you. For what you did for me. And for what you could have, but didn't do. More for that, than anything."

We walked the paths in the sunlight—Holly and Jamie talking and laughing, sharing a few tears, and finally some private time before we said our good-byes.

I closed the door on my side of the Landcrusier and looked across at Jamie.

She latched her seat belt. "So tell me, handsome, in another time and place where there was no me, but there was Holly, would you?"

"Would I what?" I said.

"Don't play dumb. You're lousy at it. Would you be attracted to her."

"Alright, yes . . . I probably would be."

She smiled. "Right answer, pal."

A T SUNSET ONE evening, sitting on the deck of *The Hatch* and talking about sports over cold beers, Wes asked me—completely out of context—if I knew who Jim Crow was.

"Hell yes," I said. "Who doesn't? He played left field for the Red Sox and batted four-oh-four when they won the Series."

He glowered at me.

"Yeah, I know about Jim Crow—about the Jim Crow Laws. I went to a school where I actually learned about such things. Got a degree and everything. So, the next time you turn into a complete pain in the ass—which can happen at any moment— I'll rub burnt cork on my face and come dance a jig in your driveway—pun intended."

"Goddamn honky," he said, then sat back and laughed harder and longer than I'd ever heard him do before.

L AZARUS JEFFERSON ADDED a second physician and two medical techs to his practice in order to handle the steady increase in his case load; people came from miles around to be seen by the man who some said could cure anything.

I'd spoken with him deep in the night after the flames had died down and we'd locked the gate on the track that led from the site where the cabin had stood hours earlier.

"We owe you a great deal."

He shook it off.

"Why did you come?" I asked.

A moment passed before he answered. "I felt my heritage, Mr. Royce. I felt my roots and those of every black person in that town who'd been wronged. I found a different way to heal. Thanks to an old crazy woman, I found my pride."

M ATTIE FRANKLIN AND her grandsons never spent another night in the town of Big Hope.

On the morning after the big burn, as we'd taken to calling it, we helped them load what few things of value they had in the bed of Mattie's truck and into a trailer they hitched to the back of it.

They were setting out for Birmingham where Mattie had a cousin who said she'd be happy to take them in until they could get back on their feet.

Mattie took my arm while the others finished securing the load. We shuffled out to the picnic tables in the area behind Katie's Kabin's where we sat and watched a flock of ducks land on the lake.

"You know what happened to m'sister's little boys, yes?"

"Yes," I said. "It was an accident. A car that lost control. They were buried near where it happened—at the edge of the woods, back from the road. Conklin and the sheriff covered it up for Zachary Rhetman."

Mattie's breath caught in her throat. "I knew they were still here. Felt it all along. Rhetman. He the one that did it? He the driver?"

"No, he wasn't."

"Was it a bad person?"

"No. Not at all. Sad. Troubled. But not bad. And sorry down to her soul."

Mattie sat for a long time staring out over the lake, her leathery hands folded in her lap. "Alright, then. You tell her Mattie forgives it. It's the Lord's way. Time to heal all of it's what it is. Amen. Now, help this ol' woman up."

I helped her to her feet, then pressed a stack of folded bills into her palm. "We found this in the cabin," I said, "before it burned. It should help you get a fresh start."

She looked at the bills, then at me. "Mattie watchin' your nose grow."

"Then think of it as coming from your Dark Angel."

The furrows at the corner of her eyes deepened. It was the first and only time I'd seen her smile. "That pretty gal a' yours got her a handful."

I bent and kissed her cheek. "That she does."

B UDDY CAIN'S MOTHER died in her sleep the same night as the big burn. She never learned of her grandson's fate.

Robby and his grandma were buried alongside his father under the shade of a spreading oak in a cemetery on the north shore of the West Bay.

Luke delivered the eulogy. I'd not seen my friend cry before. It tore at my heart.

M AY WAS A scorcher. It seemed that half the Florida peninsula was consumed by grass fires as the state continued to suffer from a lingering drought. So far, we'd been lucky on the Panhandle, but that could change with one strike of heat lightening.

I sat alone on the beach near the tide pack below the deck of *The Hatch*, the evening breeze coming onshore from the blue-green waters of the Gulf of Mexico a few degrees cooler than the air on the deck above where a Friday crowd had begun to gather. The voices of the end-of-week revelers drifted down over the dunes and met the waves that rolled against the white sand in a cacophony of indistinguishable sounds.

The sun had met the horizon in a blaze of color that always amazed me, but on this evening instead brought back memories of a deadly January night in Big Hope.

I'd heard from Gerard late in the afternoon—the first time I'd spoken with him since early February.

"It's done," he'd said.

"And?"

"Fiction. Not in the first draft, but then, I saw you were right—hard for a newspaper hump like me to admit it."

"No more articles, then?" I asked.

"Just the one we already ran—the bullshit version on the accidental fire at the hunt camp. You've read it. You know the story."

"Yeah, I guess I do. So, where's your book take place?"

"Some burg I call Freedom Falls, Tennessee."

"Is it any good?"

"How the fuck should I know?"

"Thanks, Gerry," I said.

"Sure. No sweat."

"And, Gerry . . . ?"

"Yeah?"

"Thanks for what you did that night—for shielding Jamie."

"I fuckin' fainted and fell on top of her. Goodbye, Counselor. Have a good life."

***

I WATCHED LUKE APPROACH, walking the waterline in dark silhouette, his frame growing in size with each step in the last of the day's light.

He dropped down next to me and dug his heels into the white sand. "Nice evenin'," he said.

I told him about my conversation with Gerard.

"It's the right thing. There's been damage enough. I give him credit."

"Jamie wonders if maybe you should talk it out. See somebody."

"It still haunts me. I won't deny it." He smoothed a square foot of beach between us with great study. "Maybe sometime I will. Maybe not."

We sat in quiet thought. "That night," I said at length, "when I realized there was a good chance we'd die? I was afraid for Jamie, but not for me. Strange."

Luke reached into his shirt pocket for his cigarettes, tapped one out and lit up, running his thumb over the raised emblem on the side of his old Zippo as he said, "Not such a mystery, really. It's those we care about that go on before us, Cage."

I thought of my brother Billy. And of Robby. "Meaning?"

Luke got to his feet and stood in silence for a long moment, his gaze fixed on the horizon. "They light the way, partner—shoulder the fear and take it with 'em." After a moment, he flicked the butt of his cigarette farther out into the water than seemed possible. "C'mon. Let's get us a beer," he said, then turned and headed up the stairs to the deck of *The Hatch* as the last embers of the setting sun slipped silently beneath the black water.

ABOUT THE AUTHOR

MURDER IN BIG HOPE is the second in a new series by JJ Brinks, author of MURDER ON THE WHISKEY GEORGE, the highly acclaimed first installment available in ebook and print formats from Amazon.com.

An independent writer for the television series, SILK STALKINGS, airing on the USA Network, Brinks followed his long-time passion to become a novelist when the series ended. In the course of developing and writing MURDER ON THE WHISKEY GEORGE, the author was introduced by the Editor-in-Chief at William Morrow to Richard Marek, a legend in New York literary circles who among other accomplishments in an illustrious career served as editor for nine Robert Ludlum bestselling novels.

Marek and Brinks worked together for over a year in what Brinks describes as an "amazing experience; an intense, indispensable education for which I am deeply grateful. Dick's sense of character development and his ability to drive plot and pace are unbelievable."

JJ Brinks is a graduate of Syracuse University where he studied drama and creative writing at the School of Speech and Dramatic Art, and television at the Samuel I. Newhouse School of Communications.

The author is a member of the Writers Guild of America/East.

For more information about the author, visit JJBrinks.com.

Coming Soon!

MURDER ON CARLITA CAY

A novel

by

JJ BRINKS

Empire Mystery Press

PROLOGUE

"LIPS, SWEETHEART. MOISTEN. (Click) Head back . . . a little more . . . . Good. (Click) Okay, last few shots. (Click . . . click) And . . . that's a wrap, precious."

Three long days. Twenty different outfits. Stills and videos. First the exteriors—on the beach, in the water. Up and down Ocean Drive. Window shopping. Sitting in dimly lit restaurants with a collection of pretty boys.

Then, into the studio. Twist this way. Turn that way. Smile until your face cracks.

She was beat.

SHE SLIPPED A robe over her bikini and collapsed into the salon chair, closing her eyes as the makeup artist opened a jar of cold cream and prepared to remove in seconds what had taken a full hour to create.

The photographer rushed over. "No, no! Don't touch a thing! The client's coming down from Atlanta tonight to go over the videos and still files. Remember? He wants cocktails and dinner with his new signature model. Eight-thirty. The lobby of your hotel."

She'd forgotten. Cocktails and dinner with some haughty fashion magnate—correct that, meal ticket. Okay, so tough it out. If this new line of sportswear hits? . . . we're talking money. Piles of it.

S HE CAME DOWN to the lobby five minutes late. A heavy-set black man in a black cap with a short visor stood near the front desk.

"Good evening," he said as she approached. His eyes shimmered. "My, my, my."

She followed the driver out of the hotel to a stretch limousine where he opened the rear door.

A gloved hand was extended to her from within the darkened interior.

Odd, she thought, given the warm night—but elegant, too. She accepted the assistance, lowering her head as she stepped inside.

"I am indeed fortunate to be in the presence of someone so lovely." His voice was soft, nearly musical. He sat in the shadows, face obscured, muted light seeming to gather in a halo around his silver hair.

The door closed. She looked back at the sound of it—out through the deeply tinted window where oblique shapes floated by on the crowded sidewalk like ghosts; when she turned again in his direction, her eyes fell on the crystal glass filled with champagne that sparkled in his hands.

"Shall we celebrate?" he said. "The photos. Congratulations. They are extraordinary."

She smiled demurely, took the proffered flute and clinked it lightly against its mate. "To dreams," she said.

"Indeed," he responded.

SHE RUBBED AT her eyes, scratching the lids with the ragged edges of broken fingernails.

Sunlight washed over her, spearing her pupils and piercing her brain.

She winced at the brightness, drawing her naked body into a fetal position, hugging her knees to her chest and willing herself into silence.

Every inch of her felt bruised. She rolled onto her back, certain as she did that strips of flesh were being ripped from her ribs, then forced herself to a sitting position with legs splayed out in front of her.

Her blond hair was a nest of knots; she touched herself in the place where a constant ache gripped her like a cruel fist.

Later, she told herself. *It won't help to think about it now.*

She closed her eyes and steadied her breathing, then opened them again on a room with metal walls thirty feet tall. The place was cluttered with discarded boxes and barrels, except for a space of several square yards around her.

Rectangular windows worked by long chains were set just below the open-steel grid work that supported the flat roof of a building of the same shape.

On one side was a garage door large enough to accommodate a truck; next to it, an entry door that looked ridiculously small in comparison.

Alice through the looking glass.

She struggled to her feet and took a few tentative steps, the sensation like walking on jagged stones. Her joints protested each shift in body motion as she began a slow search of what felt at that moment like a prison.

Her clothes, shoes, and purse were gone.

She rummaged through the debris in several barrels until she found a tattered work shirt that covered her to mid-thigh. On the pocket was embroidered the name, KEN. She managed a pained smile—abating fear with humor.

Right, she thought, and I'm Barbie.

A trash can yielded a sweat-stained baseball cap with a stitched-on logo for Snap-On Tools. She stuffed her hair up under it, pulling the brim low over her eyes, then walked in old lady-steps to the entry door.

THE BUILDING WAS part of a complex of four similar structures, all abandoned, artful graffiti spray-painted on their rusty corrugated walls. Weeds grew tall through the pot-holed asphalt of the parking area; a hot breeze blew litter against a chain link fence topped with razor wire that formed the perimeter of the compound.

Beyond the fence, over the rooftop of indistinct buildings, she saw the raised level of an expressway perhaps a half-mile away; a jet roared by overhead at low altitude, its landing gear extended.

I T TOOK THIRTY minutes to search the other buildings. In one, she found a pair of coveralls; in another, worn out work boots. She stuffed rags into the toes to make them fit snugly enough for her to walk.

It was the best she could do for clothing. Now, she had to get going—had to find help before . . . .

Before they come back for me.

She ducked through a hole in the fence, then slouched and shuffled her way to the street having no idea where she was, knowing only that the neighborhood was rundown and felt dangerous. With luck, she might pass for a bum or a drunk and be left alone as she made her way toward the expressway where there was sure to be help.

S HE WALKED SLOWLY and without incident until, without warning, she was blasted by a collage of images. Bright lights. Metal bars. A cell. A man—two. And a woman. She couldn't move her arms or legs. She was . . . suspended. Someone hurt her. Again, and again.

No more. Please oh please, no more.

Her head spun and her knees gave as she sank to the pavement.

***

W HEN SHE CAME around, it was dark. She lay on a sidewalk, trembling, the noise of the traffic on the overpass above her rolling like thunder.

I made it to the expressway. But how? I don't remember what—

She realized then that she *wasn't* trembling at all; someone was shaking her.

"Girlfrien'? You keep those eyes open. No white woman gonna make it long in *this* place. We got to get you off the street. Come on now, Lytella get you straightened out."

"South Beach," she croaked as the woman helped her to her feet. "I have to get to South Beach. Can you help me?"

"Exactly what do you suppose I'm tryin' to do here? Fuck you up? Looks to me like somebody already did a fine job a' that. You're a pretty one, too. Who did this shit to you?"

"I . . . I don't know."

"No matter for now. Lytella'll get you cleaned up some and see if we can't get you where you need to be."

"Maybe you should . . . call the police."

"Now you talkin' crazy. I'll *help* you, child, but I ain't fool enough to get messed up in no po-lice business."

T HE HOUSE WAS small, the shower, hot. The woman combed her hair for her and helped her into a too-tight dress, and shoes with high heels. She gave her water. And pills.

Then they were in a car—a big car, but not the limousine that came back in a flash of memory.

Music boomed all around her.

They crossed a bridge with a long string of lights that nearly hypnotized her as they streaked by the window.

In time, the car stopped, the door was opened, and she was on a sidewalk. It was crowded; people jostled her. She recognized the front of the hotel—art deco, blue neon.

SHE HAD TO sign to get a key, explaining to the clerk that she and her boyfriend had gotten a little drunk. They'd fought. He'd hit her where it didn't show. Hard. She left her purse behind.

No, thanks, she'd be okay—no doctor, just needed a hot shower and to get to bed. It took all her strength to sound convincing.

SHE LAY IN her room fighting the fatigue of fear and physical assault.

After a few minutes of rest—when she could think more clearly and make some sense out of what had happened to her—she'd call her father. He'd know what to do . . . could drive down and get her.

But in seconds, consciousness began to slip away.

If nothing else, at least she felt better—or maybe what she *felt* was nothing.

The pills. Must be the pills. Linda? Lucille? Did I say, thanks?

She hoped so, but couldn't force herself to remember. She was floating, drifting, and then she was gone—safe for the moment, lost to the caress of a deep and painless sleep.

CHAPTER 1

I WORKED MY WAY from table to table on the wooden deck of *The Ship's Hatch Café*—a cozy little Panama City Beach bar and grill I inherited from my murdered brother—emptying ashtrays, collecting glasses and bottles, wiping up the remnants of sandwiches and side orders consumed by the lunch crowd who'd hurried down the stairs and onto the beach to lay and play under the blaze of the Florida sun.

I cleared the last of the tables, then hoisted an overloaded tray of plates and beer mugs to shoulder-height and started toward the entrance to the kitchen. A partial eclipse of the sun suddenly darkened the deck in front of me.

A barrel-chested voice spoke its origin. "Stealin' glassware's a crime, ya know."

I turned and looked up at whatever angle six-two regards six-six—into the ruddy face of the mountain of a man known as Luke Carey, my deceptively gentle law partner and guide along a path of life where right and wrong are matters of degrees, not absolutes.

"I'm on duty," I said. "Two no-shows. It's the hardest part of this damn business—finding good help."

"Hardest part of life," Luke said.

"A morsel of scholarly wisdom, so noted. Now, how about grabbing the stuff off the stand. That's the last of it."

Luke scooped up the remaining tray of dishes and raised it overhead like a seasoned busboy.

"I see a new career in the making."

"How's the pay?" he asked.

"What pay?" I said, heading toward the service door.

WE STACKED THE dishes and glasses on the sideboard, then went back out to the deck. The early-June afternoon was brochure-perfect—a cloudless sky the color of faded denim, the waters of the Gulf of Mexico a palate of aqua-blues and greens, the beach an endless white ribbon stretched along the shore.

"So, what's up?" I said to Luke.

He fished out a cigarette from the constant pack in the pocket of his shirt and struck the flint of his old Zippo. "Need to borrow the Whaler— you too, if you're available." He lit up and inhaled deeply. "Couple of young lovelies beached their Hobie Cat in front of our place. They need a tow back to Seaside."

The waters off Panama City Beach were dead calm. "A little short on breeze, aren't we?"

"That would be the problem."

"I'll have to check with—"

"I smell a conspiracy in the making," Jamie, my live-in Irish lovely who sports no ring but owns my heart and everything attached thereto said as she crossed the deck. She planted a kiss on Luke's temple. "Helping Cage plan his escape?"

"Won't take long," he said. "A bit a' marine salvage."

"Just get your buddy here to fill the ice tubs before he takes off, okay?"

WE LAUNCHED THE Whaler and headed west. Four minutes later, I turned toward the beach and adjusted the tilt of the engine, then powered onto the sand next to the Hobie Cat, her colorful sails limp as wet Crepe Paper in the still air.

I followed Luke across the sand and up the stairs to his house—a two-story, weather-grayed cedar square built on poles ten feet off the ground.

LuAnn—Luke's second wife and our paralegal—reclined on a lounge, her auburn hair pulled back in a ponytail.

Seated facing her—one each at five and seven o'clock—were a pair of fair-haired heartbreakers in matching white bikinis, their smooth skin tanned to a light mocha.

Seven o'clock held a beer can in one hand; she used the other to shield her eyes from the sun. "Hey, Mr. Carey."

"It's Luke, darlin'. No need to make me feel older than I look. And this gentleman . . . this is Mr. Royce."

"That's Kelly," Five O'clock said. "I'm Kim. Nice to meet you."

"Same," I said, glancing at Luke. "And it's, Cage. Mr. Royce was my father."

"I thought the girls might like to come by The *Hatch* tonight—meet some of the local beach bums," LuAnn said to me.

"Punishment for the shipwreck?" I said.

"Ha, ha," Kelly said. "LuAnn already told us what a great place you've got. Besides, we want to meet Jamie."

Kim stood and stretched, a move not easily ignored. "And a guy or two wouldn't hurt, either."

IT TOOK THIRTY minutes to tow Kim and Kelly back to Seaside—a third of that to return to Luke's house, drop him off in the shallow surf and run the outboard home at full throttle.

With the Whaler back on its balloon-tired trailer and muscled back to its spot among the small dunes, I climbed the stairs to *The Hatch*.

Everything on the deck was in order—bar stocked, glasses washed and slotted in the overhead rack, the bandstand set up for the night's entertainment.

The inside bar and tables were in the same state of readiness.

I went up to our residence above the cafe; Jamie was in the big, open air shower. I stripped off my swimsuit and tee shirt and joined her, cranking on the water and adjusting my spray head to needle points.

"And . . .?"

"Pair of young lovelies ran out of wind," I said. "Needed a tow."

"How young, and how lovely?"

"Too young, and not in your league," I said.

"Liar."

"See for yourself. They're coming by tonight."

Jamie pulled me against her wet warmth. "You're such a good boy for helping them out that way. I should do something nice for you. We've got some time. Wanna play?"

"You ask the hardest questions."

"That's the idea, sport."

Adult games can be such fun.

Depending—I would learn in the weeks ahead—on who's playing.

And by what rules.

CHAPTER 2

THE FOURTH OF July holiday started with twenty-four hours of steady rain. When the weather finally broke, the crowds quickly moved out of the bars and onto the beach.

I was in the cramped office of *The Hatch* totaling the mid-day receipts when the phone rang.

I made no immediate connection with the voice, or the name.

"Kim? . . . Kim Sanders? You towed us to Seaside—Kelly and me. A few weeks ago?"

"Kim. Yes, of course. Sorry. I had my mind on business."

"Maybe I shouldn't be bothering you." Her tone was flat.

"It's no bother at all. How are you? You sound . . . . Are you okay?"

"Actually, no. I'm not. I was going to call my father, but then . . . . Well, I thought better of it. I remembered your talking about being an attorney—you, and Luke." A short silence, and then she said, "I might be in some kind of . . . trouble."

"Where are you?"

"In South Beach. In a hotel."

"If you need a lawyer, I could recommend someone in the area who—"

"Actually, it's not a lawyer I need—at least not right now."

"What kind of trouble are we talking about?" I asked, suddenly on alert.

"It's crazy. All I really know is that . . . . Is that I've been raped. And I think beaten, or like, tortured or something."

I pictured her face, remembered her easy smile. Anger at whoever had assaulted her built quickly. "Kim, I'm *so* sorry. Do you need a doctor—to go to the hospital?"

"I should see someone, I suppose. But I don't think it's urgent. I don't, you know, hurt as much. Besides, I can't right now. There'd be too many questions—ones I'm afraid I couldn't answer. They stole my purse. Got my credit cards. I don't have any identification. I'm not so sure anyone would believe what I say. I . . . I need help, Cage. I wish there were someone here that I knew—someone I could trust."

I answered on impulse—without thinking. "I'll come down and do whatever I can."

Relief brought instant animation to her voice. "Would you? Oh, god, that would be *so* great. I've been cowering in this room, afraid that someone might be looking for me."

Control the situation; my questions could hold. "First, we need to get you out of there." I thought for a second. Then it clicked. "A man named Brian will call you in a little while. He works for Jamie and me. I might have mentioned him to you when you were here."

"The boat, right?"

"Right. Brian and Deanne are down in the Keys. They were planning to spend a couple days there before starting back from a charter. I'll send them to Miami tonight."

"No. I don't want to mess up anyone's—"

"You won't be. You'll be safe aboard. I don't want you to worry about anything, okay?"

" 'Kay," she said.

"And that includes the hotel bill. I'll have Brian take care of it when he—"

"That's part of it—how totally unbelievable this is. Money's the one problem I *don't* seem to have. I . . . I found an envelope. There's twenty-five thousand dollars in it—in cash."

"Your attacker dropped it?"

"No, nothing like that. The envelope—well, it was in my room. When I got back. With my name on it. And there was something else, too. A contract. Signed by me. For an acting role in a movie. An *adult* movie. What I apparently agreed to do—I guess I earned every penny." Her voice broke. "*Now* what am I supposed to do? My god, what's happening?"

I CAME OUT OF the office and went to the bar where Jamie had just finished drawing a pitcher of beer for a waiter.

She drew a mug for me and brought it over. "What's up, doc?"

"I just a got call. From Kim Sanders. One of the stranded sailors?"

"Yeah, really sweet kid. What's the matter? She beached again?"

"In a way, actually yes. She's down in South Beach."

Jamie studied my face. "You look concerned. Is she alright?"

"She's— I guess she's okay. Or will be, anyway."

"Plain English, babe."

I sipped my beer, framing my thoughts. The money. The contract. "Apparently, she's been raped."

Jamie's eyes widened. "What do you mean, *apparently*? My god! If she was, she was!"

"It's not that simple," I said.

Jamie looked at me quizzically, clearly at a loss.

"There's a contract, Jamie. An adult film. She was paid. Twenty-five grand."

"A *porn* movie? That's ridiculous! There's no way. Not Kim."

"That's what she says, too. But how well do we really know her?"

"What's she going to do?" Jamie asked, her conviction a degree less resolute.

"I told her I'd come down. I really didn't know what else to say."

"I could go with you. Give her someone to talk to—a woman."

"Let me get a better read on the situation first, okay?"

"Keep emotion out of it? Great. She's hurt, and you're talking like a lawyer."

I knocked back the rest of my beer, avoiding her eyes. "Last time I checked," I said, "I believe that's what it says on my business card."

CHAPTER 3

THE RISING SUN slowly pressed the blackness off the horizon as I sat on the deck of *The Hatch* with Luke and Wesley Harland, a former cop—the ex-Panama City Beach Police Chief who'd became more and more disillusioned with the rules and regulations that favored the bad guys. He'd left the force following the unraveling of my brother's murder, and came to work for us as an investigator. And as a trust officer, of sorts.

Brian and Deanne had Kim stowed safely aboard *The Free Spirit.* Soon, I'd be on my way to Miami to do what it was I could for her.

We sat for a time in silence, drinking coffee as dark as our thoughts.

"She wouldn't be the first wannabe to get suckered into a film like that because someone promised to make her a star," Wes finally said.

"Okay, so assuming that to be the case, why would she call me for help if she'd gone into it willingly?" I asked.

"She was going to call her father, right? And then changed her mind? Think about it," Wes said. "What would she have said to him? 'Hi, Daddy! It's your little girl. Guess what? I'm a porn princess! Only, it got messy and I don't like the way things turned out. So can you please, please come punch out the bad guys and give me a big hug?'"

"But you don't buy into that, now do you?" Luke said.

"No. I don't. At least I don't think I do. Or I don't want to. Whatever. I can't sort out my thoughts sitting here with you two lugs."

THE FREE SPIRIT—INHERITED from my brother Billy, its history of drug running buried along with him— was moored two slips away from a big Bertram Sportfisher at a small marina forty minutes up the Miami River from Biscayne Bay—twenty minutes by cab from Miami International.

When I arrived, I saw two men standing in the cockpit of our fifty-two foot Hatteras Convertible: Brian, and someone I didn't recognize.

I boarded through the transom door.

The stranger was Dr. Enriquez, an angular man in white slacks and flowered shirt—a physician Wes had contacted through an intermediary.

"These were not nice people." The doctor spoke with the second-language accent of the well-educated. "There are badly bruised ribs, skin abrasions, markings that suggest she was bound limb and torso. However, this and the damage to her other tissue will heal. My concern is the thought of AIDS, or another sexually transmitted disease. I suggested to her that she be tested twice—at six month intervals."

The way Kim had apparently been used turned my stomach. Still, the ugly question remained. "In your opinion, Doctor, could this have been . . . consensual?"

Enriquez shook his head sadly, his eyes, weary. "I offer no opinion. To do so would be pointless, yes?"

What had I expected him to say? Like Wes, he'd seen this, and worse, and kept his head glued on by maintaining a distance. "Anyway, I appreciate what you've done." I reached for my money clip.

Enriquez held up a delicate hand. "Please, that is not necessary. Consider it a favor for a friend of a friend who has made a most generous but anonymous contribution to my small clinic." A brief smile touched his eyes. "And for which I thank you. Good day, gentlemen."

Wesley had taken care of that, too.

WE SAT IN the salon aboard *The Spirit*, Brian's lanky frame splayed on the couch as if he'd been dropped there from a great height.

The door to the master stateroom below had remained closed for the hour since Dr. Enriquez had left. I had better sense than to go knocking.

"No hassle at the hotel?" I asked.

"Just a nasty look from the desk clerk," Brian said. "Must have thought I was the offending boyfriend."

"And you're certain no one followed you here?"

"You can't get here from there the way I did."

I got up and went into the galley. "Beer?"

"Sure." But it was Deanne, not Brian, who'd answered. She came up from below with Kim, slapped me on the butt and took the cold bottles from my hands.

"Thanks for being here," Kim said to me with a little hug. To glance at her, you'd never guess what she'd been through; there were no visible marks. But on closer inspection the acid burn of pain and anger were clearly etched in the thin lines around her blue eyes.

"The doctor says you'll be okay."

She took a step back and looked at me. "I will be. I really will be." Her words were clipped and defensive, as though mine had been accusatory. "It's just a mistake— some kind of mix-up. It wasn't supposed to be me—or it was, and I didn't understand what I was getting into. I mean, why pay me all that money if they didn't think I'd be willing to. . . ." Kim slid into silence, her eyes becoming unfocused.

I held her gently by her shoulders, digging for the words Jamie might say, but failing. "It wasn't your fault," I said lamely. "You did nothing wrong."

Her mouth hardened as our eyes met. "Didn't I? Do you *really* believe that? Because I've been over this a million times in my head, and I'm starting to doubt my own sanity."

Lawyers, so it's rumored, measure truth and intent with a third eye—one blind to emotional nuance, one focused by intuitive sense.

I pushed away thoughts of my brother—of what I'd known about him, or *thought* I had—then offered Kim words of reassurance that sounded cut from tin. "Of course I believe it," I said. "I have no reason not to."

www.ingramcontent.com/pod-product-compliance
Lightning Source LLC
Chambersburg PA
CBHW062017170626
46813CB00001B/190